T0279061

TRESPASS AGAINST US

LEON KEMP

HARPER TEEN
An Imprint of HarperCollinsPublishers

HarperTeen is an imprint of HarperCollins Publishers.

Trespass Against Us
Copyright © 2024 by Leon Kemp
address HarperCollins Children's Books, a division of HarperCollins
Publishers, 195 Broadway, New York, NY 10007.
www.epicreads.com

Library of Congress Control Number: 2023943961
ISBN 978-0-06-332485-5

Typography by Jessie Gang
24 25 26 27 28 LBC 5 4 3 2 1
FIRST EDITION

For everyone chasing ghosts that won't rest

TRESPASS AGAINST US

ONE

Riley is being watched.

He's felt it for at least half an hour now, the insidious crawling of unwelcome eyes along his spine, prickling every inch of his skin. It takes everything he has to ignore it, monotonously stabbing orders into his register and doling out coffee without blinking.

Riley is accustomed to staring. He has to be, looking the way he does. There's a difference, however, between being stared at and being *watched*. He's hoping if he ignores it for long enough, the latter might regress to merely being the former.

Unfortunately, his co-worker doesn't take the hint.

"Hey," Chantelle says as Riley hands her an empty cup, "I think you've got a fan over there."

At two in the afternoon on a Wednesday, the store is dead. There are maybe two other customers lingering about, and the street outside is barren of pedestrians. With nobody and nothing to act as a distraction, it's hard to play at ignorance, but Riley is nothing if not stubborn.

He doesn't look up. The register buttons clack beneath his fingertips. "That'll be three fifty," he says to the businessman he's serving. The man gives him a sweaty ten-dollar bill. Riley gives him the rustiest coins in the till in exchange. "Thank you for your patience."

Chantelle waits for the man to walk away before continuing. "So, you wanna tell her that stalking the staff is against policy, or should I?"

Finally, Riley glances up. Chantelle's staring unabashedly over his shoulder, not in the least concerned by the paper cup awaiting filling at her elbow. "Leave it be," he says. "If she wants something, she knows where to find me."

Chantelle makes a thoughtful noise. "I don't know, doesn't she seem familiar to you? I feel like I've seen her somewhere before."

Against his better judgment, Riley looks.

It's a woman. Dark skin, tightly coiled hair reddened like blood to match her lipstick. The dim cafe lights glint off her impractical sunglasses, a real movie-star-in-disguise vibe. Her black halter top shows off her toned arms, and when she catches Riley looking at her, she dips her sunglasses down her nose and smiles.

She does look familiar. Riley can't place her for the life of him. Going by the way she's looking at him, she doesn't have the same problem.

Realization seems to hit Chantelle and she latches on to Riley's sleeve, pulling frantically. "Oh my god," she wheezes. "Riley, why didn't you tell me you knew *Jordan Jones*?"

Riley can count the number of people he knows on one hand. The name rings a bell, though. "Who?"

Chantelle slaps at his arm hard enough to bruise. "Jordan Jones? As in Jordan Jones of *Spirit Seekers*?"

Riley's heart plummets to his feet.

Used to be he could name every major ghost-hunting show on every network in America. These days, he does his best to stay out of paranormal chasing entirely. Too many associated triggers, as his government-mandated therapist would have said.

Jordan Jones, though? *Spirit Seekers*? You'd have to live under a rock to not have at least heard of them. They'd been up-and-comers when he was still obsessed with the scene; three years devoted to streaming their show independently on their own website. Right before he'd stopped following industry news, he'd heard a rumor that they'd been signed by Netflix. Looking at Jordan's expensive glasses and Hollywood-glamour attitude, he can only assume that it had more than panned out for them.

"We've never met," he says. "I don't know the first thing about her."

"Are you sure?" Chantelle hisses, fingernails biting into his skin. "Because it looks like she's coming over here, and I don't think it's for me."

Jordan slides smoothly out of her booth, approaching them before Riley can decide whether it's worth it to retreat to the back room. She leans on the counter and says, "I hope I'm not interrupting anything."

"Nope," Chantelle breathes, starstruck. "I mean, can we help you, Ms. Jones?"

She smiles again, the shiny whites of her teeth ghostly in the fluorescent lights. "I was just hoping for an espresso, if I could."

The businessman Riley had served earlier—who's been waiting for his drink for five minutes now—pointedly checks his watch.

Chantelle ignores him, fixated on Jordan. "Of course! For here or to go?"

"Well, that depends." Jordan's gaze slips to Riley. "I'd rather hoped I could borrow your colleague for a small chat, if it's not too much trouble."

"He would *love* to," Chantelle says at the exact moment Riley blurts, "No thanks."

Chantelle shoots him a look, but Jordan doesn't seem fazed. "It wouldn't take longer than a few minutes, I promise. I'll have you back behind the counter before your boss even knows you're gone."

"I'm my boss today, actually," Riley says. "That'll be five fifty."

One of Jordan's perfectly plucked brows climbs. "For a single shot of espresso?"

"Sure."

"Your board says it's an even four bucks."

"The board is wrong," Riley says. "Six fifty please."

Chantelle hisses his name, but Jordan merely laughs. She slips her wallet from her back pocket and drops a twenty on the counter. "Keep the change," she says. "Consider it a gesture of goodwill."

Riley doesn't touch the bill. "I don't need your money."

"Are you sure?" Jordan asks. "What about twenty-five thousand dollars?"

Riley doesn't blink. "That sounds like a very expensive coffee, even for us. If we're charging prices like that, maybe you should be buying elsewhere."

Jordan doesn't take the bait. "Just hear me out, Mr. Fox. I can promise you won't regret it."

Riley doesn't need to hear her out. From the second he realized who she was, he knew exactly what she'd come here for, and it wasn't a fucking espresso.

He doesn't say anything. Beside him, Chantelle maintains a death grip on his arm. If she's hoping to bully him into agreement, she'll have to try harder than that.

Jordan flashes him one more of her endless smiles and slips back to her booth.

"What," Chantelle says, "the *fuck* was that about?"

Riley sighs. Chantelle is just that little bit younger than him—young enough that the gossip of the town from two years ago has probably blown right over her head. He liked that. It allowed him the pretense of anonymity, something he wasn't always afforded these days.

People don't often approach him in public. Not anymore. But Riley is well accustomed to being a public spectacle of pity—well-meaning glances from the corner of grim eyes, curious stares when they catch sight of his scars, his name tag, his apathy.

He's out of practice with confrontation, but he supposes there's no better time to relearn what was once second nature.

5

He takes Jordan's twenty and drops the change in the tip jar. Then he slams the register closed, unties his apron, and says, "I'm taking my fifteen minutes, okay?"

"You can't just— Oh, would you stop clicking your tongue? I'm getting to you!"

Riley passes by the businessman, ignoring the dirty look he shoots him as Chantelle finally starts on his latte.

Jordan's booth is tucked into the corner, where nobody can rubberneck over the seat backs. The choice of it is so intentional it rankles Riley something fierce. He drops onto the edge of the seat across from Jordan, arms folded tightly over his chest. "All right. You have three minutes. Go."

She slides a manila folder across the sticky tabletop toward him. When Riley doesn't open it, she says, "I'm sure you know who I am, so let's cut to the chase, Mr. Fox. My team and I have been given permission—*finally*—to investigate one of the most interesting paranormal cases in modern memory."

Riley's stomach turns at her words, at the impersonal ring of them, as if everything that happened to him and his friends is nothing more than prime-time entertainment. He stares at her. "Cases."

To her credit, she seems to immediately realize her misstep. "We can call it whatever would make you the most comfortable, but the fact remains that an opportunity like this doesn't come around every day, not even for people like me."

"That's nice," Riley says. "Two minutes twenty."

"You can understand, I'm sure, why I had to approach you."

"I wouldn't call it approaching so much as staking out my workplace. Didn't anybody ever tell you it was rude to stare?"

Brutally, Jordan says, "I have to believe that you're quite used to staring at this point."

Riley is. He doesn't look in mirrors much anymore, but he feels his scars every time he speaks, the unkind pull of them over his cheek, across his mouth. The burn of them on cold nights.

"Is this how you want to win me over?" Riley says. "By reminding me of the worst thing that ever happened to me?"

Jordan reaches out. Her nails tap on the folder, a stuttering rhythm like footsteps in the dark. "Open the file, Mr. Fox."

Riley doesn't blink. "No."

"I think you would agree that twenty-five thousand dollars for one night of your life is a generous offer."

"And I think you're well aware that most of us have made our stance quite clear by now," Riley says. "We just want to be left alone."

"Interesting you say that," Jordan says, "because Miss Cho disagrees."

Riley is caught off guard. "What?"

Sensing an opening, she continues, "I talked to Miss Cho before reaching out to you. She was quite amenable to our terms. Providing, of course, that you agreed to the proposition too."

Riley opens his mouth. He can't think of what to say. He closes it again.

Jordan pushes the folder nearer to him. Kinder this time, she repeats, "Open the file, Riley."

Trepidation eating at his heart, Riley does. What he finds inside does not surprise him, but it still steals his breath like a gut punch.

It's been two years since he last saw Dominic House, but the photo in front of him burns the passage of time away in a moment. The main building sits atop its hill, a sentry over the woods that surround it. Stretched twice as long as it towers tall, it boasts shattered windows and cracked roof tiles. It's a recent picture; Riley can tell by the police tape wilting across the rusted iron of the front gate, browned with age.

Behind the first building, a second one peeks out, riding the crest of the hill it calls home. The chapel's cross pierces the sky, blackened at the edges but still standing, resilient and immovable.

Dominic House looms like a monolith; it looms like a god.

Riley's fingers tremble against the paper. He stuffs his hands in his pockets, but not quick enough. The smug look that flickers across Jordan's face tells him she saw it. "How did you even get permission for this?" Riley asks. "Last I heard they still considered it an active crime scene."

"Actually, they officially designated it a cold case a month ago," Jordan says. "And if you have the right connections, you can get anywhere."

Riley barely hears the second part of her sentence, he's so busy tripping over the first. "They— What?"

Jordan pauses in her spiel. "Oh. You didn't know?"

"I— No." Riley's throat feels thick. "I didn't . . . I didn't know."

Jordan looks at him silently. Then she gets to her feet, slinging her purse over her shoulder. "I can see that you need time to think about things," she says. "My phone number is in the folder, as are all the details you need. I'll be waiting to hear from you—sooner is better than later."

Riley doesn't look up. His gaze sticks on the photo of Dominic House. He stays quiet.

Jordan sighs. "It was good meeting you, Mr. Fox. I'll speak with you soon."

It's a presumptuous thing to say, but Riley doesn't correct her. She sweeps out of the booth and away. A moment later, there's the tinkling of the bell at the door, and she's gone.

She'd been right. The whole conversation had been three minutes, maybe less. In her absence, Riley feels unmoored. He's a shipwreck, sinking fast, and solid land feels an entire ocean away.

Footsteps approach, and then Chantelle says, "So, what did she want?"

It takes effort, but Riley rips his gaze from the photo. The afterimage of it lingers behind his eyelids. "Nothing. It's fine."

He's not quick enough to cover up the contents of the folder. Chantelle glances down at the picture in front of him and immediately pulls a face. "Oh, gross. That looks like something out of my nightmares."

A laugh bubbles in Riley's chest. He spreads his fingers over the photo, but even half-hidden, it stares back at him, a blemish beneath his skin.

"Yeah," he says. "Yeah, mine too."

BEFORE

"When you said we should take a road trip during summer break, this isn't what I pictured." Colton sounded as unimpressed as he looked, feet kicked up on Vee's coffee table.

"What *did* you picture?" Ethan asked curiously. He had an arm tossed around Riley, the pair of them squeezed into an armchair meant for one. His free hand kept the laptop balanced precariously on Riley's knee steady. Twice now, it'd nearly fallen, and both times, Ethan had been the one to save it. Two years of football had given him reflexes like a snake. Two years of no football and little exercise at all had given Riley no reflexes, period. "I mean," Ethan continued, "you don't even like long trips. You get carsick."

Colton scowled, flushing. "I don't know. The beach, maybe? You know I've lived in Maine my whole life, and I've never been to the coast. Surely they have ghost stories by the sea."

"You're barely going to manage an hour in the car without moaning about it, and you wanna take a trip across the state just to see the sea?" Riley asked skeptically.

"Not stories like this one," Vee said, ignoring Riley. She patted the top of the TV beside her. The slideshow Riley had painstakingly prepared glimmered across the flat screen, incongruent with the fine china and chintz of her living room. "This is our chance at really getting something good. Aren't you sick of posting the same generic bullshit over and over again? How many times can we really make a video sneaking through a cemetery or rambling about the Amityville house before it starts going stale?"

Riley might have put the largely unnecessary slideshow together, but Vee had been the spearhead behind all the carefully cited research, as if their friends were going to shoot them down if they slapped a Wiki link at the bottom of the page and called it a day.

To be fair, Colton looked like he might do it anyway, his sour face pinched. "I know this YouTube channel is your baby and all—"

"Don't call it that," Riley protested. "It's more than just a 'YouTube channel.'"

Colton continued as if he'd never been interrupted at all. "—but do we really have to waste our summer break on it?"

They'd wasted a lot more than summer break on it at this point. Ghost Hawks had been up and running for nearly six months, and they hadn't even broken the coveted hundred-subscriber milestone Vee had optimistically set for them on launch day.

By now they'd filmed every haunted location around town from every possible angle and shared every urban legend or ghost story they could find from extensive trawling through Google.

Ghost Hawks had gone from being a fun pet project with Riley's best friends born of a mutual curiosity for the paranormal to something that kept him awake at night, wondering how long it'd take before they found something *real*. Something more than a few cheap scares in basements and cemeteries or the morbid retelling of another person's tragedy a whole country away.

So maybe his slideshow was unnecessary, and maybe Vee's perfectly cited research was overkill, but if they ever wanted Ghost Hawks to be more than just a "YouTube channel," as Colton had said, they needed to start venturing a little farther out than their own backyards.

"It's an hour out of town," Vee wheedled. "It'll take two days out of your busy schedule, max."

"You know that's not true," Colton said. "You'll have us filming B-roll until all I dream about is the fucking scenery. Besides, who's driving?"

Vee smiled sunnily, hands clasped together. "I'm glad you asked."

Colton had been the first of them to turn sixteen and the only one to obtain his own wheels since. Something he was fond of reminding them at every available opportunity. The way Riley figured, if he was going to be unbearable about it, he might as well be unbearable in their favor.

Catching on, Colton groaned. "Come on, really?" He turned to Ethan. "You wanna spend your break ghost hunting?"

Ethan shrugged, the picture of benevolence. "Why not? It's been fun so far, hasn't it? Besides, Riley wants to go."

As simple as that. "Riley wants to go." So they would. Riley tried not to look too smug.

Vee said, "Riley, change the slide."

Riley did. The title card slipped away. In its place was another, this one accompanied by a picture of a building so old and crumbling, Riley was amazed it had stayed standing long enough to be photographed at all. *Saint Dominic Savio's School for Troubled Youths* read the heading. On the next slide, Riley had transcribed its history in neat twelve-point font with accompanying WordArt. Outdated, maybe. But fun.

It was quiet for a second as the others read through it.

"Huh," Ethan said. "The WordArt's nice."

"You know what's not nice? The five missing kids and the priest." Despite his words, Colton migrated his feet from the coffee table to the floor. He leaned forward, squinting at the TV.

Riley tried not to be smug about that too. Sometimes Colton liked to complain just for the sake of complaining. Beneath it all, he was just as invested as the rest of them. He'd been the one to suggest starting the channel, after all.

Riley clicked to another slide. This one had photos of the missing kids, complete with matching bios. One photo was significantly larger than the other.

Colton whistled. "Who's the kid who looks like he just lost a fistfight with his own authority issues?"

The boy glowered out of the screen, sixteen at most but built like a tank. Bruises darkened his blue eyes, and his cheekbones were scraped red from punches he'd taken rather than thrown.

"That's Jacob Smith," Vee said. "He was the eldest of the missing kids and the prime suspect in the case. Newspapers said he had no friends and butted heads with all the teachers, not to mention the priest."

"And who's the priest?" Ethan asked.

Riley flipped a slide. A young man stared back at them, eyes big and solemn, white collar nestled around his throat. His dark hair was neatly brushed aside to make way for his kindly face. "Father Thomas," Riley said. "He stayed behind to look after the kids who didn't go home over break. Disappeared with them."

"And they have no clue what happened?" Colton asked skeptically. "Nothing at all?"

"This *was* decades ago," Vee said, quite sensibly. "You think the police are incompetent now? Imagine what they'd have been like then."

Ethan said, "Their parents wrote them off as 'troubled kids.'" The face he pulled as he bookended that with air quotes made his distaste of the term clear. "I'd be surprised if they investigated much at all."

"They shut Dominic House down after the disappearances," Vee added. "I guess the reputation was too much to deal with."

A shiver spun down Riley's spine. From the screen, Father Thomas stared back at him, patient and benevolent in his frozen moment of time. Riley clicked once more, and the photo vanished into darkness, just like the man within it. Unnerved, he cleared his throat. "So? Haunted enough for you?"

Colton pretended to consider it, fingers tapping at his chin in thought. He heaved a put-upon sigh that sounded disjointed in such a young body, a sound he'd picked up from somebody at least twice his age and made his own. "I *guess*. At the least, we'll get some interesting footage of a creepy house. That always makes for good content. You were right, we're just rehashing the same things over and over on the channel at this point; we need something new."

Vee and Riley high-fived. Riley turned to Ethan with pleading eyes.

Ethan smiled at him. "You know you have my vote. What else would we do with our summer break?" he teased. "Besides, where you go, I go."

Colton made gagging noises in the background, but Riley scarcely noticed—he was too dizzy with affection.

"Yeah," he said, and it felt true then—would feel true two years later, even if he didn't know that yet. "Where you go, I go."

TWO

Ethan's mom hadn't even shown up after the cops called.

It's funny, of everything that happened that night, Riley remembers that the clearest. Sitting in the back of an ambulance as paramedics tried to piece his face back together, Vee sobbing in the distance, Colton already en route to the hospital. The unlucky officer who'd found them pacing up and down the cracked sidewalk, phone to his ear as he said, "I understand, Mrs. Hale, but your son is— No, I can't call back. We need you here. There is the possibility that we could be looking at a missing person case. We need you to— Mrs. Hale? Mrs. Hale?"

That's what Riley takes away from Dominic House. That's what he takes to his nightmares. His face falling from his skull and a stranger parroting "Mrs. Hale? Mrs. Hale?" over and over and over again for the rest of his life.

Nobody had told him the case was cold. He wonders if they'd even told Ethan's mom. If she'd even cared.

When Riley gets home, the apartment is dark. He hangs his keys on the empty hook by the door, kicking his boots to a puddle by the faded welcome mat. "Mom?"

Nobody answers him.

Riley heads down the hall, flicking every light switch he passes. In the kitchen, he finds a note pinned to the fridge.

Working night shift. Will be home tomorrow xx

Beneath it is a set of instructions for cooking dinner that his mother, quite ambitiously, thinks Riley ought to follow. Instead, Riley slaps together a sandwich. The bread's stale; his mother has been too busy to go grocery shopping lately, and Riley keeps forgetting. The sandwich hangs from his mouth as he scribbles a reminder on the bottom of the note for whichever of them sees it first, leaving it pinned where it is.

The kitchen table is a cluttered mess of magazines and unclean plates. Riley pushes aside the debris, dropping Jordan's folder into the free space, and then sits in one of the mismatched chairs.

He takes a bite of his sandwich. It tastes about as appetizing as it looks. At least, he supposes, he won't have to worry about losing his appetite.

He opens the file.

He's more prepared this time. He flicks past the initial photo without pausing, Dominic House a fleeting glimpse of shadows and no more. Behind it he unearths a collection of media releases from the immediate aftermath, and somehow, even more than the photographs, looking at them makes him uneasy.

He thumbs through everything. His own name jumps out at him, Vee's name. Colton's most of all.

Unsurprising. Colton had been the only one unable to keep his mouth shut when the tabloids came knocking.

Colton's role in the media circus that haunted them after Dominic House is an old wound by now, just like everything else. All the same, it doesn't stop irritation souring his mood, and Riley tosses the press releases aside, finally finding Jordan's proposition. It's written in neat little bullet points, concise and informative. Above, the *Spirit Seekers* logo leers, the spooky font incongruous with the official report it heralds.

- Permission for access to the retired Saint Dominic Savio's School for Troubled Youths has been granted for August 17 to August 18, 2022.
- All team members will undergo a safety induction prior to filming and—

That was a solid month later than they'd gone last time. Riley can't help but wonder if maybe production wanted to avoid the stigma of the Spirit Seekers heading out on the anniversary of a very real tragedy. Or maybe Jordan Jones just didn't like filming during the peak of summer. Who knows.

Riley finishes his sandwich and flips the page. The next one doesn't make him feel any better.

—agree to pay the designated fee of $25,000 USD to the nominated beneficiaries (Miss Evelyn Cho, Mr. Riley Fox, Mr. Colton Pierce) for their agreement to return with *Spirit Seekers* to Saint Dominic Savio's School for Troubled Youths.

Riley closes the folder. Seeing it written out does not make it feel more real. What does feel real is the ghost of fingers on his face—the drag of his flesh ripping apart, blood warming his skin.

Riley presses a hand to his cheek. It comes away clear, like he'd known it would.

His therapist, back when he had one, told him that the scars would fade with time. Not the physical ones but the phantom ache of them bleeding into life across his skin.

It wasn't the first thing she'd been wrong about. Not the last, either.

Riley gets to his feet, abandoning Jordan's folder on the tabletop, bracketed by dirty mugs and ancient magazines. He leaves the lights on as he goes, as he slips into his room, closing the door behind him.

Unlike the rest of the house, Riley's bedroom is orderly to the point of military precision. Shoes lined up like soldiers beneath his sagging clothes rack, desk tucked in the corner boasting a stack of pristine, unopened community college magazines. His mother has spent the past year pointedly dog-earing tech courses in every college pamphlet she could find. They sit atop the magazines, equally untouched.

Riley throws himself onto his bed. As he goes, his elbow knocks against his bedside table, and he scrambles to keep it from sending everything scattering to the floor. His lamp wobbles but remains upright. The photo frame tucked behind it isn't so lucky. It topples to the carpet before he can make a grab for it.

For a moment, Riley holds the table steady, staring at the fallen frame. He lets out a shaky breath, loosens his grip on the table, and reaches for it.

The glass is smudged but unbroken. Beneath it, a younger Riley smiles out, face smooth and unblemished. His hair had been shorter then, barely curling past the nape of his neck, and his right ear boasted a single piercing instead of several.

He's so young and bright that it's like staring at a stranger. His arm is tossed around the person next to him, and Riley swallows, gut lurching.

Don't, he coaches himself. *Not tonight, not after today. Don't do that to yourself. Don't, don't, don't—*

He can't help himself. The only thing worse than Riley's impulse control is his self-destructive streak. He looks.

Ethan grins back at him, the impossible blue of his eyes bright in the camera flash. His dimples are on full display, blond hair windswept. Boy-next-door handsome and clinging to Riley like it was as natural as breathing.

Riley's heart hurts, and even after two years, the ache of loss that has eased but never vanished sets its hooks into him and rips anew.

His hands are shaking as he sets the frame back on his bedside table. The glass glints in the lamplight, turning the white of Ethan's skin sallow. Riley hesitates, then reaches over, turning the frame face down. The relief is instant and palpable.

He settles against his headboard, pulling his phone from his pocket. His call history, when he opens it, is bleak. Other than his mother and work, there's only one number within, and Riley dials it immediately.

The phone rings. Once. Twice. The line clicks.

"I was just thinking about you," Vee says.

"I'll bet," Riley says. "Do you know who came by my work today? I'll give you three guesses. The first two don't count."

"I'm not sorry."

"For what?" Riley asks. "The list of things you could potentially be not-apologizing for is kind of long right now; you're going to need to clarify."

"For not warning you. I knew if I did, you'd find a way to weasel your way out of seeing her."

Probably not wrong. It doesn't make Riley feel any better. "So you thought Jordan fucking Jones propositioning me in the middle of my workplace would go over so much better?"

"Propositioning you? Sounds like we had very different conversations."

Riley's patience, which has withstood enough today already, is dangerously close to fraying. "Vee."

Vee sighs static down the line. "Did you let her explain herself at all, or did you just immediately kick her out?"

"The folder sitting in my kitchen indicates I more than let her explain herself."

"Have you read it yet?"

"Twenty-five thousand dollars to the nominated beneficiaries for their agreement to return to Saint Dominic Savio's School for Troubled Youths," Riley drawls. "Yes, I read it."

Vee doesn't immediately respond. Riley can practically hear how carefully she's sorting through her words, trying to string together a sentence gentle enough not to tip the precarious balance of their conversation over the edge.

She didn't used to have to tread so carefully around him. It's amazing what trauma can do to a person.

Be gentle, Riley coaches himself. *Don't lash out. Don't start a fight.*

Vee says, "I think this could be good. For all of us. Think it through."

"I don't need her fucking money," Riley snaps, and then grits his teeth. So much for gentle.

Vee is unperturbed and, without missing a beat, replies, "Yes, you do. And so do I. College is right around the corner, and it'd be a big help. But that's not what I meant, and you know it."

"You know what *I* know?" Riley says. "That all three of us agreed we'd rather die than go back there again."

"You can't hold me to something I said when I was sixteen," Vee says. "We were kids, Riley. We were just scared fucking kids."

Riley doesn't want to think about that. He's worked hard over the years to push that part of himself away, that terrified sixteen-year-old who was just that: a scared fucking kid.

Sometimes he doesn't feel as if he's succeeded at all.

Instead, he asks, "Have you spoken to Colton?"

"Have you?" Vee shoots back.

"I'm not the one meeting with TV crews, selling the rights to our life story."

"This isn't our life story. This is one thing that happened to us years ago."

Riley laughs. "Right. So it's wrong when somebody else talks to the media but fine when you do it?"

A lingering pause. When Vee speaks, her tone is chilly. "Jordan spoke to him. He already signed on. Said he'd be there even if we weren't."

"Colton going where the money is. Big surprise there," Riley says.

"Don't act like you're above it," Vee warns. "I've seen your apartment. You're not exactly set to rise through the tax brackets, are you?"

Riley's mouth twists into something approaching a smile. "If you're hitting to hurt, try aiming lower than that."

Silence. Vee sighs again, less tense, more exasperated. "You know I don't want to do that. I don't want to hurt you at all."

"Of course I know that," Riley says, and he does. Vee isn't like him—it's why he's always loved her the way he does. The last defensive edge of his irritation flakes away beneath that reminder. "It's fine. I was taking it too far."

"I don't care if you insult Colton," Vee confesses. "I was just . . ."

"You want me to agree to come," Riley says.

"No," Vee says. "I want *you* to want to come. Does that make sense?"

It does. Riley doesn't reply.

Vee continues, softly, "I wouldn't ask if I didn't think it was worth it. For all of us. Even Colton."

Weary, Riley grinds the heel of his palm against his eye and asks, "What could possibly make it worth it, Vee?"

"How much do you remember about what happened? *Really* remember, I mean."

Claws in his face—the flash of fire climbing the walls. Blue eyes glimmering in the flames. Fingers, white like bone, drawing Ethan into the shadows of the cross above.

Riley squeezes his eyes closed. The memories flicker, unreliable. "Sometimes too much," he admits. "Sometimes . . . Sometimes not enough."

"I want to know what happened," Vee says. "I want to know how much of what I remember from that night was real. What do you want, Riley?"

There's a list of things Riley wants to remember about that night. A list of things he wants to know. Things he thinks about when he lies in bed, staring at the ceiling and waiting for the nightmares to set in, waiting to be sitting in the back of that ambulance once more, listening to the endless circle of *Mrs. Hale? Mrs. Hale?*

Mostly, what he thinks about is this: Four people walked into that house. Three people walked out.

Riley should be going to college next month. He hasn't told anybody that he never even applied. He doesn't know what he's planning to do otherwise. He does know eighteen is too young to spend every day of your life getting up to go to a job you hate, unable to think about anything but all the chances you missed.

Riley wants the same thing he has always wanted. To find out the truth of what happened to his damn boyfriend.

"It won't just be us there," Riley says.

It's not a capitulation, but Vee rushes toward it eagerly nonetheless. "It'll just be Jordan and the other two Spirit Seekers. They're a small team. It won't be all that bad."

"Doesn't matter if there are three people or a thousand; we're going to be all over the TV."

"Isn't that what you always wanted?" Vee teases. "Sixteen-year-old Riley would be delighted."

"Sixteen-year-old Riley thought a YouTube channel with thirty subscribers was the big leagues," Riley says dryly. "It didn't take much to impress him."

"Well, as somebody who was actually friends with sixteen-year-old Riley, I can tell you that's factually untrue; he was just as much of a snob at sixteen as he is at eighteen."

Despite feeling like he's gone ten rounds with an emotional heavyweight, Riley can't help but smile. "Thank you for putting up with him for that long. It sounds like he's lucky to have you."

"He can be a pain in my ass, but I guess he's worth it." Vee pauses. "So . . . ?"

"Yeah," Riley says. "I'll sign Jordan's stupid contract. I'll do it."

"Thank you," Vee says. "Really, thank you, Riley."

"I'm not doing it for you," Riley says, honestly.

"I know. I'm grateful anyway."

"Yeah, yeah," Riley says. "You should stop while you're ahead, before you talk me out of it."

Vee laughs. "All right. I haven't seen you in a few weeks. It'll be nice to see your face again, at least."

Riley stamps down on the way his stomach turns. "Yeah, you too. Good night, Vee."

"Good night, Riley."

He hangs up. After making his decision, he expects his world to look different somehow. It doesn't. He's still just Riley, alone in his empty room, in his empty apartment.

He glances back to his bedside table. After a second of hesitation, he rights the downed frame. Ethan smiles back at him—young, now and forever.

Riley waits for his hands to shake. For his scars to ache. They do not. Somehow he isn't surprised.

Deep down, Riley had always known Dominic House wasn't done with him. Deeper than that, he'd always known the opposite too.

He wasn't done with Dominic House either.

His hand white knuckles around the photograph. The glass is cold to touch.

He wonders if it's cold in Dominic House. It's summer now. Summer again, even. Somehow he thinks that matters very little.

Riley has spent the past two years being told that Ethan is gone. The internet called him missing, his parents called him a runaway, and their friends called him dead.

Ethan Hale is *gone*, the world said, and Riley should just move on.

Is Ethan cold? Is he lonely? Does he think about the night Riley left him behind half as much as Riley does?

Ethan isn't missing. He isn't a runaway. He isn't *dead*.

None of them had been there that night. Not in the end, when it was just Riley, Ethan, and one more awful, awful thing as the chapel burned down around them. None of them fall asleep at night picturing blue eyes and fire.

Riley sets the frame down with a clatter. The shakes are back finally. Riley had known it was only a matter of time.

He rolls over, staring out the window to the quiet night.

Is he really going to do this?

He's not looking, but he feels Ethan's smile all the same. Time has drained the warmth from it, but he remembers it still.

Fuck, he misses it still.

Riley rolls over again. He grabs up his phone. He dials. The phone picks up on the first ring. "Hello?"

"I'll do it," he says, no preamble at all. "Don't make me regret it."

Jordan makes a delighted sound. "I'm glad to hear it. If you could come by the address in the file tomorrow, we can do the safety induction, sign some contracts. Is that okay with you?"

Riley's meant to be working tomorrow. "That's fine by me."

"Excellent. I look forward to—"

He hangs up. Something tells him Jordan won't take it personally.

Drawn like a magnet, he looks to the photo.

Yeah. He's fucking doing this.

BEFORE

The night before they were due to head to Dominic House, the group piled together into Ethan's tiny, empty house.

His parents were out for the night, as they usually were. Ethan's relationship with them had been strained since he'd stopped accompanying them to church as he got older, but after he and Riley had started dating, it'd deteriorated into no relationship at all.

Ethan claimed this didn't bother him. Riley knew better.

But that night was a good night. They ordered pizza and spent a couple of hours going over their game plan—what they wanted to film, where they planned to go on the grounds, what Vee would say when she narrated their adventure.

All of Vee's careful research had been clipped down to the most salient points—the missing kids and priest, Dominic House's use as a semi-halfway house, the overbearing Catholicism of it all. The stuff that would sound great as they walked its haunted corridors, showcasing all its ancient, imposing glory.

Not for the first time, Vee protested being the designated face of Ghost Hawks. "Make Ethan do it," she said. "I do it every time, and he's good at stuff like this."

"No, I'm not," Ethan said. "If you put me in front of the camera, I'll be reading off cue cards the whole time."

"You can't do that," Vee snapped. "We need to appear educated!"

"And that's why *you* should do it," Ethan said. "It's good for consistency if you remain the face of the channel, too. Besides, I thought you bought a new skirt for this."

Vee flushed and shoved a piece of pizza in her mouth to avoid answering.

At some point, they tossed old horror movies on the TV, sprawled across the living room as they chattered back and forth. Riley had gotten a new camera a few weeks back; this trip was the first time he'd be able to use it for the channel. Ethan very patiently let Riley show him all the fanciest settings and specs even though Riley knew the tech side of their little production bored him. Ethan was good like that.

Eventually, enthusiasm petered out under exhaustion. Vee fell asleep on the sofa with half a slice of pepperoni in her hand. Colton was out like a light atop the patchwork rug on the floor, the TV painting glimmering blue pictures of murderers and monsters across his skin.

Ethan got to his feet, finger to his lips for silence. He pulled an afghan from the back of the sofa, shaking it out over Colton like a snowdrift, and then took Riley's hand, hauling him up, tripping over Colton's socked feet as they rounded the couch again and rushed to Ethan's room. Inside, Ethan clicked the door closed, drowning out the soft murmur of the TV. There was just enough moonlight seeping through the open curtains to see the glint of his grin. "Just because the others are going to spend all of tomorrow tired from sleeping like shit doesn't mean we have to as well."

Riley snorted. He hooked his fingers in Ethan's belt loops, walking them both back until Riley could drop onto the end of the bed. "How selfish of you, Mr. Hale."

Ethan flopped down beside him, stretching out on his back. "I had a good teacher."

"Did you just call me selfish?" Riley asked incredulously.

Ethan's stomach flexed with silent laugher and when he smiled his hair fell into his face, boyish and charming. "No. Of course not."

"Good," Riley said. "Because I can still go sleep on the couch with Vee."

"You know that couch can't take two people." He paused to give Riley a pointed look.

Riley ignored him. Last week, they'd tested their luck and nearly wound up on the floor for their troubles, but it takes two to tango. Instead, he said, "You know, you don't have to go along with everything I say, right? I know you're not all that interested in this paranormal stuff. Interested in the channel, I mean."

Ethan sighed, hauling himself up on his elbows. "Riley, I really don't mind. Colton and Vee both seem into it, and you love it."

Riley pulled a face. "Before you met us, your idea of a good day was throwing a football around and scoring home runs."

"Those are two very different sports and I know you know that," Ethan said patiently. "And it's also not true. I was listening to Colton ramble about all this freaky paranormal stuff long before he introduced me to the rest of you."

30

Riley had never fully understood how Colton and Ethan even became friends, given how little they had in common. He supposed the same could be said for him and Ethan as well, though, so maybe Ethan just had a thing for guys who didn't know the difference between one ball game and another and considered ghost hunting to be a good time.

He'd asked Ethan about it once, how he and Colton had hit it off, and Ethan had just said, "We sit next to each other in Home Ec."

That was it. They sat next to each other in one class. So naturally they had to be best friends. It was so quintessentially *Ethan* that it made Riley exasperated and fond at the same time.

Ethan had come late to their group, Colton only dragging him into their fold a month into sophomore year. Colton and Vee had known each other since preschool, treating each other more like siblings than best friends, and Riley had been adopted by Vee a week into high school.

Initially, Riley had been slow to warm to Ethan, wary of being replaced. Ethan hadn't had the same problem. Once, Ethan had told him he'd had a crush on Riley since the moment Colton had introduced them.

In hindsight, it was obvious. Ethan was a lot of things, but he wasn't subtle. Riley, however, had been too busy being irrationally jealous of the handsome quarterback encroaching on his friend group. Even after that feeling had morphed into something entirely different and Riley had begun making increasingly stupid excuses just to get a moment alone with Ethan, he still hadn't picked up on the fact the feeling was mutual.

Probably, they'd still be dancing around each other now if Vee hadn't taken Riley aside one day and said, "Put that man out of his misery one way or another, Riley, I swear to god. If I have to watch this stupid pining for much longer, I'm going to hurl."

That had been that. Riley and Ethan had been inseparable ever since, and Ethan had been the sort of boyfriend that somebody like Riley could only ever dream about. Handsome, funny, and utterly devoted to him, even if was only quietly and behind closed doors, where small-town homophobia couldn't sink its teeth into them.

And it was exactly things like that which made it hard to not sometimes feel like he was taking advantage of Ethan's willingness to dote on him, happiest making Riley happy.

Riley eyed him dubiously. "If you're just saying that—"

"I'm not," Ethan interrupted. He looped one arm around Riley's waist, dragging him down to the mattress. "Really. I know I couldn't tell the difference between EMF and ESP when I first met you, but I'm all in on this ghost-hunting thing now." He gave Riley an affectionate shake. "Now, tell me more about this house, because I know you held back on the slideshow and you're probably bursting to show off."

Riley was, but he had hoped he was doing a better job of hiding it.

Ethan's arm over him was warm, almost too warm in the summer heat. His bedroom was small, and the remains of the late-evening sun stuck in all the corners of it like glue. If they stayed like this all night, Riley would boil alive.

There was a crucifix above Ethan's bed. His parents had gifted it to him as kid, and even after all this time, it remained. When they were sprawled together like this, Riley couldn't help but be overly conscious of it watching over them.

Still, he didn't move—shifted only enough so he could card his fingers through Ethan's hair. "All right, but it's going to be boring as hell," he warned.

"Great," Ethan said sleepily. "Boring as hell. Just how I like my ghost stories."

Riley tugged his hair in gentle admonishment. When he soothed his fingers through it immediately after, Ethan made a contented noise Riley knew he'd remember for the rest of his life.

Sometimes, it was hard for him to believe that Ethan had only been in his life for the better part of a year. He fit so naturally at Riley's side that Riley couldn't imagine going back to a life without him.

"Okay," Riley said. "You asked for it."

He talked about Dominic House—the building, the history, the horror. He talked until Ethan was long asleep, and when sleep reached for Riley too, only then did he shut up.

In his dreams, Dominic House waited for him.

It would not be the last time.

THREE

The "address in the file" Jordan had so kindly asked Riley to come to belongs to the ritziest hotel for miles.

Riley stands on the sidewalk, looking up at it with both hands tucked in his pockets. It's four stories tall—among the tallest in town—made up of metal struts and shiny glass windows. Through them he can see the lush reception area littered with plush couches and fancy men and women in suits.

He remembers when they built this place. They'd had to demolish a rusty old playground to do it, and Vee had corralled him into signing a petition against the project.

The hotel gleams at him now. Riley sighs and shoves his way through the revolving door.

Inside, the air-conditioning slaps him in the face, at least ten degrees cooler than outside. Riley hadn't even realized he was hot until he was abruptly too cold.

He beelines to the reception desk, and a woman in a prim black dress glances up with a smile. "May I help you?"

"Yeah," Riley says. "I'm looking for Jordan Jones?"

Her fingernails clack on the keyboard in front of her. "Your name?"

"Riley Fox."

More clacking. "Ms. Jones is in room 406. There's a note here that she's expecting you."

"Wonderful. Thanks." Riley strides away from her plastic smile before it can sink its claws into him.

The elevator takes forever to climb the meager four stories. It spits him out in a claustrophobic corridor, and Riley gets so turned about looking for the right room that it leaves time for more doubts to creep in. He dithers in the hallway, and it's only the ding of the elevator that spurs him back into action.

Room 406 is two doors from the end of the hall on the right. The placard above the peephole is chipped, and the burnished metal of the door handle has started to dull with age.

Riley scrounges up his courage, steels his shoulders, and knocks.

The door opens, and Riley is confronted with a freckled, sunburnt face framed by a wash of strawberry blond hair. The man beams at him. When he speaks, the lilt of his Irish accent is strong. "Riley, yeah?"

"That's me," Riley says. "Joshua, right?"

The man sticks his hand out. "Josh is fine. You watched much of us, then?"

"Sure," Riley says.

He'd stayed up until nearly three in the morning bingeing *Spirit Seekers* on Netflix. Jordan Jones and her two-man team really were streaming TV's dream: professional but with all the drama of a Vegas show.

Honestly, Riley really thought their shtick about investigating houses alone or not at all was just a bit for the camera, but when he peers over Josh's shoulder, the hotel room seems largely empty.

"I'm glad you showed up," Josh says cheerfully, stepping back to let him in. "Even if you cost me twenty bucks."

From the sitting room, another voice calls, "That's your fault for taking a losing bet."

Josh ushers him forward and inside. Compared to the neatness of the rest of the hotel, the sitting room is a disaster. Equipment is stacked all over the carpet, tripods guarding the heavy drapes that in turn guard an ajar door to a balcony with a perfect view of the Target across the street.

Two couches face each other across an expansive antique coffee table covered in paperwork. A man sits on one of them, methodically cleaning a set of camera lenses that look like they're worth more than anything Riley owns. Unlike Josh, he's clean-shaven, with warm brown skin and dark hair, and seems perfectly content where he is. He barely looks at Riley as he says, "My name's Alejandro. Thanks for winning the bet for me."

If Riley remembers right, Alejandro Diaz is the oldest of the group, nearly forty, according to Wikipedia. Compared to Josh's blatant enthusiasm, and Jordan's overly sleek professionalism, Alejandro's quiet disinterest is a breath of fresh air.

He reminds Riley of Colton, before everything went to shit.

Riley stomps mercilessly down on the pang of nostalgia in his gut and says, "It was my pleasure. Where's Jordan?"

Footsteps come from an archway in the far wall and Riley looks up to see her entering the room, two mugs of coffee in her hands. Her expression brightens when she sees him, and she sets the coffee unceremoniously on the table to swoop in on him. "Riley! I'm so glad you could make it!"

Riley shrugs uncomfortably. "I said I'd be here, didn't I?"

"You did, you did." Jordan swats Alejandro pointedly in the side until he relents, making room for her. She rearranges the coffee, one on each side of the table, and indicates for Riley to join her. "Please, sit. I'm sure this coffee isn't as good as yours, but we've got a lot of paperwork to get through, and we might as well do it with something to keep us warm."

The air-conditioning in the room is worse than the lobby. Goose bumps tremble down every inch of his exposed skin. Riley cautiously sinks onto the opposite couch. The cushions are soft like butter beneath him. "How much paperwork are we talking about?"

Jordan picks up a stack, taps it on the table for neatness, and slides it across to him. "A standard NDA, the predicted filming schedule, some insurance and liability forms, so on and so forth. Tedious but necessary, I'm afraid."

Riley thumbs through the stack. Perfect white paper, twelve-point font. His name over and over. Dominic Savio's on every other page. "Last time I broke into a haunted house, I didn't have to sign jack shit."

Across the room, Josh coughs to smother a laugh. Jordan tries and fails to sweep a pained look from her face before Riley can see it. "Yes. Well. This is what happens when you take the proper legal channels."

There's a fountain pen on table beside him. Riley eyes it and asks, "You got a ballpoint? If you want me to sign anything with that, it'll be more ink than paper."

Jordan sighs. "Of course."

Alejandro extracts one from god knows where, handing it to Riley without ever once taking his eyes from his camera lenses. Riley looks back to his paperwork. "Walk me through this."

Jordan does. She'd been right; it's as tedious and time-consuming as she'd predicted. Riley will be covered by the *Spirit Seekers'* insurance should anything go wrong. Riley is prevented from disclosing any events of the filming until the episode airs. Riley agrees to waive his rights to sue *Spirit Seekers* and any affiliated parties in the event of an incident. In the event of an incident, Riley will—

By the time he's done signing, his hand hurts and so does his head. His coffee is cold at his elbow.

Jordan piles the papers together with a bright smile. "That's about it."

"You sure you haven't got anything else you need me to sign?" Riley asks. "Maybe a life insurance policy?"

Josh, who's helping Jordan sort through the papers, grins. "Why? You think you'll need one?"

Riley doesn't answer that. The levity of the group rubs him wrong.

Last night, watching them on TV, he'd been impressed with how seriously they took it all. Dramatic but never boisterous. Whenever their flashlights flickered, or their cameras caught a spectral orb, their enthusiasm seemed genuine. When they tried to commune with any possible spirits, their invitations were respectful and eager.

It'd made Riley feel better, if only a bit. If nothing else, it seemed like they'd treat Dominic House with the seriousness it demanded. Now he's starting to second-guess himself.

Jordan sees his expression and rushes to say, "He's joking, of course. We've taken all the proper precautions. In fact, I need to walk you through the standard safety induction for filming now."

Riley doubts there's anything she could walk him through that would stand up to whatever Dominic House throws at them. Still, he says, "Sure. Knock yourself out."

It's worse than the signing. Jordan rattles through her induction at light speed. Riley yawns and sips at his cold coffee. Once she's done, she pauses for breath and asks, "Any questions?"

"Don't wander off," Riley says. "Don't go anywhere off-limits. Don't leave the property. Seems fairly straightforward."

"I'm glad," Jordan says. "But really, if you have any questions, now's the time to ask them."

Riley feels if anybody should be the one offering to answer questions, it's him. Instead, he gets to his feet, tucking Alejandro's ballpoint in his back pocket. "No, I'm fine. I guess I'll see you next week, then."

"Of course," Jordan says. "We'll pick you up from your apartment around seven, so we can get to Saint Dominic Savio's before sunset."

"Can't wait," Riley says and turns to leave.

"Here, I'll walk with you," Josh offers, palming his paperwork off to Jordan.

Riley levels him with an unimpressed look. "I know my way out of the building."

Josh flashes him a charming smile, holding the door open. "Maybe I just want to pick your brain a little. Ask what there is to do in this town."

"Nothing," Riley tells him and strides outside.

Josh hurries after him. He beats Riley to the elevator and hits the call button before putting his shoulder to the wall. "You're kind of prickly, aren't you?"

Riley offers him his sweetest smile. "You would be too in my position."

"And what position is that?" Josh asks, playing dumb.

The elevator dings. Riley pushes past Josh and inside before turning to face him. "The position of somebody who can't get ghost-obsessed idiots to leave him alone," he says and jams the close-door button.

Josh's face is briefly surprised before it breaks into a smile. As the elevator slides closed, he calls, "I'll see you next week!"

Riley ignores him. Music starts up. Something cheery and bland like a dime-store jingle. The carriage rattles to the foyer and dings once more. The doors slide open and, standing on the other side of them, is a face Riley hasn't seen in over a year.

To his credit, Colton looks as caught off guard by Riley as Riley is by him. Colton wipes the expression from his face quick though, replacing it with a cool look that doesn't suit him in the slightest. "Move. You're in the way."

Riley steps out. "It's all yours."

Colton glances to the elevator and then back to Riley. "Didn't think you'd actually show up."

He looks different. The years will do that, Riley supposes. He's over six foot now, although it's hard to tell with the way he slouches. He's dyed his hair black at some point, but Riley can see the dishwater roots peeking through.

He puts all his weight on his left leg. You'd only be able to see it if you knew to look for it. Riley does.

It's like staring at a stranger. "Yeah," Riley says. "Heard that a few times today already. Can't say I'm surprised you're here."

Colton's lip curls. "What does that mean?"

"Just that it must be hard running out of tabloids to sell the story to," Riley says. "Guess this came at a good time for you."

Colton's hands clench into fists before he makes the deliberate effort to uncurl them. "Wow. Glad to see your attitude never improved."

"My therapist says it's the PTSD," Riley says.

Colton laughs. "You don't have a therapist. You dumped her the moment the court-ordered therapy was over."

"That makes two of us," Riley says.

Around them, the world continues on, oblivious to the rising tension between them. When Riley glances over his shoulder, the receptionist is still there with her prim dress and practiced perfection.

He sees movement in the window behind her, and his heart skips a beat, but it's just a pedestrian passing by outside, eyes glued to their phone.

God, he wants to be out of here more than he's wanted anything in his life. Away from the glass and smiles and Jordan Jones and her Spirit Seekers haunting his every footstep. Riley grits his teeth and glances back to Colton. "Look," he says. "If we're going to do this, can we at least be civil? This is going to be bad enough without making it worse."

Colton's eyes flash dangerously, and his mouth snaps open on a reply that's probably as nasty as it is automatic. After a second, he closes it. His shoulders sink as the wind blows out of his sails. "You didn't have to come," he says without heat. "Vee and I would have been fine on our own."

"First of all, like hell I'd leave you alone with Vee after what you pulled," Riley says. "Secondly, I don't have to do anything."

Colton rolls his eyes but hits the button to open the elevator again. It dings cheerfully and he steps inside, his back to Riley. For a second, Riley thinks that's going to be it, but after a brief hesitation, Colton turns around. As the doors slide shut, he sticks his hand out to stop them. "Why *did* you decide to come? Can't have been for the money."

"It wasn't," Riley says.

"Then why?"

The elevator doors on either side of Colton are so shiny, Riley can see his own reflection. His face is tight with unhappiness. Nobody stares back at him but himself. It's not at all as comforting as one might think.

Riley's scars burn. He thinks of the fire, the cross, the blue eyes watching him from the shadows. He thinks of Ethan, smiling up at him as they lay sprawled on his bed in the summer heat, the gleam of the moonlight on his skin.

The last time he got to see him like that. The last time they were uncomplicatedly happy.

"None of your fucking business," Riley says and strides out of the building.

BEFORE

Colton's car was a clunky two-door junker. It looked as if it'd survived two wars through sheer grit alone, and yet another mile of road might be what unraveled it entirely. It'd been Colton's mother's before it was his. The beige seat covers clashed admirably with the band stickers freshly gleaming on the dashboard.

Standing in Ethan's driveway with a backpack each slung over their shoulders, Vee said what they were all thinking. "I know I've asked before, but are you sure that thing is even street legal?"

Colton unlocked the car manually; it was too old for automatic locks. Colton said, "You were the one who elected me driver."

Vee looked as if she were deeply regretting that decision now. Ethan, however, rounded the car to the open trunk, slinging his bag inside without a care. "It's either Colton drives or we walk," he said reasonably. "I know which I'd prefer. Do you?"

Vee bit at her lip. "Maybe I could—"

"Ask your parents? Let them know you're planning on sneaking out of town to an abandoned building with three boys and no supervision?" Ethan suggested.

"Well, that's not fair," Vee said. "Two of you are gay, and the third's Colton."

"Hey!" Colton protested from the driver's side. "I'm standing right here!"

Riley rallied. "Ethan's right. It's this wreck or nothing." He dropped his bag in the trunk and came to a stop beside Colton, realizing he didn't know his next step. Up close, the situation was even more worrisome. He realized they'd never all had to cram in here at once before. "Are we all going to fit?"

"That was a short-lived bout of optimism," Colton said wryly. "And sure we will. Here, hold this." He thrust his bag into Riley's stomach, nearly winding him, and leaned into the car. His skinny fingers wrapped around the driver's headrest, and he wrenched the whole seat forward with an earsplitting shriek. "Voilà!"

Riley eyed the exposed space with some concern. "Aren't you meant to use a lever to do that? A button? Something? Doesn't seem very safe."

Colton sighed and snatched his bag back. "Get in the car, Riley."

Riley did, with all the grace of a newborn foal. An empty can of energy drink crunched beneath his foot. It stank of cigarettes in the back despite the fact that Riley knew Colton's mother didn't smoke and Colton swore up and down he didn't either. "Jesus, Colton. Clean your fucking car sometime. I signed on for a haunted house tour, not to go dumpster diving."

"If you don't stop your griping, I'm going to leave you on the road," Colton said as Ethan wormed his way in. The moment they were both settled, Colton yanked his seat back, locking them into place.

There was no legroom. It was worse than flying economy on a full flight.

Riley had never been claustrophobic before. He felt it now.

Ethan nudged his shoulder, brow raised. "Are you okay?"

"Fine," Riley replied, even though he wasn't so certain it was true.

Ethan frowned, but before he could say anything more, the other two slid into the car. Their doors slammed shut with twin thumps.

"So," Vee said, holding her phone aloft, "I know you don't usually let me touch the stereo, but I made a playlist for this trip. I found some interesting podcasts about the history of horror, haunted buildings, stuff like that. I thought it would get us in the mood."

Colton twisted the key in the ignition and the car grumbled to life. "Sorry to break it to you, but my baby doesn't have a CD player, let alone an aux jack."

Vee looked fit to tear her hair out. "What *does* this car have?"

Colton smiled sweetly. "A radio," he said and flicked it on.

They pulled out of Ethan's driveway with the Top 40 blaring from the speakers, four kids crammed like sardines in a car easily ten years their senior, on their way to ghost-hunt an hour out from any true civilization. Their parents didn't know where they were going, and even if they had, half of them wouldn't care.

Anything could happen.

That's the point, Riley reminded himself sternly. Anything could happen, and if it did, he'd get it on camera.

Colton took the turnoff to the highway. "Y'all ready?"

"Baby, I was born ready," Vee said, turning up the music. "Let's go, Ghost Hawks!"

In unison, they all screamed, "Let's go, Ghost Hawks!"

The sick feeling of dread in Riley's gut dissipated. In its place was something warmer, something settled.

Anything could happen. And when it did, Riley would be ready.

FOUR

The day the Spirit Seekers are due to set out is hot as hell.

Riley stands on the sidewalk outside his apartment, baking beneath the sun. They've got only an hour or two of daylight left, and the last of it is punishing him brutally while Jordan takes her sweet time. His watch tells him Jordan and her crew are approximately fifteen minutes late. His phone tells him it's closer to twenty.

If it weren't for the confirmation text he'd received only this morning, Riley would think he'd gotten the day wrong.

To be sure, he checks his phone again. The time remains unchanged. For once in his life, Riley isn't the issue in this equation.

As far as omens go, this one is hardly auspicious.

He'd told his mother he was spending the night at Vee's. She'd been so delighted at the prospect of him out socializing, even if it was with the same friend he'd had for most of his teens, she hadn't even questioned him. If she woke up for work to find him standing outside on the sidewalk like his prom date stood him up, Riley's willing to bet those questions would appear real quick.

He's just debating heading back inside when he hears the crunch of tires approaching. A van pulls past the no parking sign, sleek and white. Expensive. He can tell just by looking at it. It rolls to a stop right in front of him, and the door slides smoothly back to reveal Jordan's smiling face. Today she's wearing a leather jacket that is far too hot for the heat. It matches the blood red of her lips.

"Riley!" she says. She'd been quick to do away with "Mr. Fox" as soon as Riley's name was on the dotted line of her contract. "So good to see you!"

"You could have seen me a whole half hour earlier if you'd been on time," Riley says.

"Well, we're here now, and that's what's important," she says, leaning out of the way so Riley can duck his head and clamber inside. "Where's your bag?"

"No bag, just me." The van is spacious, with two bench seats facing one another. Most of the gear is piled in the back, but a lone handheld camera, as shiny and expensive as the car, sits beside Jordan. Other than Jordan and Josh behind the wheel, the car is deserted.

"Where're everybody else?" Riley asks

"We dropped Alejandro, Evelyn, and Colton at the house first," Jordan says. "We needed to get a head start on filming some day-of B-roll if we want to have any half-decent shots by the time night hits." Something must show on Riley's face, because Jordan asks, "Is there a problem?"

Maybe. Yes. Riley had thought Vee would be here for this part. He hadn't thought he'd be returning to Dominic House *alone*.

"No," Riley says. He slides the door closed. "It's fine. Let's get going."

Jordan grins. "That's the spirit!" She turns, rapping Josh on the shoulder. "You heard the man, let's get moving."

Josh, who'd been in the middle of lighting a cigarette Riley isn't entirely sure he's allowed to smoke in the car, sighs. The cigarette goes back behind his ear, and he shifts gears. "All right, all right. Don't rush me, woman."

Jordan says something back, bickering easily, but Riley isn't paying attention. He's watching his apartment block shrink out the windshield, vanishing down the street.

"Hey," Jordan says, snagging his attention. "Seriously, are you okay over there?"

Riley folds his arms across his chest, sinking into his seat. "Peachy."

"Good," Jordan says. She snaps open her video camera. "Then you won't mind if we get started, will you?"

Riley stares at the blinking red light, unimpressed. "You don't waste any time."

She smiles. "When you run on a skeleton crew, you learn to take your chances when they come. Now, how are you feeling about tonight?"

The recording light flashes at him over and over. Riley can't look away. "What do you want me to say?"

"Just be honest. Don't worry about the camera. Pretend it's not here."

Easier said than done. "I don't feel anything about tonight."

Jordan looks put out for a moment, but she rallies. "Are you nervous? You haven't been back since your dramatic rescue. Surely there are a lot of conflicting feelings."

There are. Riley says, "It's been two years, not twenty."

Jordan is undeterred by his reticence. "Have you ever thought of going back?"

All the time. Some days it's the only thing he thinks of. He's not certain all of him ever left. "No."

In the driver's seat, Josh laughs, but when Jordan shoots him a glare, he turns it into a badly disguised cough. To Riley, Jordan says, "You do realize you signed a contract to be involved in the filming of this, yes?"

"I signed a contract to be filmed," Riley says. "I didn't sign a contract to make it easy for you."

This time, Josh's laugh can't be quashed by Jordan's look. "Kid has some serious gonads."

"Don't *encourage* him," Jordan snaps.

Riley looks out the window. He lives on the far side of town, so they're still a good hour out, maybe more. The idea of being stuck in this van with Jordan and her camera the whole time makes him want to open the door and throw himself to the road.

Back in the day when he had his camera glued to his hand, was he this bad? Would he have been eventually, given the chance?

"Fine," Jordan says. The blinking red of her camera vanishes. "I can see that we'll need to take it slow with you. We can do that."

"Thanks," Riley says dryly. "Your consideration warms my heart."

Jordan sets the camera back on the seat, swinging one leg over the other and nearly catching Riley with the sharp heels of her boots. "What about off record?"

Riley frowns at her. "Off record?"

She has an elbow to the window, leaning against her knuckles as she considers him. "A little chat. No cameras, no notes. Just the three of us killing time."

"No offense," Riley says, slowly, "but you must think I'm a total fucking idiot. Is anything ever off record with you?"

She smiles, pleased. "Usually, no. But when I say it, I mean it. Nothing we say here will be put on camera. I promise."

Riley considers that. "And what exactly do you want to talk about it?"

"I think you know."

"The same thing everybody wants to talk about," Riley says. "Color me shocked."

"Let's not pretend I'm just anybody else." Jordan raised a brow at him. "Don't you think if anybody out there could understand what happened to you, it'd be me?"

Riley can't help but laugh. "Wow, I've never heard that line before. Do you know how many ghost chasers and wannabe psychics have reached out to me over the past two years? You want to impress me, do better than that."

"Okay," Jordan course corrects without missing a beat. "Let me try again. The truth is, I *don't* believe you—I don't believe any of you."

Riley blinks. "What?"

"I don't believe that Dominic House is haunted. I don't believe you survived *ghosts*. I don't believe in ghosts *at all*."

Riley stares at her, speechless. In the front, Josh startles, twisting in his seat. "Jordan, what the *fuck* are you—?"

"Eyes on the road, Josh. Besides, I don't think Mr. Fox is going to be the one who breaks the news that Jordan Jones is a nonbeliever."

Riley can barely comprehend what he's hearing. "You don't believe in ghosts?"

"No. I don't believe in ghosts, spirits, zombies, heaven, hell, or limbo either. I don't believe there's an afterlife." She smiles. "I believe when we die, we stay that way. For good."

"Christ," Josh murmurs and reaches for his cigarette once more.

"You're the host of the most popular ghost-hunting show in America," Riley points out.

"I know," Jordan says, and the red of her mouth splits into the most honest grin Riley's seen from her yet. "Isn't it hilarious?"

Smoke curls from the front seat as Josh winds a window down. "Don't listen to her, kid. She's just trying to get a rise out of you."

"She's lying?"

"No." Josh sighs, flicking ash to the road. "She really doesn't believe in any of this shit. That's true, unfortunately."

Jordan ignores him. "Are you satisfied now?" she says to Riley. "A bit of equivalent honesty."

Riley eyes her. "What do you want to ask in exchange?"

"I'll settle for an answer to the same question," she says. "Tell me, Riley Fox: Do *you* believe in ghosts?"

The memory of a hand on his face, inhumanly sharp and twice as cruel. From the front seat, Josh's smoke smells like a bonfire, and Riley feels the invisible heat of it on his skin.

Riley looks back out the window. "I don't know."

"That doesn't sound very honest."

Riley doesn't have to tell her anything. He gave up on telling people the truth a long time ago now. It never helps; it just hurts.

"I don't know," he says again. Then, "I don't *want* to."

Jordan smiles, satisfied. "There we go. Was that so hard?"

Riley looks away. "I'm done with this chat now," he says.

"That's fine," Jordan says, relaxing into her seat. "We have all night, Riley. We have all night."

✗ ✗ ✗

Dominic House rolls into sight just as the sun is beginning to sink at the horizon.

It sits like a fat, ungainly lord atop its hill, bloated with too many peaks, windows, walls. The path that wends its way through the forest to its gates is overgrown, and the van bounces every inch of the way up, unwelcome and aware of it.

Once, it'd been a pretty thing, back when it was first built close to 150 years ago as the summer home of a wealthy family. But the building had never stopped, and each time it changed hands, new additions sprung up like summer daisies. Finally, it'd landed in the hands of a well-intentioned patron who generously donated its use to the state for a higher purpose.

It'd served its time as a community center for the nearest town about a half hour away, and its chapel had been erected in the courtyard, surrounded by watchful statues of long-dead saints. At last, in the 1980s, its ultimate purpose was realized. Officially, it was christened Saint Dominic Savio's School for Troubled Youths, but the locals who sent their wayward children into its care had another name for it.

"There she is," Jordan says indulgently. "Dominic House in all its beauty."

The van rocks to a stop just inside the rusted iron gates, monolithic in their own way. Riley leans forward, clutching the back of Josh's seat, unable to keep himself from staring.

The police tape from the photos is gone, but he can see the fraying remains of it stuck in the gate's hinges. The fountain in the wretched yard leading to the front door is dry as a bone, thick with weeds and other ancient debris.

Riley can't see the chapel from here, but he feels it watching him all the same, hiding in the shadow of the house like a wraith.

It's not the only one watching him. He feels Josh's eyes on the side of his face.

"What's it like?" Josh asks.

"What's what like?" Riley says, as if he can't guess exactly what he means.

"Returning after all this time."

Riley sits back. "Like a nightmare."

Jordan is outside, pulling bags from the back to sling over her shoulder. "Most of the big stuff is inside already," she says, catching Riley looking. "Hopefully, if your friends haven't distracted him, Alejandro should have finished double-checking the setup and filming some B-roll by now."

Riley takes one of the bags off her hands. "Let's go find out."

Josh stays behind, checking on the chunky battery-powered LED lights outside. Jordan leads the way to the front door, her heels clapping heavily over the flagstones circling the fountain and arrowing to the building. Riley follows, pretending like he's not feeling every inch of the vanishing distance between himself and the house.

Jordan fumbles in one of the bags for a moment before coming up with an old-fashioned set of keys. Wrought iron, to match the lock. Riley eyes them. "They really gave you the keys?"

"How else were we going to get in?" The lock squeals as it turns. She casts him a sidelong look. "What did you do? Climb through a broken window like animals?"

Riley turns away from her. "Kicked in the back door, actually."

Jordan laughs. "They warned me the back door was broken. I didn't think that was *you*."

"Are we going in or not?" Riley asks.

Jordan smiles, setting a hand on the rotting door and giving it a gentle push. It yawns open, baring the guts of the house with reluctance. Jordan steps over the threshold. "So long as you're ready."

Riley's opening his mouth to reply when something darts by in the corner of his eye. He lurches backward, but Jordan's not quick enough; it squirms over her feet in a writing mess of fur. "What the *fuck* was that?!"

Riley's not listening. He's crouched down, hand extended. "Hey, hey," he says quietly. "You're all right."

The most disgusting cat he's ever seen meows at him.

"Oh my god," Jordan says. "Don't touch it. It looks diseased."

It does. It also looks more afraid of Riley than he could ever be of it. "It's not going to scratch me."

The cat eyes him distrustfully, slinking back toward the flower beds. Riley doesn't follow it, and after a second, it leaps away. Out-of-season poppies line the walls of the house beneath the filthy windows, bloodred and vibrant, and the cat vanishes into the wild bushes they spring from with a rustle.

Jordan presses a hand to her chest, staring after it. "I can't believe I didn't get that on film."

Riley gets to his feet. "It was just a cat," he says. "Not exactly spook material."

"Tell that to my heart," Jordan mutters, but she's stepping through the threshold and Riley has no choice but to follow.

The entrance is a barren room, bracketed on either side by stretching hallways and headlined by the massive staircase that climbs to the second floor. Beneath the staircase is a solitary door. The carpet is filthy, and it shows recent footsteps cutting through the dust clear as day.

Despite clearly having been here earlier, Jordan looks around curiously. "The entrance doesn't really live up to the scale of the exterior, does it?"

There's a bloodstain on the ripped wallpaper right next to where Riley is standing. If he looks closely, he can see the shape of a hand. He can't remember who it belongs to, but something tells him if he set his palm to it, he'd find out quick. He looks away. "Where are the others?"

Jordan steps forward and opens the door beneath the stairs, revealing an auditorium that has all the grandeur Jordan had been denied in the hallway.

There's no carpet here; the naked floorboards are shiny even beneath the dirt. Despite its intended purpose, there are no built-in seats. It'd been a gymnasium once, after all, before Dominic House decided otherwise. Instead, folding chairs from half a century ago lean against the far wall, waiting for assembly to be called.

The ceiling soars, and windows line the walls, letting in the last of the fading sunlight. A single door punctures the wall of windows, leading to the grounds beyond. Through the murky glass, Riley can see the hint of another building.

The chapel's bricks are blackened and crowded with ivy, and the dirt path leading to its doors is thick with weeds. Statues stand guard in the courtyard around it, their faces crumbling into anonymity after decades of duty.

Compared to Dominic House itself, the chapel ought to be underwhelming. An afterthought crammed into the back-yard. It's half the height, and a fraction of the size. If it weren't for the cross upon the steeple jutting into the sky, it'd be over-shadowed entirely.

Riley's body doesn't care about any of that. Every inch of him goes tight at the sight. Sense memory runs riot through him. He smells smoke, and he knows he's a moment away from the shakes taking his hands.

Two years. Two years and here he is, struck to stone by fear, just like the ruined statues outside.

"Riley!"

Riley startles at his name, turning to see Vee sprinting toward him. Behind her, Alejandro is setting up a tripod, LEDs cutting through the gloom and a collection of chairs somebody has rescued from the side of the room dotted about. Riley has barely a moment to register this before Vee collides with him, spinning them both in a circle.

"Fuck, Vee," he wheezes, giving a brief squeeze before easing her back. "Do you think you can give me five minutes before you break one of my ribs?"

She grins, unrepentant. Her short dark hair is slicked out of her face, and her girlish outfit looks better suited to a relaxing evening stroll than ghost-hunting. "Sorry," she says. "It's just been too long since I saw you last."

Jordan demands, "Did you get that on camera?"

Alejandro hoists a camera he'd been setting on a tripod. "Who do you think you're talking to? Of course I did."

Reality reasserts itself. Riley wipes the smile off his face. Behind Alejandro's shoulder, a rumpled figure lurks near the gear, shoulders hunched, hands tucked in their pockets. Riley says, "Colton."

Colton doesn't even glance at him. He unearths a pack of cigarettes from his pockets, and shakes a lighter free. "Riley."

He looks even worse than last week. His pale face is narrow, cheekbones sharp ridges beneath his gray eyes. His hair hangs in a greasy curtain over his face, and when he blows out a mouthful of smoke, it covers him like a shroud.

Whatever he may think about returning here, the time he had to dwell on it hasn't done him any favors.

Riley can relate. His hands aren't shaking, but it's close. He's so incredibly conscious of the chapel only a single wall away.

Again, Jordan hisses, "You're still filming, yes?" and Alejandro taps pointedly at the mounted camera between them.

Colton rolls his eyes, turning his back to it. "Now that the final musketeer has deigned to show up, can we get this show on the road?"

Riley ignores him. "This is home base, then?"

"It has to be, unfortunately," Jordan says. "I wanted to set up in the chapel, but insurance wouldn't sign off on it. Apparently, it's too big of a safety hazard. They don't want to take a risk on fire damage."

Relief makes Riley's knees weak. He does not glance out the windows. "Yeah. Unfortunate."

"All right," Jordan says, glancing at her watch. "We're hoping to get some interviews in with all of you first. After that—well. I guess you'll find out when we get there. Everybody okay with that?"

Colton shrugs, tapping ash onto the floor. Riley doesn't answer. He has a sneaking suspicion he knows what comes after their interviews. He's seen enough of *Spirit Seekers* by now to know how Jordan likes to start off her shoots by interviewing more than just her crew.

Vee says, "You're the one calling the shots. Just let us know what to do."

"Excellent," Jordan says. She snaps her fingers and points to one of the folding chairs. "You'll be first, then."

Vee rolls her eyes when Jordan turns her back. She turns to Riley, hand still on his arm, and asks, "Are you doing okay?"

"Sure," Riley says.

"No, not 'sure.' Give me something more than that."

Riley glances past her. Jordan and Alejandro are arguing about where to set the chair to get the best light. Colton watches them silently, already onto his second cigarette.

Riley says, "I don't know. I just got here. None of this feels real yet, I guess."

Vee's mouth pinches. "I know what you mean. I've been here over an hour, and I'm still waiting for it to click. It doesn't feel . . ."

"It doesn't feel like last time," Riley agrees.

Vee's shoulders droop in relief. "Yeah, exactly. I don't know. I thought it would."

Nothing has gone wrong so far. Everybody's accounted for; nobody's hurt. When Riley checks his phone, he's getting a full three bars of signal.

Dominic House shows no signs of being anything other than an extraordinarily creepy house. Riley knows better than to be fooled by that again. After all, it's still early.

"Well, wait until the sun goes down and Jordan has us walking around trying to talk to ghosts, then we'll see," he says.

"Evelyn!" Jordan hollers.

Vee sighs. She looks him up and down. "Don't go far, okay?"

"I won't," Riley lies.

"Evelyn!"

"I'm *coming*!" Vee calls. To Riley, "Try talking to Colton. It's not as bad as I thought it would be."

Riley doesn't even bother lying in response to that. He watches as Vee crosses the room, letting Jordan direct her into the chair, fussing over Vee's perfectly crisp outfit and flawless hair.

Despite himself, Riley glances to Colton to find his sallow gaze looking back at him. Immediately, Colton glances away. He turns and limps to the wall, his back to Riley.

Colton had always excelled at the fine art of the cold shoulder. It's less amusing to watch when Riley's on the receiving end of it. He thinks about going over. He doesn't.

By the time Jordan is eagerly asking Vee her first question, Riley's already on his way out the door they just came through.

BEFORE

Forty minutes into the drive, the enthusiasm had dampened significantly.

The air-conditioning had given out six miles back, and half the radio channels followed not long after. They rattled down the road in a cramped, boiling car, the stereo warbling Bible verses at them in the voice of a Nowhere-No-Town preacher.

An hour in a car didn't feel like a long time until they were over halfway through it with no promise of relief at the end.

"Seriously," Vee said, dabbing sweat from her brow with the back of her wrist. "Why is it that music never makes it out past the edges of suburbia, but you can find a channel sermonizing in the Bermuda fucking Triangle?"

Colton drummed his fingers on the wheel. He'd been doing that off and on the whole trip. Riley would be annoyed if he had the energy for it. "You know why," Colton said. "The same reason every truck stop on the interstate is manned by a grubby white guy with a shotgun underneath the counter."

"—the Lord will guide his lost sheep," said the radio. "As a shepherd does to his flock."

"Can you turn that off?" Riley asked. He had his forehead smashed against the window, the glass a cool wash of silence against the static the heat made of his nerves. "Please?"

Colton did. The car went quiet, and Riley breathed out for what felt like the first time in hours.

There was a tap on his elbow, and when he turned, Ethan was offering him a water bottle, still sweaty from the fridge an hour ago. Riley took it gratefully. The water was a relief, and the feel of the bottle pressed against his damp cheeks was even better. "How far out are we now?"

"We should see it soon," Colton answered, and then, like a prophecy, a speck appeared on the horizon.

Ethan and Riley leaned forward, clinging to the seats in front of them as they squinted against the sun. It was impossible to make out any details from this distance, but it didn't stop Riley from trying. The building loomed over the woods surrounding it, just like he'd known it would.

Anticipation clawed at his stomach—the whole car was silent with it.

They drew closer. The speck resolved into a specter, more the memory of a structure than the reality of one.

Colton pulled them to an idle stop out front of the gates that blocked the path into the property. They were iron, rusty after so many years of neglect. Colton crossed his arms atop the steering wheel and said, "Damn. That's one mean-looking building."

It was. Riley hoped any footage they took would be meaner still.

"All right," Vee said. "Colton, go open the gates."

Colton sent her a disgruntled look. "Why do I have to do it?"

"Ethan and Riley are trapped in the back, and those gates are ten times my size," Vee said.

Colton heaved a sigh, throwing open his door as he stepped out of the car. He looked tiny approaching the gates despite nearly clearing six feet at sixteen. Riley was seized by an illogical conviction that once those gates opened, Colton would disappear behind them, leaving the rest of them behind.

He was wrong. Of course he was wrong. Colton unwound the slack chain from the latch, dragging the gates open as they squealed like slaughtered pigs.

"Christ," Vee said. "Maybe you should be filming this part, Riley."

"I would," Riley said, "but this is technically breaking and entering. Also, my camera's packed in the trunk."

"Let's save the filming for when they can't prove that we were trespassing," Ethan suggested.

Colton climbed back in the car, wiping his grimy hands on his shirt. "It's hot as hell out there. You couldn't have picked a haunted house with air-conditioning?"

"Who knows, maybe we'll get some cold spots," Ethan said. "Would that make you feel better?"

Colton grunted. "They'd have to be pretty fucking cold."

There was just enough space between the gates for them to slip through, and the dirt driveway crunched beneath the wheels as the car struggled up the last few dozen feet. They passed a retired fountain and scraggly bushes before coming to a final stop by the overrun flower beds, weeds spilling across the splintered planters.

This close, Dominic House didn't just look mean. It looked ghastly.

Vee twisted in her seat, grinning. "You ready?"

Riley glanced to Ethan who smiled back at him. "Yeah," Riley said. "I was *born* ready, baby."

Vee laughed, a bright starburst into the late-afternoon heat, in the dim shadows that fell over them like a shroud. "Project Dominic House is a go."

FIVE

In the kitchen, Riley stands behind the gaping wound where the back door once stood. In its place are a half dozen solid planks, hammered into the walls on either side, crisscrossing. Riley stares at them, hands in his pockets. After a moment, he turns, surveying the kitchen.

It's just like he remembers. Long benches run the length of the walls, and kitchenware several decades out of date has rusted brown. There's a nest in one of the ajar cabinets, and when Riley stoops to investigate, he finds a lonely dead bird rotting among the twigs. There's a stray cloth on one of the benches, and Riley flaps it out, draping it over the nest before closing the cabinet firmly.

When he stands, he's put at eyeline with the window.

Outside, there's nothing. Some trees. Flower beds rife with bramble and weeds. The glass baring it all is so smudged that everything beyond it is smeared into an indistinct sepia.

He can just barely see his reflection. The mess of his hair, his gray eyes turned to hollow hints of darkness, as if somebody has plucked them clear from his skull.

Something moves in the reflection behind him. A hand lands on his shoulder.

Riley's heart drops like lead. On instinct alone, his elbow sails backward, only to hit something distinctly human.

"It's me! It's me!" Josh yelps.

Riley lets out a breath. His heart refuses to rise from the floor even as he turns around to find Josh hunched over, an arm wrapped firmly around his middle as he wheezes. "Josh?"

"Who did you think it would be?" Josh gasps. "No, actually, don't answer that. I'm too winded to hear horror stories right now."

Riley's not in the mood to tell them. "You should have said something."

"I didn't get a chance!"

"Sorry." Riley does not feel sorry.

Josh winces, straightening up. "It's fine. Good to know you can defend yourself if you need to, at least."

The scars on Riley's face say otherwise. Ethan would have too. "What were you doing in here?"

"I'm checking on the thermal cameras we have in the main rooms," Josh says, reaching out to tap a camera positioned in a nearby corner. "They're supposed to—"

"I know what a thermal camera is," Riley interrupts.

Josh grins. "I guess you would. You used to do this yourself, yeah?"

The camera Riley had two years ago was solidly midrange. He'd saved for months to buy it. It burned with the chapel, and the police had taken what was left as evidence.

"I was sixteen," Riley says. "I couldn't afford a thermal camera."

Josh fusses with the tripod, checking something on the camera screen. "I bet you wanted one."

Riley had. Vee had promised to split the difference with him if he found one in his budget. Despite only just buying a camera the month before their original trip to Dominic House, Riley had already started researching one with thermal specs. "What are you hoping to catch on it?"

"You've seen our show," Josh says. "Sometimes we manage to get some pretty compelling stuff."

Two years ago, Riley would have agreed with him. Now the "compelling stuff" the Spirit Seekers catch reads a lot more like coincidence and good editing.

"Do you really believe a ghost is going to leave a heat signature?" Riley asks skeptically.

Josh laughs. "Why not? What do you think?"

Riley's lip curls and he glances away. "It doesn't matter what I think."

"That's where you're wrong," Josh says. "Jordan is paying a fortune specifically because it matters a *lot* what you think. You're the whole reason we're here, after all."

Riley's stomach tosses like a ship in a storm. "Thanks."

Josh looks up, catching his expression, and winces. "That's not what I meant."

"It's not like you're wrong," Riley says. "I was the one who wanted to come here. Last time, I mean. And if we hadn't, then Ethan wouldn't . . ." He can't make himself finish that sentence.

"No, hey." Josh lays a hand on Riley's arm, and Riley's taken so off guard, he lets him. "That's not what I meant." Josh contemplates something for a moment. "Look, I know asking you to come here was . . . in bad taste. Fuck, this whole episode is in bad taste, honestly speaking. We don't usually touch tragedies this recent. But when Jordan heard they'd labeled the case cold, and that all of you were—" He jams his mouth shut. Not quick enough. Realization sets in.

"I wondered why she'd reached out now," Riley says. "It's because we're all eighteen, isn't it?"

Josh sighs, dropping the hand from Riley's arm. "It's nothing personal, kid. It's just, things go easier when we don't have to fight for parental consent."

Riley bristles at being called "kid." "And if something happens to us now?"

"That's what we buy insurance for," Josh says. "But nothing is going to happen to you. I've done a hundred of these things by now, and nothing has *ever* happened to anybody. We're pros, okay?"

Riley had thought he was a pro too.

We were just scared fucking kids, Vee had said.

It's funny how quickly time changes the perception of everything.

"It's fine," Riley says. "Let's just get out of here."

"You can head back to the others," Josh says, twisting back to his camera setup. "I've still got to hit a few more rooms." Riley turns to go, but Josh says, "Oh, Riley?" Riley looks at him. Josh smiles wryly. "No more wandering off, yeah?"

70

"Sure," Riley lies, and Josh's laugh as he leaves the kitchen tells Riley he's fooled nobody.

✗ ✗ ✗

Back in the auditorium, Jordan seizes Riley like it's been a century instead of a half hour. "Oh thank god," she says. "We're less than an hour out from sunset. We have a schedule, Riley, and I don't want you messing with it."

Amused, Riley lets her lead him over to a folding chair. She fusses with his hair, then, giving that up for a lost cause, tries to get him to sit at an angle to show off fewer of his piercings. "It's not that they don't look good," she assures him, "but we've already played up the bad-boy angle with Colton, and we really can't have two people in the same niche, you know?"

Riley snorts, stealing a glance to the corner of the room where Colton is sprawled, back to the wall as he tosses his lighter in the air over and over, steadfastly pretending he's not paying attention to anything. Vee is sitting next to him, silent.

"Bad-boy angle?" Riley asks.

"There's not much else we could lean into when he came to set dressed like *that*," Jordan says, gesturing at Colton's ripped jeans and baggy black hoodie.

Riley eyes her. "You're not a very nice person, are you?"

"Nice people don't win Emmys," she informs him. "Here, show off your scars. It'll make you look more sympathetic."

"It won't make me look sympathetic; it'll make me look mutilated," Riley says.

"Well, there's not much we can do about them, so this is just how it's going to be."

Well. He supposes she isn't wrong.

After what feels like far too long of working out his best angles—of which he has very few, it turns out—Jordan finally retreats, joining Alejandro beside the camera. She folds her arms, looking him up and down. "Not bad. Are you ready?"

Riley's never been less ready for anything in his life. "I guess."

Jordan flashes him a smile. "All right, let's try again. How do you feel being back in Dominic House after everything that happened to you here?"

It's instinct to play the question off again, but Riley holds back. He knows by now that Jordan will have him in this chair until she gets what she wants out of him, and her questions are only going to get worse the more he pushes back. He grits his teeth. "Not great," he says.

"Is it bringing back bad memories?"

"What do you think?" Riley snaps, then takes a deep breath, forcing himself to relax. "It's not bringing back great ones."

"Anything specific?"

Riley thinks of Ethan smiling at him like the sun. He thinks of fingers at his face, fire, a cross bearing down like judgment from above. "That's private."

Jordan changes track easily. "Why did you come here two years ago?"

Riley shifts uncomfortably. "We came here to try to film a video for our YouTube channel," he says. "We'd heard it was haunted after what happened in the eighties. We thought we were— We *wanted* to be ghost hunters."

"Understandable," Jordan says, grinning. "It's a very compelling career."

Riley doesn't reply. He won't stroke her ego.

"If you came here to film a video, what went wrong?"

Riley shrugs. The camera's light is winking at him, hypnotic. He feels overexposed beneath it. His hands are shaking. There's nowhere to hide. "I don't . . . I don't know."

Jordan is like a dog with a bone now, unrelenting. "What *do* you remember about your time here? Your friends have said that they consider their recollections unreliable; do you?"

"I told you, I don't know."

"When Miss Cho called the police, they arrived to find two of you seriously wounded and a third missing. What happened?"

"You've seen the reports," Riley says. "You know what happened."

"Right," Jordan says. "Ghosts happened, didn't they?"

Riley doesn't answer.

"Isn't that what you told the responding officers? Actually, I have a quote here." She opens a file, flicking through, finger chasing down the sentences. "When one of the paramedics asked what happened to your face, you told them—"

"Stop it," Riley says.

"—'Death touched me. He wouldn't let go.'"

73

There are fingers on his face, ripping through the skin. Riley struggles not to flinch. "I was confused," he says. "I didn't know what happened."

Jordan snaps the file closed. Beside her, Alejandro looks uneasy. "Hey, Jordan, maybe you should back off a bit, yeah?"

She doesn't. "What about your friend? The one who went missing? Ethan Hale?"

"I know his fucking name," Riley snaps.

"I'm sure you do," Jordan says.

A chill goes down Riley's spine. "What's that supposed to mean?"

Jordan says, "Well, he was your boyfriend, wasn't he?"

Riley's breath catches. His blood turns to ice.

That hadn't been public information. He hadn't told her that. He knows Vee sure as hell didn't either.

The auditorium plunges into darkness.

"Hey! Hey! The fuck is going on?" Colton calls, just as Vee shouts, "What happened to the lights?"

"Shit," Alejandro hisses. There's just enough remaining light streaming through the windows for Riley to see him abandoning the camera, beelining for the perimeter of the auditorium. "The LEDs went down."

"All of them?" Jordan asks, but she doesn't sound worried; she sounds delighted.

"Yeah! Fuck! They're all brand-new, too!"

"The camera's still working though, right?" Jordan demands, fussing with it. She hoists it off the stand, turning it to face her as she says, "As you can see, we've just experienced a total blackout. Clear evidence of electromagnetic interference—"

Riley barely hears her. The darkness seems secondary. "Excuse me," he says to nobody in particular. He gets out of his chair and heads across the room.

Vee sees him coming first. "Riley, are you—?"

Riley bypasses her, seizes Colton by the front of his shirt, and punches him in the face.

Colton reels back, hand flying to his cheek. "What the *fuck* are you—?"

Riley punches him again. His knuckles split like paper. "Fuck you," he spits. "You can never keep your mouth shut, can you?"

"Riley!" Vee gets between them, shoving them apart. "Calm down! What's wrong?"

"Why don't you ask him?" Riley snarls. He can feel blood dripping down his knuckles to the floor.

Colton has one hand to the wall, the other to his face, flexing his jaw like expects it to be broken. "How the fuck am I meant to know? You just came at me like a total *psychopath*!"

"What did you say to Jordan?" Riley demands.

"What—?"

"Why does Jordan fucking Jones know that Ethan was anything more than my best friend?"

Colton blinks, taken aback. "Shit, Riley—"

"You outed me on national TV! You outed *Ethan* on TV! I always knew you were a piece of shit, but this really is a new low, even for you."

"I didn't think it mattered!" Colton protests. "It's not like you guys were secretive about it."

"Sure. With people I *know*. I don't want the choice to share it or not to be taken out of my hands. You ever think about that?"

Colton's mouth snaps shut.

"Yeah," Riley says. "That's what I *thought*."

Vee stares at him for a split second before spinning to Colton. "You *what*?"

Jordan is heading right toward them, camera glued to her hand. "What is going *on* over here?"

Riley's done talking. He turns, brushes by her, and heads for the auditorium door they'd come through. Vee calls his name but doesn't chase him. He passes Alejandro on the way out, but he takes one look at Riley's expression and lets him go.

Riley leaves, trailing blood along the floorboards the whole way.

BEFORE

The front door wouldn't open.

Riley thought they perhaps should have anticipated that. The local cemeteries they usually slunk through were locked too, but Riley and his friends had long since perfected the art of hauling ass over the fence. Dominic House wasn't like that, though. It was a mammoth of a building, fortified against vandals and vagrants. Why make things any easier for them than it had to be?

"Come *on*," Colton grunted as he slammed his shoulder into the door, willing it to pop free of its frame. "Did we really drive all the way out here for nothing?"

"We better not have," Vee said darkly, both hands on her hips as she observed his frantic efforts. "I'd rather die than climb back into that wreck you call a car."

"That can be arranged," Colton muttered under his breath. He gave the door one more definitive shove before stepping back. "The lock's not giving. I don't know what it's made of, but we don't stand a chance."

Riley stood on the porch, bag over his shoulder and a sense of growing disappointment in his gut. He hadn't even had gotten his camera out yet.

A crunching noise came from around the side of the house, and all three of them looked up to see Ethan poking his head around the clapboard siding. "There's another door back here," he said. "I think it might lead into the kitchen."

"Do you think it'll open?" Colton asked, trying and failing to be discreet as he rotated his shoulder. Riley gave him an hour, two tops, before he started moaning about it.

"Only one way to find out," Ethan said cheerfully and vanished back out of sight, leaving them scrambling after him.

Ethan's door was half the size of the one at the front, a sad thing made of flaking paint and peeling wood. A window stretched the length of the wall next to it, and when Riley peered through, he could faintly see a countertop, linoleum floor, pots and pans. What looked like a dead rat, maybe two.

Colton tried the handle. "It's locked. Stand back; I've got this."

Vee and Riley exchanged a skeptical glance, but they all obediently shuffled out of the way. Colton reared back before lashing out with a kick that would not have looked out of place from a donkey. The door groaned but did not budge, and Colton staggered madly before managing to right himself.

Vee clapped slowly. "Congratulations. You've saved us all. What *would* we do without you?"

"If you're just going to be negative, maybe you should go sit in the car," Colton said primly.

"Sitting in your car is excessive punishment for the crime of stating the obvious."

Ethan stepped between them, hands up to still their familiar bickering. "Here, let me have a go."

"If I couldn't get it, I don't see the point in you trying," Colton said.

Ethan smiled warmly. "What can it hurt?"

Colton considered that and sighed, stepping aside as he waved his arm in a grand gesture. "All right, go ahead. Your funeral."

"You're too kind," Ethan said dryly. He stepped forward, bracing himself with one hand on either side of the doorway, and pulled his foot back. When he kicked, it was with the full force of many long nights of football practice and endless sprints.

The door had no hope. It bounced out of its frame and ricocheted off the inside wall. By the time it swayed back to them, there was a splintered hole in the middle, right where Ethan's sneaker had punched through.

Colton took one look at it and announced, "I weakened it for you."

Ethan laughed. "I know, I know. Thanks for your help, Col."

"Don't call me that," Colton grumbled, shrugging past Ethan and inside, but it was good-natured. Vee followed after, teasing Colton mercilessly as she went. Riley moved to follow, but he'd barely begun to trail after his friends when he saw something moving in the window in front of him.

The pane was so filthy, it was nearly impossible to tell, but the longer Riley looked, the more it seemed as if there was something looming in the glass.

Unnerved, he glanced over his shoulder, but there was nothing there—just Ethan, who was looking at him with a concerned frown. "Riley?"

Riley glanced back at the window. Whatever he was seeing, it was gone now. "Shit," he said. "I think some of those rats might not be as dead as we thought."

Ethan pulled a face. "Well," he said, gesturing toward the doorway, "after you."

"A gentleman," Riley said, and Ethan laughed again. Riley stepped forward, linking their arms. "C'mon. Together, asshole."

The smile Ethan blessed him with made Riley warm all over. "Together," Ethan agreed, and as one, they stepped into Dominic House's welcoming embrace.

SIX

There is nowhere in Dominic House that feels safe, so Riley retreats outside.

The edge of the fountain is dusty and crumbles when he sits on it, but he's too mad to care whether it gives out beneath him. His knuckles are stinging like a bitch. Gingerly, he unfolds his fingers, testing the stiffness of them.

Nothing feels broken, but they're going to bruise. One of his rings had split his skin, but he's stopped bleeding now, at least. Riley never could throw a decent punch.

Once, Ethan tried to teach him.

"You should know this," he'd said, gently folding Riley's fingers into a fist.

"Why?" Riley had teased. "You need me to protect you? I thought you were the big, bad football player?"

He hadn't taken the bait. He never did when Riley teased him like that. Patient to a fault. "Just in case. I want you to be able to protect yourself."

"Isn't that what you're here for?" Riley asked.

"I hope so," Ethan said. He closed his hand over Riley's fist. Gentle. Warm. "I really, really hope so."

Heels clack against the stone of the courtyard, and Riley stiffens, hiding his bruised, bloodied hand out of sight. Somebody settles next to him and he turns, expecting Vee. It's not.

"You know," Jordan says, "we need to talk about your tendency to wander off."

Riley scowls. "Where's your camera?"

Jordan holds up her hands. "It's just you and me."

Riley rolls his eyes, glancing away. "Sure."

Silence lingers for a long moment before Jordan speaks again. "I spoke to Evelyn. She told me what happened."

"Great," Riley asks. "Let me guess. You want me to re-create it so you can get it on film this time?"

"Actually," Jordan says, "I wanted to tell you I was sorry. I didn't realize that your relationship with Ethan was a secret."

Riley's shoulders draw tight. "It's nobody's fucking business."

"Not if you don't want it to be," Jordan agrees, catching him off guard. "What I asked you, and what Colton shared— all of it will be cut. I promise you."

Riley stares at her. "I don't know if I can trust that."

"That's fair," Jordan says. "If you want, I can have our legal team draft up a contract for it, if it'll give you peace of mind."

Riley tries to find the lie in her expression, but she meets his gaze unwaveringly. "Why?"

"Because it's the decent thing to do," she says. "You said I wasn't a nice person, and you're right. But I'm not a monster,

Riley. I'm not looking to out anybody here; I just want to hunt some damn ghosts."

"Ghosts you don't even believe in," Riley points out.

Jordan laughs, leaning back, hands propping her upright. It's dark now, well and truly, and the LED pointed at the porch outlines her in gold. "What's that term for when you don't believe in God, but you don't *not* believe in him?"

Riley raises a brow. "Agnostic?"

Jordan snaps her fingers. "That's it. How's this: I'm agnostic toward ghosts. I don't believe in them, but I'd like to. I just need something a little more sustainable than wishful thinking."

"Why do you care so much?" Riley asks. "What does it matter to you if they're real or not? You dedicated your life to chasing something you're not even certain exists."

"Maybe it's the money," Jordan says. "You have to know our viewership is staggering. We've trended on Netflix every day since they signed us."

"You weren't always signed to Netflix," Riley says. "I saw your old website you used to stream through. You didn't even have ad space. You can't have made anything off that."

Jordan's brows climb. "I didn't know you did so much sleuthing," she says. "Maybe I should be the one asking *you* why you care so much."

Riley stares her down. Jordan smiles at him. A genuine one that creases the corners of her eyes and smooths the steel from her expression. "You'd make a good reporter or something. Maybe a ghost hunter again, if you ever feel like returning to your roots."

"I'll pass," Riley says. "Are you going to answer me?"

"I'm afraid you won't be impressed by it," Jordan informs him. "It's not all that interesting. No tragic backstory. No missing boyfriend. Very, very boring."

"I love boring," Riley says.

Jordan looks him up and down. "Not sure I believe that," she says. "But if you must know, I graduated valedictorian. Went to college on a full ride, majored in mathematics, although my mom used to say I should have majored in law or journalism because I loved asking questions so goddamn much."

"You majored in math?" Riley asks, surprised. "That's not on your Wikipedia page."

"Well, I don't tell most people," Jordan says cheerfully. "It doesn't really fit my persona, does it? Consider that another piece of equivalent honesty." She crosses her ankles, the heels of her boots just tall enough to straddle the border of impractical for such an excursion. "My mom was right though. I did like asking questions; that's what drew me to math to begin with. I like *knowing* things. I don't like uncertainty. If there's something out there to discover, to know, I want to be the one to know it."

Riley has an inkling he knows where this is going. "And death is the great unknown."

Jordan snaps her fingers at him. "Exactly," she says. "You get it. So I could be stuck in a boring office my whole life, discovering new things like that, or I could tackle the greatest mystery of humankind and look damn good doing it."

Despite himself, Jordan's enthusiasm pulls a wan smile from Riley. "You got into ghost hunting because math was too boring for you and you like to show off," he observes. "Wow. I don't even know what to say to that."

Jordan looks unperturbed. "I told you it was boring, didn't I?"

"Boring" isn't how Riley would describe it. "Wild," maybe. The more he thinks on it, the more it fits. Jordan's interesting dichotomy of showmanship and professionalism. Most people would be satisfied with dedicating themselves to one or the other, but he doesn't need to know Jordan too well to know she's an overachiever.

Riley thinks that over for a moment. "What would be enough to win you over?"

"Why?" Jordan asks. "You got something up your sleeve?"

Riley doesn't answer.

She looks away. For a moment, he thinks she's ignoring his question, but she's staring into the night, thoughtful. "I don't know. I feel like today there's so much we can explain. The LEDs going out inside? That's something, but it's also not enough, you know? Batteries go out, electronics malfunction, things break. It's fun in the moment, but now that I'm sitting out here, I can think of a half dozen things that could have made it happen."

"Doesn't sound like you're very open to believing," Riley says.

Jordan snorts. "Okay, why don't you tell me what you think happened inside?"

Riley glances away. "I don't know. I wasn't paying much attention at the time."

"Yeah." She glances over her shoulder back to Dominic House and adds, "Between your spat with Colton and the lights going out, Evelyn seems pretty shaken up, if you want to talk to her."

"Did you shove a camera in her face right after it happened?" Riley asks.

Jordan gets to her feet, dusting her hands off on her jeans. "We talked, yes. If we want to stay on schedule, I'd like you to come back in soon so you have half an hour to calm down and get back on your best behavior."

"If you think I've ever offered you my best behavior, you're mistaken," Riley informs her, and Jordan shakes her head, but she's smiling. She vanishes inside, leaving Riley alone but for the poppies warming the beds around him.

When Riley returns to the auditorium, Josh has beaten him there.

He's standing with Alejandro, both of them fussing over the LEDs. Josh looks up when Riley approaches, offering him a grin. "Heard I missed a lot of excitement in here."

"If you can call some lights going out exciting," Riley says.

"When you're hunting ghosts, you can call *anything* exciting," Josh says. "But that isn't all I meant." He casts a meaningful look to Riley's raw hand.

Riley tucks it into his pocket. "Any clues what happened with the lights?"

They're out still, and Alejandro pops up, looking frazzled. "At this point, I'm *hoping* it's electromagnetic interference, because if it's not I'm going to have to take these back to Home Depot tomorrow."

"Of course it's electromagnetic interference," Josh argues, slapping one of the LEDs. It wobbles, and only Alejandro's grip keeps it from falling. "What else could it have been?"

Alejandro throws up his hands, ducking out of sight again. "Another nonbeliever?" Riley asks.

"Nah," Josh says. "He's just worried about his precious electronics."

"*You* tell Finance that we need a whole new set of LEDs and see how they take it," Alejandro snaps.

Riley leaves them be, heading to where Vee is pacing back and forth, her arms wrapped tightly about her midriff.

Catching sight of him, she lets out a deep breath. "There you are," she says. "I was beginning to worry."

"Where did you think I went?" Riley asks, curious.

Vee's eyebrows knit together. "I didn't know. That was what worried me."

Riley sets his hands on her shoulders and steers her to a corner. "Hey," he says, voice low. "You're fine, okay? I'm fine. Everything's fine."

Vee's brow wrinkles. "That didn't feel fine, Riley."

"I'm not sorry for punching Colton."

"I'm not worried about fucking Colton," Vee says, exasperated. "As far as I'm concerned, he more than had it coming. I meant the lights."

"Lights go out," Riley says, parroting Jordan. "Anything could have happened."

Vee looks at him. "Is that what you believe? That 'anything' happened?"

Her dark eyes are wide, staring him down seriously. Riley swallows. "Yes," he says.

Vee sighs, reaching up to set a hand to his cheek. "Riley, my dearest, dearest friend," she says. "You can't lie for shit."

Riley can't afford to think about the lights as anything other than a terrible coincidence. If he does, any courage he might have managed to scrape together is going to give out quick.

Searching for a distraction, Riley asks, "Where *is* Colton?"

Vee casts him a look that says she knows precisely what he's doing. "Jordan took him away to get cleaned up. You split his lip open."

"Good."

A smile pulls at the corner of Vee's mouth. "Hey," she says. "Are *you* okay?"

"Not really," Riley says. "But I don't want to talk about it."

She pats his arm. "What do you think Jordan's got planned for us next?" she asks, and Riley gratefully allows himself to be distracted.

It takes about another twenty minutes, but eventually Jordan and Colton return. Riley glances up as they patter back into the auditorium, and satisfaction blooms darkly in his chest when he sees the swelling of Colton's bottom lip.

"All right," Jordan says, hands on her hips as she surveys the room. "How are the cameras?"

"Still fine," Alejandro says. "Haven't had anything else break since the lights."

"How long until you can fix them?" she asks.

Alejandro opens his mouth to reply, but before he can, the lights snap back on, chasing away the gloom and bathing the auditorium in artificial brightness once more.

"That was quick," Jordan remarks, surprised. "Well done, Alejandro."

Alejandro frowns. "That wasn't me, boss. I checked them all a dozen times—I couldn't find anything wrong."

Beside Riley, Vee grasps at his sleeve, drawing him closer. Until this moment, Riley hadn't realized the return of light could be more frightening than the absence of it.

Jordan beams, her expression rivaling the LEDs. "The cameras are still rolling, yes?"

"You know they always are."

Jordan turns to Vee and Riley. "Normally this is the part where we'd head to the creepiest part of the building, but considering the chapel is out of bounds for safety reasons, we're going to the dining room instead."

Riley can't help but glance over his shoulder, out the window. Now that the sun's set, he can't see anything, but he feels the chapel's presence like eyes on his back.

"Is the dining room particularly creepy, in your opinion?" Vee asks.

"Not really," Jordan admits. "But it'll be easiest for what we do next."

She clearly expects them to ask. Riley doesn't need to.

He knows where this is going. Still, he says, "And what are we doing next?"

Jordan's grin grows. "My favorite part."

Vee says, "And what part would that be?"

"The part," Jordan says, "where we have a séance."

BEFORE

In the late-afternoon light, Dominic House seemed almost fake.

The floorboards creaked as they walked the halls, and cobwebs draped from the ceiling, curtaining every doorway. There was a chandelier full of broken bulbs hanging by the stairs, and half the doors sagged in their frames, yawning open to abandoned rooms full of abandoned things.

It was like walking through a haunted house attraction. Riley half expected a zombie to jump out from around a corner, machete in hand.

"Wow," Vee said. "Kind of a dump, isn't it?"

It was, and Riley's new camera was picking it up in high definition. In the daylight, it was just bright enough that they didn't need flashlights, but already the picture on the screen was darker than he'd like. Come night, he'd be grateful for the night-vision mode that was half the reason he'd bought this camera to begin with.

"Nobody's been here in decades," Ethan said. "What were you expecting?"

"I don't know. I feel like nowhere else we've gone has been this much of a wreck."

"Everywhere else we've gone has been abandoned for like, ten years at most," Colton remarked, neatly sidestepping a lump in the carpet. "And within city limits."

"Yeah, well." Vee sighed. Turning to Riley, she asked, "What do you think?"

"I think we should find somewhere to ditch our stuff so I can film you walking through before we lose light," Riley said.

"Yeah, let's establish home base," Colton agreed. "Any suggestions? The auditorium, maybe?"

Vee made a thoughtful noise, looking over her shoulder, down the hall to the door that led to it. "Yeah, I guess that would work."

"Or," Riley said, "we could use the chapel?"

They hadn't gone inside yet, but he could feel the presence of it looming over the building, a palpable fifth person in their space. He couldn't wait to see what was inside, to crack open the doors and film the messy guts of the place, the beating heart of the abandoned school.

Vee's face brightened and she clapped her hands together. "The chapel! You're a genius, Riley. What do you guys think?"

"Works for me," Colton said. "I love to desecrate holy ground."

Vee turned to Ethan. "Ethan?"

Ethan's face was pinched. "I don't know."

Riley was taken aback. Lowering his camera, he said, "What, why?"

They couldn't see the chapel from there, but Ethan glanced in its direction anyway, drawn toward it like a magnet. "I don't know," he said again. "It just gives me a bad feeling, you know?"

"That's the point," Vee said. "That's what haunted houses are meant to do."

Riley had never seen Ethan so torn. A people pleaser by nature, Ethan sometimes struggled to stand his ground, especially with his friends. Sometimes he worried that Ethan viewed his addition to their group as too tentative to even attempt disagreement.

It made Riley's stomach turn. *You don't have to go along with everything I say*, he'd said only last night.

"It's fine," Riley said. "Let's just stay in the auditorium."

Colton frowned. "You were the one who was all gung ho about this place," he said. "Now you don't even wanna take advantage of the spookiest part?"

That seemed to do it. The creases in Ethan's face smoothed out in a hurry. "Yeah. Sorry. You're right."

Riley didn't feel nearly so convinced. "We don't have to—"

"No, Colton's right," Ethan said. He offered Riley a smile that was only slightly strained. "Let's go set up in the chapel. I know how much you were looking forward to it."

Riley had been, but he sort of hoped it went without saying that the comfort of his boyfriend came first. Still, Vee was already turning back the way they'd come, Colton on her heels, and Riley lost his moment to protest.

When Ethan went to move past him, Riley seized his wrist, halting him. "Hey," he said, voice low. "We don't have to. We really can spend the night in the auditorium."

Ethan shook his head. "Thanks, but it's okay. I was just . . . I don't know. It doesn't matter."

It felt like it did. Ethan was not somebody who spooked easily. He was the easygoing one, the one who laughed when

93

the rest of the group jumped, the one who picked up the pieces when they fell.

"Get a move on," Vee called from the foyer. "Let's go! I want to see this place before it gets dark!"

"We're coming!" Ethan called. He turned back to Riley, pulling his arm loose from his grip and taking his hand instead. He offered Riley a smile. "Come on, Colton's right: let's go desecrate some holy ground."

How was Riley supposed to say no to that? He sighed, mouth turned up in a reluctant smile. "Lead the way."

SEVEN

Dominic House's dining room is aglow with fire.

A massive mahogany table dominates the center of the sprawling room, and atop it Jordan has erected a small shrine's worth of lit candles. Near them, a small leather notebook rests, a pen propping its pages open, waiting for a hand to take it.

The first time he was here, Riley had been surprised by the hominess of it all. It was nothing at all like a high school cafeteria, or even a dining hall from every boarding school movie he'd seen. He can only imagine how awkward mealtimes must have been at Dominic House, the kids staring each other down across the table like they had anything in common except a failure from the world at large to accommodate them.

It doesn't look so homey now. Set for the séance, it looks unwelcoming and cursed.

Riley tucks his hands into his armpits for warmth. It's colder in here than anywhere else in the house so far. Already, he wants so badly to be back in the auditorium with the big LEDs acting as a sun.

"Do we have to do the séance here?" Vee asks, no happier than Riley. Jordan ignores her, busy setting a camera at an angle to capture the dining room table in its entirety.

The *Spirit Seekers* crew have flashlights out now, modern little things that clip to the front of their shirts. The bobbing and weaving of their lights makes Riley kind of motion sick. Riley had asked for one himself, but Jordan had turned him down without batting an eye. "It's not like you're going to be separated from us at any point," she'd said. "Besides, it might keep you from wandering off."

Alejandro puts a sympathetic hand on Vee's shoulder. "We won't be here long," he says. "It'll be over before you know it."

"Don't encourage the children," Josh says, helping Jordan. "And don't lie to them either."

"I'm not lying," Alejandro protests. Colton stands in the corner, smoking, as he watches the goings-on without participating. Riley can't get a read on his mood.

Apprehension births goose bumps along Riley's skin. A chance to communicate with the dead.

There's only one person who could possibly be in this house that Riley's interested in communicating with, and if he's dead, Riley's never going to recover from it.

Josh drops a bag of gear on the table with a thump. "All right, gather round, children. I've got presents."

"You're no Santa Claus I've ever seen," Colton drawls.

"Santa Claus wishes he were as charming as me." Josh pulls free a tangle of electronics. "We're gonna mic you up. Try not to break them, will you?"

"Why?" Colton asks. "Are they expensive?"

Jordan pauses long enough to shoot him a look. "They are. And if one goes missing and turns up on eBay later, it'll void all of your contracts. They're expensive, but not twenty-five-thousand-dollars expensive."

Colton flicks his cigarette into a corner but thankfully the ember doesn't catch on the carpet. "If I was going to steal your shit, I wouldn't be dumb enough to stick it on eBay."

"Thank you. That is reassuring," Jordan says. To Josh: "Get them suited up, will you?"

The mic setup takes longer than Riley would have thought. He stands there patiently as Josh fusses about, stuffing it down the back of his shirt, explaining in methodical detail how it works and what not to do with it on.

"It's a microphone," Riley says. "It records me when I speak. It's not exactly rocket science, is it?"

Josh sighs. "Don't break it, okay?"

"No promises."

Josh pulls an agonized face, but Jordan steps back, announcing, "I think we've got the perfect angles here. Is everyone ready?"

"No," Colton says.

"Yes," Riley says, just to spite him. The look Colton shoots him indicates that he knows exactly what Riley is doing. Unable to help himself, Riley adds, "How's your face feeling?"

97

Vee sets a hand on Riley's arm, pulling him away. "Don't wind him up," she warns.

Jordan rounds the table, taking her seat at the head. "I assume we're all familiar with this."

"Yeah, yeah. We hosted our fair share of séances back in our day," Colton says, keeping a pointed cold shoulder turned to Riley. "We know what we're doing."

He says it like they'd summoned the dead on the regular. In reality, Riley remembers three, maybe four, séances held awkwardly over graves they had no right visiting and in Vee's basement. They'd yawn their way through the late-night hours for footage that got less than a dozen views on their channel.

Once, Vee's mother had interrupted them mid-séance and wrathfully ordered them all to bed when she saw they were burning her good Bath & Body Works candles. Riley had deleted that recording pretty swiftly.

Less than half a dozen séances. Some graveyard visits and a basement. In all that time, they'd encountered less than nothing. It's a streak Riley is unwilling to break.

"I'm aware," Jordan says. "But I'm also aware that it's been some time."

"Some time," Riley repeats. "Not that much."

"Let's sit, shall we?" Jordan flashes him a smile, excitement palpable. The candles on the table drool wax steadily onto the moth-eaten tablecloth.

Riley reluctantly takes a seat to her right, and Vee tags along with him. Colton ends up beside her, and Alejandro and Josh settle on the other side. Jordan asks, "Are you ready?"

"Are you sure you can't keep your flashlights on?" Vee asks.

Jordan makes a dismissive noise. "Have you ever seen a séance conducted with flashlights?"

"There's a first time for everything," Colton says wryly.

Jordan says, "Not this time. We're keeping it traditional, and that means candles." She reaches up, and her flashlight goes out; a moment later, Josh's and Alejandro's follow.

Riley takes Jordan's hand, and her fingers are steel in his grip. Vee takes his other hand, and Colton hers. Josh and Alejandro complete the loop. The table is so spacious that they can barely maintain their grip on one another. Riley can only imagine how this is going to look once it makes it to TV screens.

He can't look away from the candles. Vee's hand in his is sweaty.

They didn't do this last time they were here. They didn't have the time.

Vee squeezes his hand and Riley looks up, catching her gaze. Quietly, she asks, "Are you okay?"

"I'm fine," Riley says.

It's a lie, and he knows that Vee knows that. She doesn't push and Riley is eternally grateful.

"Are we just gonna sit here all day holding hands, or are we actually going to do something?" Colton says.

Jordan doesn't reply. Instead, she turns, giving her best side to the camera, and, voice ringing like a bell, says, "If there are any spirits in the room with us, know that we come in peace."

As far as Riley can tell, it's the same opening line she always uses. Days spent on the sofa, watching as she chased her way through one haunted hellhole or the other, Josh and Alejandro on her heels, sitting down to séance after séance with lukewarm results.

Riley could have told her that if there was ever a chance to mix things up, today would be the day. After all, it's not exactly the spirits Riley's worried about being harmed here.

They all hold their breath, even Colton. Riley, who welcomes a response like most people might welcome a bullet to the head, could cry from relief when the room remains silent but for the groans of the shifting house, its old bones weary.

"If you wish to communicate with us," Jordan says, "we are listening. Just reach out and we promise to hear you."

Across the table, Colton gives an exaggerated yawn. Alejandro chances a glance over his shoulder toward where the camera is blinking at them. Jordan remains a consummate professional. Her grip on Riley's hand is steady.

"Are the missing children of Saint Dominic Savio's School for Troubled Youths present with us today? Can you tell us what happened to you all those years ago?" She pauses. "What about Father Thomas? Are you here with us?"

Prickles trace along Riley's spine, tripping on every notch on the path down. They must tremble their way to Vee through where their hands touch, because she shoots him a concerned look. Riley can only shake his head.

Jordan doesn't even notice, too wrapped up in her little performance. "If there is anybody here with us, please reach out now." In the center of the table, the candle flames gutter.

Josh sucks in a harsh breath.

Jordan's eyes snap open. "What? What?"

"The candles," Josh hisses. "There was something in the candlelight."

"There was nothing in the candlelight," Colton says. "It's just drafty as hell in here."

Josh, unswayed by Colton's marked lack of enthusiasm, seems genuinely excited. "Jordan, keep going."

Riley fights the urge to break the circle. Jordan's hand is steel in his, keeping him anchored to the moment.

Her eyes shut again, needing no encouragement. "Father Thomas? Was that you? Please, if you're trying to communicate with us, try again."

This time, no breeze touches the candle flames. Instead, cold air brushes the bare nape of Riley's neck. Might be the wind.

Might not be.

Unable to help himself, he peers over his shoulder. Through the archway, he can see clear into the filthy hallway. There's nothing there.

Last time he was in this house, Riley had thought that too.

He turns around, squeezing Vee's hand hard.

The table sits in tense silence, and, after a suitably long amount of time, Colton says, "I don't think any ghosts want to talk to you."

Jordan isn't put out in the slightest. She drops the hands she's holding, and everybody else follows suit. From the corner of his eye, Riley sees bands of red around Vee's palm from the tightness of his grip. His relief is short-lived.

"All right," Jordan says. "We have other ways to reach out to you."

Riley has a sneaking suspicion he knows where this is going. The lone book waits. "Spirit writing? Really?"

"Hey," Josh says, as Alejandro rises from the table to fuss with the cameras. "It's a respected medium."

"Speaking of respected mediums," Colton says, "are you planning on sticking the pen in Jones's hand? Because something tells me even if there's something in this house, it's not *her* it wants to chat with."

Colton's words set fresh chills along Riley's skin, but if Jordan picks up on the loaded statement, it doesn't show. She reaches out, pulling the book across the tablecloth to rest before her, dramatic fountain pen poised between her fingers. She glances back to Alejandro. "How are the cameras?"

Alejandro turns a lens, settling one of the tripods so Jordan is the central focus. "Good to go, boss."

"Excellent." Jordan turns back to the book. Ink bleeds out where the nib graces the paper. "If any spirits of this house wish to command me, you have my permission. We only wish to communicate."

Riley sits back in his chair, jaw tight and arms crossed. As he watches, Jordan begins to write. It's nothing more than nonsense scribbles, looping across the page idly. The black ink glimmers like blood in candlelight.

"Have you ever had a success with this before?" Vee asks, low enough so as not to disturb Jordan's focus.

Josh shrugs. "I guess it depends on your definition of success."

"Feels like a fairly definitive definition," Colton drawls. Alejandro shushes them with a pointed glare, and they all fall back into the uneasy silence, broken only by the scratch of Jordan's pen. She turns a page.

"This isn't working," Riley says.

She doesn't raise her eyes. "Have more faith. There's a few things I can try yet."

This time, she doesn't scribble. Words pour from the pen, and Riley's sitting just close enough to catch them.

Dominic Savio, House, Haunted, Ghosts, evidence, lights, blackouts, dining room, candles, darkness—

"What's she doing?" Vee asks.

"Stream of consciousness," Josh answers. "The idea is, if she writes whatever comes to mind, maybe we'll find something in it that didn't come from her." There's a silence, then: "It's probably the most subjective form of spirit writing," he admits.

Jordan flips a third page. She hasn't stopped writing. *Outside, chapel, windows—*

"Not to be rude," Colton says in the voice of somebody who doesn't much care about being rude at all, "but none of this is screaming 'ghosts' to me."

Vee pursues her lips, but even she doesn't comment.

Jordan writes for a moment longer and then sighs, setting down her pen and flexing her hand. She slides the book over to Josh without glancing at what she's written. "Thoughts?"

Josh pages through it. His expression is disappointed. "If I'm being honest . . . I think the kid with the bad attitude might be right."

"Hey," Colton objects.

Jordan glances wistfully out the doorway to the hall. "If we'd been permitted access to the chapel—"

"The chapel is likely to come down with one wrong step," Alejandro interrupts. "Even if they'd given us permission, you couldn't drag me in there if you tried."

"You're right." Jordan sighs, but it's grudging. She glances to the table and seems to perk up a smidge. "At least we have the footage of the séance. Viewers love it when they can't tell if something else is in the room or not. The candles flickering will make fantastic television."

"Great," Colton says. "Didn't realize the wind had such an effect on your ratings."

"If you're determined to be unpleasant, maybe you should just keep your mouth shut," Vee suggests sweetly.

Colton looks taken aback, but Josh sweeps in before he can reply. "All right, I think we're done here, kids. We need to get moving. We have a filming schedule to follow and we haven't got all night."

"We very specifically do have all night," Riley points out.

Josh rolls his eyes skyward and joins Alejandro in the corner to help with the equipment. "God save me from the know-it-all attitude of teenagers everywhere."

Riley considers pointing out that he's eighteen—barely a teenager at all—but it doesn't seem worth the effort. The others are splitting away from the table now, Jordan and Vee chatting amicably at the doorway, and Colton lingering by the cameras, craning his neck to watch the footage Alejandro is rewinding through.

Riley gets to his feet, intending to join Vee and Jordan, but then he notices the book lying forgotten on the table. Frowning, he glances at Jordan. "Do you need this?"

"Oh! Yes. Sorry, could you grab it for me?"

Riley leans across the table to do just that, but is drawn up abruptly short when he sees the last page Jordan has written.

Chapel, it reads. *Chapel, chapel, chapel, chapel—*

On its own it makes a chill go down Riley's spine, though it's not the reason that his stomach drops to the floor.

He glances over his shoulder, but Jordan is still chatting with Vee, utterly oblivious to him. Utterly oblivious to the fact that the words in the book might very well be her own, but the hand that had written them wasn't.

Riley would recognize this handwriting anywhere. The print so neat it could have been measured by a ruler, the delicate swoop on the tail of the *p*.

Ethan used to write him letters, back before they got together. Sweet secrets left in Riley's locker for him to find at the end of the day. In the years that he's been gone, Riley has missed them more than he could ever explain.

He lays his fingers atop the page. *Chapel*, it says, and when he swipes his thumb along it, the ink smudges like a bloodstain. *Chapel, chapel, chapel—*

There's a window across from the dining table, pointing right to the front yard. Riley's gaze is drawn to it without his permission.

It's dark outside. With the candles alight and the flash-lights on, Riley's unable to see anything but his own reflection staring back at him. Behind him, the others are hazy, insubstantial figures. Looking at them all now, Riley is struck by the feeling something is off. It takes him a moment to realize what it is.

Besides Riley, there are five people in this little group.

In the reflection in the window, he counts six.

"Riley?" Riley startles. Jordan is nearer now, frowning at him. The others are lingering at the doorway, waiting. "What's wrong?"

Riley glances to the window once more. When he counts again, there's only as many reflections as there ought to be and not a single one more. He takes a deep breath and turns back. "Nothing's wrong."

Her frown deepens. "If there's something—"

Riley stuffs the book into her hands. "There's nothing," he says and sweeps from the room without a backward glance, heart in his throat.

BEFORE

The chapel was everything Riley had hoped it would be.

It sat in the rear of the courtyard, surrounded by crumbling statues guarding it with their stone eyes and impassive faces. The iron fence encircling the property broke at one of its walls and resumed at the other. Once, it had been skillfully masoned with care. Now its stone flaked to dust in the overgrown grass.

The double doors were set into an arch, and on either side of them beautiful stained-glass windows glittered in the sun. At the roof's peak, a heavy wooden cross pierced the sky.

Standing below it, Riley contemplated how heavy it must be—what dark magic must be keeping it erect after all this time.

Beside him, Colton was peering up at it too, hand cupped against the sun. He asked, "You think it'd crush us if it fell?"

"I think I don't want to find out," Riley said. "Let's head inside."

"It's going to be locked," Colton warned.

It wasn't. Ethan was first in, preparing for more resistance than just the rusty hinges, but the doors gave easily. The rest of them followed only a pace behind, Riley with his camera held steady an inch from his face.

The room was split down the middle by a bloodred carpet runner. The ancient wooden pews stank of mildew and stood in disorderly lines, and stray Bibles and hymnals littered the ground, fallen from their shelves on the backs of the pews in front of them.

The pulpit was a modest thing atop the chancel, one step up from the ground, with a stand carved from ancient wood. Above it, Jesus hung from his cross, his eyes sorrowful as they surveyed the ruins of his kingdom, bereft of worship.

Candles lined the windowsills, the pulpit, the walls. Their wax had melted into frozen pools of red on the ground, bloody like a sunrise heralding foul weather.

Colton whistled and the sound bounced from wall to wall. "Fuck me, this place is creepy as hell."

Riley zoomed in on the crucifix on the wall. It made a great shot, but something about it turned his stomach. He zoomed out just as quickly.

Vee's heels clicked as she crossed the room, climbing the chancel to the pulpit. Even with the added height, she looked tiny up there. "There's nothing on the podium," she said, disappointed. "I guess they managed to finish their last Mass before everything happened."

"How many times a day do you think they made the kids come here?" Colton asked curiously. "I bet they could recite prayers in their sleep."

"I bet you can't recite a prayer at all," Vee said.

"Joke's on you, I've played enough video games to know the big ones," Colton said. He sucked in a deep breath, and then, like he was trying to prove something: "Our father who art in heaven, hallowed be thy name. Thy kingdom come, thy will be done, on earth as it is in heaven—"

Riley tuned him out. He circled the chapel, filming the fallen Bibles and hymnal books, the candles, the pulpit.

"—lead us not into temptation, but . . ." Colton faltered. "Uh. Lead us not into temptation . . ."

"But deliver us from evil," Ethan said, startling them all. He was standing three feet into the chapel but no farther, hands in his pockets, staring at the crucifix. "Amen."

"I would have gotten there," Colton protested, scrubbing a frustrated hand through his hair. "You're always stealing my thunder, man."

Riley waited for Ethan to smile, to brush aside Colton's grumbling with ease, the playful back-and-forth that was the foundation of their friendship.

Silence.

Ethan was still staring skyward. Riley followed his gaze, but whatever it was that had snagged Ethan's attention eluded him. The crucifix was just that: creepy as fuck but nothing more. "Ethan?"

Ethan blinked as if coming out of a daze. When he looked toward Riley, a flicker of confusion passed over his face—as if he couldn't figure out where he was or *who* he was looking at.

Riley went cold.

The moment passed. Ethan smiled. "Sorry," he said. "Haven't been in a church in a while. Think I need to give a confession?"

Riley strived to keep his concern out of his voice. "I think you only need to do that when you practice what they're preaching."

Ethan laughed. "Probably for the best. I'm not sorry enough about anything to offer any worthwhile penance."

Across the room, Vee called, "Riley, come over here. There's a spider as big as my head. I want to get it on film."

Colton took several very quick steps backward. "As long as it stays over there."

Riley moved toward her, hefting the camera back up, but hesitated. When he turned around, Ethan hadn't moved, eyes aimed upward again.

Staring at the crucifix.

Riley opened his mouth to say Ethan's name, but nothing came out.

The look on Ethan's face when Riley had called to him before flickered through his head—and Riley wasn't so prideful that he couldn't admit he was afraid to see it again.

"Riley!" Vee shouted.

Riley headed to the pulpit. When he chanced another glance over his shoulder, Ethan was right where he'd left him, staring, staring, staring.

EIGHT

Jordan is not at all put out by the apparent lack of success with her séance. In the auditorium, she rolls out the blueprints for Dominic House along the floor for all of them to see, fingertip chasing out the veins that make the thoroughfare of its beating heart.

"We're going to do a walk-through," she says. "Josh has already set up static thermal cameras in most rooms, so don't worry too much about staying in line of the handhelds. Riley, stay to the front. I don't want you wandering off again. Colton, try and keep that bruise on your face out of line of the camera. It'll mess with continuity, and I don't want to have to explain how it got there. Evelyn, try to keep the boys in line."

"Ms. Jones," Vee says seriously, "if Riley takes another swing at Colton, I'll be cheering in the background."

Jordan sighs, rolling up the blueprints once more. "This is why I don't like working with teenagers. Everybody stay close. Remember, mic packs are on, and so are the cameras.

Whatever you say or do now *will* end up on TV. This is your only warning for the night, clear?"

"Crystal," Riley says.

"All right," Jordan says, and the cameras behind her wink on as one. "It's showtime."

✗ ✗ ✗

Dominic House has two wings on the ground floor. The first holds the kitchen, the dining room where they'd conducted their séance, and the private rooms the scant few teachers and accompanying priest had slept. The second wing is entirely dedicated to the dormitory, where the worst of northern Maine's teenagers had laid their heads.

Jordan leads them down the hallway to it now, monologuing to the camera with professional ease. ". . . when all else failed. Desperate parents shipped their children here, to Saint Dominic Savio's School for Troubled Youths, an isolated boarding school, heavy on the Catholicism and, supposedly, heavier on the punishment for not adhering to it. On average, it housed anywhere between ten to fifteen children at a time who would spend their days here sleeping, eating, learning, and living in each other's pockets under the minimal guardianship of Dominic House's accompanying teachers and priest."

Riley lingers behind her with Vee, conscious of Josh at his elbow, his camera steady with a professional hand. Colton sticks behind Alejandro, a fleeting shadow darting in and out of frame.

Voice low, Vee says, "Sounds like she's reading off the Wikipedia page."

Riley raises a brow. "Critical, Miss Cho?"

Vee pulls a face, folding her arms around herself. "I did *so much* research when we came here. I know things about this house that Jordan couldn't even dream of."

"Did you offer to share any of that with her?" Riley teases.

Vee glances away. "Isn't that wallpaper lovely?"

Riley smothers a grin in the sleeve of his jacket, straightening up as Josh's camera turns his way, striving for seriousness. "Something you want to share, Riley?"

"Watch your step," Riley says. "There's a hole beneath that rug."

Josh stumbles but not quickly enough to avoid his heel snagging in a cracked floorboard. He catches a hand on the wall for balance, nearly putting it through a nearby window as he goes. "Fuck!"

"Are you okay?" Riley asks, but Josh isn't paying attention to him. Instead, he's frowning out the window. "Josh?"

"Hold on," Josh says, aiming his camera through the glass. "I thought . . ."

"You thought what?" Riley prompts.

Josh shakes his head. "Thought I saw something," he says. "Camera didn't seem to pick anything up though."

Riley exchanges a glance with Vee. "What did you think you saw?"

Josh sighs. "Thought I saw somebody walking past the flower beds," he says, sounding disheartened as he rewinds his camera footage and comes up empty. "Hell, this house is really getting to me, man. I usually don't start to see things until at *least* three a.m."

Farther down the hall, Jordan glances over her shoulder. "What are you doing back there?"

"It's okay, I've got you," Alejandro says. "Keep going. You're on a roll."

Jordan turns back, resuming her trek down the narrow corridor. "It functioned until 1982, when an unimaginable tragedy occurred. Seemingly overnight, five students, as well as the priest who'd stayed behind to supervise them over winter break, vanished without a trace."

"It wasn't winter break," Vee mutters as they resume walking. "It was summer break."

Without skipping a beat, Jordan corrects: "Seemingly overnight, the students and the priest supervising them over summer break vanished without a trace."

Colton snorts, but when Riley glances his way, he doesn't look up. The blue of his bruised cheek looks ghostly in the flashlights of the Spirit Seekers.

"Here it is," Jordan announces, coming to a stop. "The dormitory."

Riley looks at the door. Compared to everything else he's seen today, it's unassuming. The crystal doorknob is cracked, coated in a thick layer of dust.

There's a scar on his palm. Minuscule compared to his face. Riley rubs his thumb over it, staring at the missing chips on the glimmering doorknob, remembering how sharp it'd been as it cut into his skin.

He'd barely felt it at the time—didn't realize it'd happened until much later, when the adrenaline of the night had worn off.

Josh's camera blinks at him. "How are you feeling, Riley?"

"Fine," Riley says. "Are we going to stand out here all day, or are we going inside?"

The look Jordan shoots him could flay a man alive. "Have you never heard of suspense?"

"It's just a fucking door," Colton says, and before anybody can stop him, he reaches past Jordan to turn the knob.

The crew's flashlights paint the room silver. Iron bunk beds are lined in even rows, stripped of sheets and baring filthy mattresses. At the end of each bed, a wooden chest stood sentry. More than one is open, exposing a mess of cobwebs and dust. A single desk is crammed into the corner. How a dozen children were meant to share it, Riley has no idea.

Jordan's flashlight beams across the carpet, the walls, the boarded windows. "Here it is," she says, hushed. "Hard to believe that nearly half a dozen of the children who once slept here laid down one night, not knowing it'd be their last."

Alejandro and Josh swoop in, rounding the room with cameras, capturing every angle they can. Riley stays in the doorway, hands tucked into his pockets, and watches Alejandro zoom in on a chest.

"It's smaller than I remember," Vee says, making him jump. Riley turns to find her beside him, watching the crew with a pinched expression. "I could have sworn it was bigger."

"It's exactly as big as it always was," Colton says. He's still in the hallway, leaning against the wall as he lights a cigarette. "You just remember it wrong. As usual."

Riley grits his teeth. "Why don't you tell me how *you* remember it, then?"

Colton flicks a glance at him, then away, back to the room. He taps ash to the carpet. "Doesn't seem like you wanna hear my opinions, so why does it matter?"

"Doesn't seem like you're capable of being a decent human being, so why would I *want* to hear your opinions?" Riley replies.

Colton's jaw tightens. "You don't know shit about me."

"Oh, get off your high horse," Vee says. "I was there when you pissed your pants in third grade."

The look Colton shoots her is acid. He drops his cigarette, crunching it under his boot as he pushes off the wall. "There's no point talking to you two. I'm here for the money, and that's it."

Riley goes to respond, but Vee's hand shoots out, tugging his sleeve. With effort, Riley bites back his response, and Colton shoulders past him, into the room.

"Thought you were going to cheer me on if I took another swing at him," Riley mutters.

"If he deserves it," Vee says. "Don't go picking fights for the sake of it."

Riley shoots her an incredulous look. "For the sake of it? You of all people should—"

"Don't," Vee says lowly. "What happened between Colton and me is between us. I don't need you fighting battles I don't even want to wage, especially not on camera."

From within the dormitory, Jordan calls, "In here, please. Stop wearing holes in the carpet outside."

Vee drops his sleeve, and Riley has no choice but to follow her.

Stepping past the threshold, a chill ghosts down his spine. Riley doesn't glance over his shoulder, even though he very much wants to. There's nothing there, he knows. Nothing but bad memories.

Colton is sitting on one of the beds, talking to Alejandro in a low voice, unbothered by the camera in his face. Josh isn't anywhere in sight, and Jordan walks the length of the room, but her earlier cheer has mostly dissipated.

"Not what you were hoping for?" Riley asks.

"I thought there would be more left behind," Jordan allows. "They cleaned up all the personal effects of the residents, by the look of it."

"Parents wanted the reminders of the kids," Vee says, although she doesn't sound convinced.

"More like they didn't want the fact that they'd sent their children here getting out to their communities. It doesn't seem like any of the kids who vanished were wanted much back home," Jordan says. "The lead suspect in the disappearances was one of the boys who stayed here for the winter. He was—"

"For the summer," Vee corrects. "And yes, his name was Jacob Smith, I know. You're not the only one who's read up on this place."

Jordan smiles at her, pleased. "Why don't you tell me what you read up about, Evelyn?"

Vee shoots Riley a look, but Riley holds his hands aloft, backing away quickly before Jordan can turn her attention on him too.

There's an open door to the right, one that was locked when Riley was here last. Curious, Riley peeks inside.

It's a bathroom. A set of communal showers crowd a corner, and toilet stalls line a wall. The massive mirror that headlines the sinks is spiderwebbed with cracks, fracturing Riley into a dozen people, all carrying their own scars.

Josh looks up from the sink he's steadily filming. "Welcome to the creep zone."

Riley peers over his shoulder. Rust has colored the drain like blood. "You don't think a sink is maybe a waste of footage?"

Josh grins, turning the camera to him. "Maybe. How about you give me something interesting instead."

Riley stares down the camera, unimpressed.

Josh laughs, sweeping it back over the mirror instead. "I knew it was a long shot, don't worry."

"You're not going to ask me some more ridiculous questions?"

"Nah." The camera whirs as Josh zooms out. "That's more Jordan's thing. I'm just here to make sure I capture all of the house's worst angles for our dedicated viewers."

"Does it have any *good* angles?"

"Well, I can't say for sure because the one place I *really* wanted to film is totally off-limits." He gives Riley a pointed look. "Something about fire damage, I heard."

It's not meant to be a dig. It feels like one, catching Riley in the gut. "Trust me," he says. "You don't want to go in that chapel."

Josh raises a brow. "Why? Something in there I should be afraid of?"

Riley is conscious of the camera in Josh's hand. "How did you even get in here? It was locked."

"You see, when you come to places like this on legitimate business, they usually give you the keys," Josh says. He takes a step toward the door and winces as one of the tiles cracks beneath his boot. "Christ, this place really is a shithole, isn't it?"

Riley is looking over his shoulder to the empty corner where a second camera stands stationary over a clogged floor drain. "That your thermal camera?"

"Why? You wanna see how it works?" Josh grins.

Riley's interest in cameras and filming of any kind has been dead for years now, but the ghost of it flickers like an ember in his chest. "Is it any good?"

"Come and see, hotshot. Here, hold this." Josh passes off his handheld camera, and Riley takes it obediently while Josh fusses with the thermal. "I'm going to turn the flashlight off. You good?"

The door to the bathroom is ajar, and he can see the faint glimmer of the rest of the team in the dormitory beyond. He presses his back against the wall. The reassurance of it eases the knot in his gut. "Yeah, go for it."

Josh winks at him and then reaches up to flick off his light. The bathroom plunges into darkness. Riley blinks as his eyes adjust, aided by the ribbon of light from the doorway.

"All right," Josh says, and Riley squints at the camera he's holding out to him. "What do you think?"

The room is painted blue with shades of light green at the door. Details are more suggestions than fact, and when Riley waves his hand in front of the lens the screen lights up in red. "Not bad."

"'*Not bad*,' he says," Josh mocks. "Shut up, it's cool as hell. I know you think so."

With the dark to hide behind, Riley allows himself a smile. "Can I—?"

"Sure," Josh says, and they trade cameras, fumbling in the dark.

The weight of it is unsettlingly familiar in his hand, and for a second, Riley freezes. How long has it been since he touched a camera?

Stupid question. He knows the answer.

"Hey," Josh says. "Still good?"

Not really. "Sure."

A pause. "If you want to see anything on it, you're going to have to film more than just the floor, buddy."

It's enough. Riley's shoulders sag and he lets out a breath. He aims the camera up, catching the glimmer of the mirror. He and Josh are reflected in it, bright specks in a dark space. Josh waves cheerfully. Riley slowly sweeps the camera away, and everything slips back into violets and blues.

"Anything interesting?" Josh asks.

"No." He passes over the showers. Riley freezes. Slowly, he angles the camera back. "Wait."

"What do you mean, 'wait'?"

"I . . ." Riley stares. The shape on the screen does not move. Red flickers at him, fire-bright. "There's something there."

"In the *showers*?" Josh snatches the camera from Riley's hand, and Riley lets him. "Holy shit, what the fuck *is* that?"

Riley steps back to press himself into the corner. It's dark. He doesn't have a flashlight. He can see the shape of the showers, but inside is like a black hole.

"Hello?" Josh asks, voice low. "Is there something in here with us?"

There's no answer. Outside, the sound of the others in the dormitory echoes. The showers are between Riley and the door.

"I'm going to check," Josh says.

Don't, Riley thinks but doesn't say. *Don't, don't, don't—*

There's a clatter as Josh sets his main camera atop the sink and, slowly, eases his way toward the shower bank, thermal camera in hand. From where Riley is, the shape seems dimmer—dimmer, but not gone.

"There's something in the corner here," Josh says. "I'm going to turn my flashlight on, okay?"

"Okay," Riley says.

The room flickers with light. Instantly, Josh recoils. "Jesus!"

"*What?*"

Josh has a hand to his chest, the other to the floor holding him up as he gets back to his feet. "Christ. I think . . . I think it's an animal."

Riley stares at him. "An animal?"

"Yeah. It looks like a cat."

All the tension leaves Riley at once. He droops against the wall, and a laugh bubbles in his chest. "A fucking cat."

Josh isn't nearly as amused. "Yeah. It's dead."

The bubble of laughter bursts against the sharps of ribs and sinks out of sight. "What?"

Josh is shaking his head. "It must have been pretty recent if it was showing up on the thermal camera still."

Riley peels himself away from the wall. Josh shuffles over to make room for him, and Riley bends down, following the beam of light.

It's the cat from outside. The one that ran by as Jordan opened the door. Riley recognizes its matted coat, the missing ear. "What killed it?"

"You mean how'd it die?" Josh shrugs. "Probably starved to death, poor thing."

Riley reaches out. Realizing what he's trying to do, Josh snags his wrist. "Whoa, don't *touch* it. Who knows what it's infected with."

He hadn't been quick enough. Its side had been warm under Riley's palm, and the belly beneath it thin but healthy. "It didn't starve. I can't feel its ribs."

Josh makes a noise of disgust, dragging him up and away. "You're going to be the death of me, kid." He sets his thermal camera down on the edge of the sink and fishes a packet of disinfectant wipes from his back pocket. "Here. Don't tell Jordan you touched it, either. She can wait until editing to find out I can't wrangle one teenager."

Riley's staring at the showers, at the cat that was very much alive only a few hours ago. "How did it get in here?"

"What?" Josh asks, distracted as he resets his thermal camera.

"The door was locked. You had the keys. How did it get in here?"

"How do cats get in anywhere?" Josh asks. "They're Houdinis, man."

Riley tears his gaze away. "Yeah. I guess."

Josh glances at him, then sighs. Setting a gentle hand to Riley's shoulder, he steers him back to the door. "Come on. Jordan will be *thrilled* I got that little scene on film, at least."

BEFORE

The first thing Vee wanted to try out was the spirit box.

"Come on," she wheedled, "we always get something good on it."

"You know I hate that fucking thing," Colton said. "Besides, why am I always the one who has to hold it?"

"You're the one who built it," Vee said. "If something goes wrong, it stands to reason you'll know how to fix it."

They were still in the chapel, even though the longer they stayed, the more Riley wished they would leave. They sat two to a pew, with Colton and Vee in front, twisting to face Riley and Ethan. At Vee's cajoling, Riley had reluctantly set his camera up on the podium atop the pulpit so it could film all four of them and the chapel in its entirety; he felt its absence like a hole in his heart.

"I can do it if you don't want to," Ethan offered. "I don't mind so much."

Ethan, at least, seemed more his old self, less distracted.

Colton pulled a pained face at the offer. "I can handle it. It's fine."

"It's settled, then." Vee shoved the gadget into his hand. "Let's get this rolling."

The spirit box had started life as a portable radio, liberated from its grave in Colton's shed. It'd taken some tinkering, and at least three different wikiHow articles, but eventually they'd managed a decent if not perfect facsimile of the same gear all the best ghost hunters used.

It looked like shit. It sounded worse. Even Riley, who always held his breath in anticipation when they switched it on, admitted it could be . . . frustrating.

As best as he could understand it, it worked by switching between radio signals at light speed. If a ghost wanted to communicate with them, all it needed to do was borrow the words of a thousand people jammed into the little miracle humanity called a radio.

Colton sighed, unwinding the cheap earbuds from around it, tucking one in his ear, where he'd get the brunt of the noise. "You all owe me," he warned. "This is going to give me tinnitus."

He flicked it on, and immediately the chapel was full of the screech of static. A few garbled sounds slipped through it, but they were unintelligible.

Loudly, so as to be heard over the static, Vee asked, "Is there anybody in here with us?"

No answer. The spirit box shuffled through its channels. Across the room, Riley's camera blinked at them, strangely in tune with the wash of white noise, drowning them like an ocean.

Vee said, "We mean no harm—if there are any ghosts in Dominic House, we wish to communicate." She paused. "We have a platform; we'd love to share your story with our sub-scribers."

"All thirty-six of them," Colton muttered, wincing when Vee punched him in the arm.

Vee turned to Riley. "You say something. Ghosts like you."

"What do you mean, ghosts like me?" he asked incredulously.

"Remember when we walked through that cemetery last month?" she said. "The spirit box wouldn't shut up for you!"

"It said, 'Apples, apples, apples,'" Riley said. "That's not a ghost, that's a toddler learning the alphabet."

The spirit box tripped on something that was almost a word, but when they looked to Colton, he frowned and shook his head. "I'm not getting anything more than the usual junk," he said. "Stray words here and there but nothing interesting."

Vee looked remarkably let down. Riley knew her aspirations for Dominic House had been just as high as his—maybe higher still. "Could be you offended them earlier when you fucked up your prayer."

"I would have remembered it if Ethan hadn't interrupted," Colton insisted. "I would have!"

Ethan said, "You're right. Sorry, sorry."

The radio choked, clicked, and said, "—hallowed be thy name."

Riley's heart stopped. The chapel was abruptly a black hole, devoid of movement, of sound. All four of them stared as the little radio in Colton's hand preached gospel like a believer.

Beyond the static, the voice sounded familiar. Riley said, "Is that—?"

"—forgive us our trespasses as we forgive those who trespass against us—"

"Fuck me," Vee breathed, sagging in the pew, hand to her heart and face sheet white. "It's that same religious dude who was on the radio on the drive over."

Just like that, air swept back into the room. The black hole receded. They were just four kids with sweaty palms and racing hearts.

"Jesus," Colton swore, rattling the box uselessly. "How is it—it's not meant to stick to a station like that."

"Maybe it overheated?" Vee suggested. "It was probably melting in your trunk on the drive over."

"Maybe," Colton allowed, but he didn't look as if he believed it. "Still . . ."

The preacher had finished his prayer and, for some reason Riley couldn't comprehend, started it again from the beginning. "Turn it off," Riley said. "I'm so sick of this guy."

For a second, Riley was convinced it wouldn't work—that the voice would drone on and on until it was all he could hear. Until it haunted his every footstep.

Colton flicked the power switch. The chapel was plunged into silence. Riley let out a deep breath he couldn't bring himself to suppress.

"Well," Vee said. "I guess if we edit out the part where Colton calls it a malfunction and curses, we might be able to get something creepy from that, no?"

"If I can't say Jesus's name in church, when *can* I say it?" Colton asked, and just like that, he and Vee were off to the races, bickering so loudly that Riley almost missed the radio preacher.

He glanced to Ethan, but whatever he had intended to say slipped his mind at the expression on Ethan's face. "Hey, are you okay?"

Ethan looked to him. He didn't seem dazed, but the furrow between his brows was deep, and there was something unsettled in the way he held himself. When he smiled, it lacked depth. "I'm fine."

I don't believe you, Riley thought, but didn't say.

Right now, if he pushed, Ethan would just shut him out entirely. For someone so well adjusted, he shared his own insecurities and issues about as well as a three-year-old shared their mother's attention.

Riley had to be patient. He just had to be patient.

He got up. "It's going to be dark soon. Let's eat dinner and figure out where we're sleeping."

"I thought we were sleeping in here?" Colton asked. "Home base, remember?"

Riley played dumb. "I don't know, I think maybe we should pick something more structurally sound. Ten bucks says that giant cross up top falls through the roof and kills us all in the middle of the night."

Colton got to his feet in a hurry. "Twenty bucks says we live through a night in the chapel and you never take me anywhere with a giant fucking cross again."

If the frustration of it didn't kill him first. "Deal," Riley said.

"Great," Vee said. "Now let's focus on the living-through-the-night part, shall we?"

NINE

The others are still in the dormitory, but even Alejandro looks sick of filming the same angles over and over again. Colton has both boots kicked up on the mattress he's sitting on, smoking like a chimney, and Vee sits at his feet, talking with Jordan about the history of the house.

They all look up as Josh and Riley rejoin them, and Jordan says, "Finally. I was wondering what could be so fascinating in there."

Josh glances at Riley and merely says, "Riley was helping me with the cameras."

Relief sweeps through Riley. He doesn't know that he has it in him right now to fight the tide of Jordan's enthusiasm over his own unsettling experiences.

Jordan clucks her tongue. "At least you're back now. I want to try a spirit box in here before we move on."

Alejandro groans. "You know I hate that thing, boss. It makes my ears bleed."

"Then it's good that your opinions have zero impact on the decisions I make," Jordan says, merciless. She raps her knuckles against the desk. "Over here, so we can get a good view of the room. Riley, Colton, Evelyn, make sure you're standing somewhere Josh can film you."

Colton rolls his eyes but slings his feet off the bed. "Sure."

Vee shoots him a look and then says, "If you want help with the spirit box, Colton can do it, if Alejandro doesn't like to."

Jordan's brows climb. "Can he?"

"No," Colton snaps, but Vee continues, "He made ours."

"Did you?" Jordan seems impressed. "I didn't realize that was part of your skill set."

Colton curls his lip. "You didn't ask."

Jordan is unperturbed by his attitude. "You know what? That'd be perfect. It'll be great footage, one of you helping with this."

Vee trails over as the others busy themselves setting up. She looks Riley up and down. "What happened?"

Riley glances over his shoulder, back to the bathroom. "Nothing happened."

"If . . ." Vee hesitates, then forges ahead. "Did you see something?"

It's such a straightforward question compared to what they've been dancing around all night that Riley is momentarily thrown off guard. "Did I— No. Nothing like that. I promise."

"Then why do you look like you've seen a ghost?"

Riley shoots her a look. "That's not funny."

Vee smiles, but it's more tired than anything. "Sorry. I don't think I'm doing so well myself."

"I'm doing fine," Riley says.

"Yeah, you look it too." Vee stands on her tiptoes, brushing her fingers through his hair. Her hand comes back sticky with cobwebs. "What happened here?"

Riley thinks of the corner he'd pressed himself into, heart pounding, throat stuck. "Stood too close to a wall."

"Sometimes talking to you is like pulling out teeth," Vee informs him.

Riley is saved from answering by Jordan calling their names. "We're about to start. I'll try asking some basic questions, but if any of you have anything you want to say, you'll get a chance, too."

Riley doesn't respond. Colton has drawn out a chair, the spirit box in his lap, one earphone in his ear. He looks incredibly sour about this whole thing, and seeing it makes Riley feel better about it, if only a bit.

"We're ready when you are," Vee says.

"Excellent." Jordan twirls a finger. "Light it up."

Colton flicks a switch. Instantly, static fills the room, making everybody but Jordan wince. Riley used to be like that. Years of absence have stolen his tolerance.

"My name is Jordan Jones. I'm a ghost hunter. Is there anybody in this room with us?"

The box continues to trip its way through radio static, silent but for the awful noise.

Jordan continues, unperturbed, "Are any of the children of Dominic House here with us? If so, please speak now."

The static ratchets up; a garbled noise spills out, indecipherable. Jordan shoots a look to Colton, who shakes his head. Josh shuffles in closer, zooming in on Colton and the box.

"If anybody has anything they wish to tell us, you may use this box to do so. We are listening. Is there anything you want to say?"

The static shrieks along. Every nerve in Riley's body feels stripped raw by it; his ears are ringing.

Disappointment curls Jordan's mouth. "I have with me three people who have visited you before—do you have anything you want to say to them?" Riley startles, shooting her a glare, but Jordan isn't paying attention to him. She's fixated on the spirit box, her hands glued to the back of Colton's chair. "If you have anything to say to them, now's your chance. Their names are Colton, Evelyn, and Riley."

The static grinds, and the box says, "*Riley.*"

Electricity rivets Riley to the floor. Everybody's head snaps to him, even Colton, one hand pressed to the bud in his ear. Eagerly, Jordan says, "Was that—?"

"I heard it," Colton says.

Delighted, Jordan opens her mouth, but the static squeals and, again, "*Riley.*"

Riley's heart is in his throat. "Turn it off."

"Do *not* turn it off," Jordan says. She leans forward, towering over Colton, and says, "You want to talk to Riley, is that it?"

"Colton," Riley snaps, "turn it *off.*"

Colton looks at him, eyes wide.

"Do not," Jordan snaps, "*dare.*"

The static roars like an ocean in Riley's ears. *"Colton."*

Jordan says, *"Don't—"*

Colton flicks the switch. The room plunges into silence.

Behind Riley's shoulder, Josh marvels, *"Holy shit."*

Jordan straightens up, hands on her hips. "Well," she says, "I believe that's the clearest feedback we've ever gotten in five years of this show. We might have even gotten *more* if you'd let it run."

Colton holds up a hand. "Didn't feel like your call to make."

"Considering I'm the one headlining this little expedition, I think you'll find it is."

"It wasn't *your* name the radio was chanting."

A hand settles on Riley's arm, and Vee says gently, "Riley?"

Riley swallows. His hands are shaking. He folds his arms, tucking his hands out of sight, refusing to look at anybody. "Are we done in here?"

Jordan eyes him shrewdly. For a moment, Riley thinks she's going to argue, but she says, "I think this room has given us everything it's likely to."

Riley lets out a quiet breath of relief.

Jordan turns to Colton. "All right, pack it up. We'll—"

A deafening squeal cuts through the air, making everybody flinch, and then the radio jabbers back to life. Hand to her ear, Jordan hisses, "What are you doing? Turn it off!"

"I am!" Colton snaps, stabbing at the power switch. The static trips over itself, catching on something that's almost a word. "It's not me!"

"Riley," the static says. *"Riley, Riley, Riley—"*

Vee pulls Riley back, jamming him behind her shoulder, as if her five-foot-nothing frame could shield him from the sound of his own name.

"Riley, Riley, Riley—"

"Colton," Riley gasps. "Colton, please."

"It's not me! It won't turn off!"

"Then break it!" Vee snaps.

Like lightning, Colton is on his feet, the spirit box soaring through the air. It crunches against the wall, plastic flying off as it spins to the ground.

The static vanishes. Silence falls like a shroud.

Colton looks at Riley. "You okay?"

"I think I'm going to be sick," Riley says and leans forward to puke on the carpet.

✗ ✗ ✗

Being back in the auditorium is a relief. The LEDs are lit up like stars, and the open space eases the suffocated feeling making itself at home in Riley's gut.

Riley sits in a far corner, Vee and Colton on either side of him. The *Spirit Seekers* crew circles together in the center of the room, talking in low voices. More than once, they steal a glance at Riley and the others.

At least they'd let Riley and the others turn off their mic packs for the time being. Probably, Riley thinks, because if the mics also started spitting out his name, he might have had a breakdown.

Colton is smoking again. The smell of it is more comforting than Riley wants to admit. He leans toward him without quite meaning to. "What do you think?" Colton asks. "Are they ready to run away yet?"

"They're not going to run," Vee says. "This kind of shit is what they came here for."

Colton snorts. "No. They came to tell spooky ghost stories in the dark."

"What do you care?" Vee snaps. "Didn't you tell the fucking media you don't believe in ghosts?"

Colton pauses, cigarette halfway to his mouth. "Don't you start with me, Vee," he warns.

Vee's hand is on Riley's back, and he can't tell if she's trying to soothe him or herself. "Which one is it? Either ghosts aren't real and I'm a hysterical liar or they are real, and if they are, we should never have come back here."

"I never called you a liar!"

"No, you just told every reporter who would listen that I was 'unstable' and 'delusional.'"

Colton drops his cigarette, crushing it beneath his foot. "You know what? I don't have to put up with this."

"Oh wow, Colton the coward returns. What a shock."

The blow lands right where she'd aimed to hit. Colton rounds on her, hands fisted at his sides, face white. "Don't call me that."

"Oh?" Vee mocks. "Did I hit a nerve?"

"You're a piece of work, Cho," he hisses. "You don't know anything."

"I know that when things get tough, you're always the first one out the door." She pauses. "Who knows? Maybe *you'll* be the one to run away."

"Fuck you," Colton spits. "Fuck you both."

He spins on his heel, stomping across the room to join the others. Riley watches him go, exhausted. "So," he says, "you learned how to aim low, huh? How long have you been holding that in?"

Vee's hand clutches at his shirt, but she doesn't look away from Colton's back. "I'm tired of him not being able to make up his mind."

Riley shoots her a look. "You have to know that's not what's happening with him."

"What?"

Riley sighs, leaning his head back against the wall. "He's just scared, Vee. He's just fucking scared. He's no different than the rest of us."

Vee doesn't reply.

"We probably never should have come back here," Riley says.

Vee's head falls to his shoulder, and Riley settles his cheek against her hair. Her arm drops around him. "We can go. I'll talk to Jordan, if you want. After . . . Well, I don't think they'd blame you."

Riley lets himself imagine it. The front door is one short hallway away, the van waiting in the drive. They could be gone before the moon even hits its peak, Dominic House and all its ghosts just a glimmer in the rearview mirror.

He thinks of the book on the dining room table—the voice from the spirit box whispering in his ear. *Riley? Riley? Riley?*

It's been two years. Riley would recognize that call of his name anywhere.

"In the dormitory," he says, "on the spirit box. You heard it, right?"

Vee's hold on him tightens. "Riley—"

"It was Ethan," Riley insists, and the relief of admitting it is almost enough to outweigh the rip of Ethan's name from his soul. "It had to be. It was." He licks his lips. "And—before. With the spirit writing. I looked at the book and on the last page . . . that was his writing, Vee. It was."

"Riley," Vee says, softer. "It's been so long. Ethan is—you know, right? People who go missing for that long. They don't usually find them alive."

Riley smiles. It probably looks as awful as it feels, but there's a relief, too, in admitting the fear that has had him in a chokehold all evening. "That's kind of my point, isn't it?"

Vee is quiet for a moment. "When we left," she says. "Last time, I mean. They had to basically lock you in that ambulance."

Riley knows where she's going with this. They haven't talked about it much. After everything that happened, they'd been too wrapped up in their own private grief to want to dissect that night in minute detail. But Vee has been his best friend for years, and she knows him better than anybody alive or dead, sans one person.

"I was so out of it, I barely knew where I was," Riley says. "I'd just had half my face ripped off and barely escaped a burning building."

"You didn't want to leave Ethan," Vee says. "Even when the cops said he was probably dead."

"And I was right," Riley insists. "They never found a body. When they put out the fire, there was nobody there."

"We both know Ethan would never have left us—would never have left you. There's only one reason he'd disappear like that." Vee looks at him. Really looks at him. "You've never believed he was dead, though, have you?"

Riley doesn't know how to answer that. He can't explain what happened—those final moments in the chapel before his life was changed forever. Every time he tries, they stick in his throat, a fear he'd never even known was possible icing every part of him to a frozen standstill.

Last Riley saw him, Ethan was alive. But that hadn't been the only thing he'd seen.

Did he believe Ethan was dead? When Vee asked, it sounded like such a simple question. Yes. No. A question that didn't lend itself to shades of gray.

The truth wasn't that simple at all. That night, Riley had learned that perhaps death wasn't such a binary thing after all.

Across the room, Jordan gestures to them, and Vee sighs, saving Riley from answering her. "Guess break time is over, huh?"

Riley hauls himself to his feet. Jordan smiles as they approach, and the electric energy of it makes Riley want to wince. Since the episode with the spirit box, she's been as radiant as a lighthouse. "Exciting, isn't it?"

Riley stares at her. Vee says, "'Exciting' isn't the word I was going to use."

Jordan forges on as if she didn't hear her. "Electromagnetic activity—twice now! We've already gotten more from this shoot than all our other ones combined!"

Colton, who's lingering behind Jordan, snorts and rubs a hand over the back of his head. "Wonder why that is."

Riley grits his teeth. "You're back on the denial bullshit, huh? That was quick."

Colton shoots him a rancid look, but Jordan talks over him. "We want to capitalize on the momentum. See what else the house might be willing to give us."

"Great," Riley mutters without enthusiasm.

Vee pats his arm and says, more diplomatically, "And what were you thinking?"

The shine of Jordan's smile could have called ships to harbor. "Think it's about time the Scooby gang splits up, don't you?"

Something must show on Riley's face, because Josh rushes to add, "Not alone; one of us with one of you. Trust me, it'll make for great footage."

"The house is only so big," Vee says. "Where do you think we're all going to go?"

"I'm glad you asked." Jordan holds up three fingers. "One of us to the teachers' wing." A finger flips down. "Another upstairs, in the classrooms."

One finger remains. Riley eyes it with trepidation. "And the last?"

"We can't go in the chapel," Jordan says, "but nothing is stopping us from going to its courtyard."

Riley's stomach turns at the very idea of being within spitting distance of the chapel. Striving to keep his nerves from showing, he asks, "Who's going where?"

"Alejandro and Vee will check out the teachers' wing. Colton and Josh can go upstairs to the classrooms—"

Colton's hand drops from his hair and his spine straightens. "No."

Jordan falters. "Pardon?"

"I said no," Colton snaps. "I'm not going upstairs."

"Scared of the classrooms?" Josh teases. "The dormitories aren't scary, but a blackboard will chase you off?"

Colton's jaw's tight enough to break. He's terrified. Riley, who sees the same expression looking back at him from the mirror daily, recognizes it intimately. Before he can help himself, Riley says, "He said *no*."

Colton glances his way, taken aback, but Riley doesn't meet his gaze. He stares Jordan down until she relents. "Colton and Josh will go outside," she says. "Riley and I will take the classrooms upstairs. Does that sound agreeable to everybody?"

Relief sweeps through Riley. He won't have to worry about being near to the chapel after all. "That sounds fine." Colton's still looking at him; Riley feels the prickle of his eyes on his skin.

"All right," Josh says cheerfully, slinging an arm around Colton's shoulders. "Let's take a little sojourn, shall we?"

"Yes," Jordan says, snapping open a handheld camera. "Shall we?"

BEFORE

They ate in the auditorium, food spread out on a dusted section of floor between them. Ethan had overseen packing, so it was mostly muesli bars and fruit—the healthy kind of shit Riley only ate when subjected to peer pressure.

"Ethan's right, an apple won't kill you," Vee said, stuffing one in his hand as he pulled a face. "C'mon, humor him."

"I feel like all I do is humor you both." Riley sighed.

"May I offer you a banana in this trying time?" Colton said, holding one out to him.

"I'll eat my own fruit. I'm not eating yours," Riley informed him.

"Hey," Vee cut in, "where's Ethan?"

Frowning, Riley turned. The spot beside him his boyfriend had occupied only five minutes ago was empty. Across the room, the door to the hallway was open an inch.

"Wow," Colton said, "I can't believe he made us eat this shit and then ran away before we could return the favor."

Vee punched him in the arm as Riley clambered to his feet. "I'll go find him," he said.

"Take your camera," Colton said. "Walking alone through this hellhole would make great content."

The last fucking thing Riley wanted to do was take his camera. Of all the things he'd been eager to film on this trip, his boyfriend's distress was not one of them. But if he said no, he'd have to explain why, and if Ethan had wanted the others to know how unsettled he was feeling, he'd have said something himself.

"Fine," Riley said.

"Take an apple too," Vee said. "I don't think Ethan's eaten anything."

"*Fine*," Riley said, again, tucking one in his pocket. "Jesus, you want to fix my hair and tell me to take a sweater too, Mom?"

Vee smiled, offering him his camera. "Have a safe trip, sweetie! Behave!"

Ethan wasn't anywhere on the bottom floor—the dormitories, the dining room, the teachers' wing. The courtyard was occupied only by the silent, watchful statues, and the chapel, when he peeked inside, was empty.

Riley eyed the stairs to the second floor they'd yet to explore. They didn't look structurally sound, and several steps were bowed beneath an invisible weight. Ethan himself had taken one look at them and firmly declared them off-limits.

But he wasn't on the ground floor. And even in a building this big, there were only so many places somebody could hide.

Resigned, Riley set a hand on the filthy banister and began to climb.

The second floor was darker than the first, and with sunset not long off, Riley wished he'd remembered to grab a flashlight. The hallway the stairs took him to was short. Only one door was open, spilling dirty sunlight onto the faded hall carpet.

"Ethan?" he called.

No reply. He couldn't even hear Vee or Colton from up there. It was just Riley and Dominic House—alone together.

Riley crept forward and, slowly, pushed the door open all the way. Inside was a classroom full of old-fashioned desks and yellowing papers that carpeted the floor. A filthy chalkboard at the front, smudged by long-gone fingers. The far wall was entirely made up of windows. Standing in front of them was Ethan.

Riley let out a breath. On the camera, Ethan was a solitary, unknowable statue, no more detailed than the wrecks littering the lawn outside. When Riley let the camera drop, though, it was just Ethan—blond hair, blue eyes, and everything familiar.

"Fuck," Riley said, picking his way across the room to join him. "Why did you wander off? You're going to give me a heart attack."

Ethan didn't answer. He was staring out the window, hands resting on the sill, uncaring of the dust. Riley frowned and followed his gaze.

The classroom overlooked the courtyard and the chapel. He could see the open doors, the cross. The moon peeking through the clouds above caused the mosaic windows to glimmer like candlelight.

Riley's reflection stared back at him from the dirty glass, translucent and smudged. Something about it unsettled him, and he pulled the sleeve of his shirt over his hand, swiping against the grime of the window for a clearer view. When he pulled back, it was just as filthy as before, his face warped.

In the reflection, something moved behind him.

Riley froze.

There was somebody behind him. He could see the hint of a face. Dark eyes, dark hair. Not Vee. Not Colton.

At his elbow, Ethan was as immovable as stone.

Fuck, Riley thought. *Fuck, fuck, fuck—*

He spun around, camera raised—whether to film or fight, he didn't know.

There was nobody there. It was just a classroom. Empty. Abandoned.

"I'm losing it," he muttered, running a hand through his hair. When he glanced at Ethan, he was still lost in his thoughts, gazing out the window.

Riley grabbed his elbow, jerking him back a step, and Ethan went with him without resistance. He blinked, and when he looked to Riley, he seemed genuinely surprised. "When did you get here?"

"I've been here for ages," Riley said. "What is going on with you?"

Ethan looked shocked. Riley could understand why. Although Riley's temper edged prickly even on his best day, rarely had Ethan been the target of it. "What?"

"What were you thinking, wandering off?" Riley snapped, gaining steam now. "And upstairs, too. You've been weird since we arrived. I told you we could leave if you wanted and that we didn't have to come—"

"Riley," Ethan cut in.

"—if you're not feeling well. *Say* something—"

"Riley," Ethan said again, firmer this time, reaching out to squeeze Riley's arm. "I'm sorry. I didn't mean to worry you."

And just like that, Riley lost his momentum. He tugged Ethan's shirt, hauling him closer so he could rest his head against the crook of Ethan's neck. "Fuck. Don't scare me like that again, okay?"

Ethan's hands settled on his back. "Sorry," he repeated. "Thanks for coming after me."

Riley pulled away to glare at him. "What else was I supposed to do?"

Ethan smiled fondly, but before he could say anything, there was the sound of footsteps on the stairs, the rise and fall of familiar voices. Colton slammed open the door a moment later. "I can't believe you came up here," he said. "Those stairs are a death trap."

Vee slid past him, eyeing the room speculatively. "Wow, abandoned classrooms just have a different vibe to them, huh?"

Riley reluctantly stepped back from Ethan. "Yeah. I guess."

Colton wended his way through the mess of the room to the front. He plucked a piece of chalk from the rim of the blackboard and grinned. "What should I write?"

"If you draw a dick, I swear to god . . . ," Vee warned.

Colton rolled his eyes. "You think so little of me." A pause. "I was thinking boobs."

"Like you know what those look like," Vee said and stepped forward, stealing the chalk from him. "Here, let me."

It squealed across the board. Curious, Riley trailed closer.

When she stepped back, he had to grin, raising his camera to record it for prosperity. "Good idea."

Colton swiped the chalk back and elbowed her aside, scrawling below Vee's perfect handwriting. "There." He tossed the chalk to Riley, who fumbled to catch it, the apple rolling free of his pocket and coming to a rest at his shoe. "Your turn, cameraman."

Riley set the camera down and scribbled across the board. Once he was done he offered the flaky stub to Ethan with a raised brow.

Despite Riley's fears, Ethan's eyes were clear as day. Whatever spell had been draining him all afternoon was gone for now, and when he took the chalk, the warmth of his fingertips brushed Riley's. Ethan stepped closer to the board, the start of his writing catching the tail end of Riley's.

Once he was done, they all stood back, admiring their work. Colton said, "If the police ever find this, we're so fucked."

Ethan laughed, setting the chalk down where they'd found it. "If the police ever need to come here, I think we have bigger problems than that."

TEN

The stairs creak beneath Riley's boots like the groaning of a sinking ship.

Up here, there's no LEDs—only Jordan's flashlight to cut through the gloom. It's edging nearer and nearer to midnight, and Riley misses the brightness of the sun like a physical ache.

Jordan leads the way like an explorer, her beam sweeping every inch of the rotted carpet that clings to the skeleton steps. Riley keeps a hand firmly on the banister.

"What do you think?" Jordan asks as the stairs squeal beneath her.

"What do you mean?" Riley says.

"What were your experiences with the classrooms last time?" They hit the second floor landing. A chandelier sways from the ceiling, its flutes fractured and foggy. "Cold spots? Electromagnetic activity? Orbs? Spectral presence?"

There's a crack in the railing that keeps the second-floor landing separate from the void space, and it's all the more obvious up here. Big enough for a whole body to fall through.

Big enough for a whole body to *have* fallen through, if you know what you're looking for. Riley steadfastly does not look.

"Riley?"

Riley glances up and comes eye to eye with Jordan's camera lens. Annoyed, he pushes it back. "Do you have to do that?"

"You know I do. Are you going to answer my question?"

"No," Riley says and elbows past her.

The hall is smaller up here. The grand height of the roof has shrunk, and the walls enclose him like a coffin. There's only two doors, and Riley pauses in front of the first one as Jordan hurries to catch up with him.

"Ready?" she asks, setting a hand on the doorknob.

"Sure," Riley says.

The door swings open. The room behind it is long and skinny; two rows of old-fashioned desks scattered about, some still bearing schoolbooks and papers. At the front, a teacher's desk looms before a chalkboard. Josh has obviously been through here, because one of his cameras is set up in the corner where it can capture the room in its entirety. The faint sweet scent of fading rot fills the air, and Jordan sweeps her camera to follow it to the source. "Is that an apple rotting beneath the teacher's desk? Seriously? They left an apple here for forty years?"

"It's not from the eighties," Riley says, drifting into the classroom.

"*You* left an apple here?" Jordan asks, bemused.

"Ethan's idea," Riley says. "He didn't like eating junk food when we went on expeditions. Said we couldn't exactly run from ghosts if we were too weighed down by trash."

"How did the running from ghosts go for you?" Jordan asks.

Riley ignores her. Paper crinkles along the floor as he walks the length of the room. When he reaches the blackboard, flaky stubs of chalk rest in the rim of it. Unable to help himself, he picks one up, and it disintegrates between his fingers.

"What's this?" Jordan says. The rap of her heels draws nearer. "There's something on the board."

"Yeah," Riley says. "I know."

In the corner, smudged by time but not lost, it reads: *Ghost Hawks!*

Beneath that: *Vee, Colton, Riley, Ethan.*

The handwriting changes on each name, Vee's name a perfect cursive, Colton's sprawling. The *y* of Riley's name catches on the start of Ethan's.

Riley swipes a thumb through the message, but the chalk is old and settled. It doesn't even smudge.

"Oh," Jordan says, "this is incredible. I can't believe the police didn't touch it."

Riley takes his hand back, burying it in his pocket. The warmth of Ethan's name lingers on his skin. "Why would they? It's evidence, isn't it?"

Jordan waits, but Riley offers her no more, and she sighs. "You know, I'm paying a fortune to have you all here. The least you could do is give me something to work with."

"I didn't come here because you were willing to pay me a fortune," Riley says.

"Then why *did* you come here?"

Riley doesn't answer. He strays across the room, away from Jordan. He skims his fingers along the desks as he goes. Unfinished schoolwork stares back at him, and he reads the names. *Lucas, John, Steven, Jacob—*

He pauses, and Jordan steps closer, aiming her camera right at the desk. "What is it? Do you see something?"

"No, it's just . . ." Riley taps the browned paper.

Jordan leans forward, adjusting the camera to film better, and makes a delighted noise. "Jacob Smith—he was the primary suspect in the '82 disappearances."

Riley remembers. Weeks hunched over his laptop, skimming the web with Vee for everything history had to offer on Dominic House, chasing ghost story after ghost story. "He disappeared too."

"The police thought he ran," Jordan says, on a roll now. "It was him, four other students, and the priest who'd stayed behind to supervise them while the rest of the students and staff returned home for the break. Groceries were delivered every week from the town, but other than that, they were totally isolated out here on their own. The prevailing theory is that Jacob, who was on record as the most troubled youth in a school for troubled youths, murdered them all and buried their bodies somewhere on the grounds."

Riley remembers black-and-white photos of Jacob, staring out from ancient newspapers. Sixteen and built like he was twice his age. A face that'd seen its fair share of breakings and bruises, souring his expression.

He had anger issues. Beat a foster brother half to death once when he was fourteen, although the article Riley had read that in had never said why. He had a bad history with the staff too, mutinous in the face of so much crushing authority.

After the disappearances, there had been a short investigation into why somebody with a such a record of violence was sent away to a glorified reform school rather than to juvie. Like most of the investigations, it'd petered out quick.

In the days before they came here, Ethan had said, *They really think a single kid could have done that?*

Trust me, Colton had said, *a kid like that? He could have done a lot worse.*

Now, Riley asks, "What do you think?"

Jordan smiles at him. "I think that whatever the truth is, it can't be half as fascinating as the mystery it left behind."

Riley opens his mouth to reply but pauses. His breath fogs in the air before him. He can't remember when it started doing that.

"What?" Jordan asks, brows raised, her words clouding between them.

Riley looks over Jordan's shoulder to the door. It's open still. There are maybe five feet from here to there. "I think we should go."

Jordan frowns. "Are you kidding? We've barely looked around. There's so much left to explore."

"It's a classroom," Riley says. "You've seen all it has to offer. Let's go someplace else."

Jordan purses her mouth, sweeping the camera over the room. Riley stays patiently quiet. Jordan rarely responds well to being pushed, he's learning.

Something moves in the corner of Riley's vision, and when he turns to look, a face stares back at him from the window.

For a moment, Riley thinks somebody's looking in from the outside. And then he remembers they're on the second floor.

He can't make out details. It's like gazing at a warped reflection in a muddy pond; the features ripple. Pale skin, bruised in death. Dark eyes. Dark, dark eyes.

They look familiar. He can't place them.

Jordan has her back to the windows. Riley opens his mouth to call her name.

In the window, the figure presses a skeletal finger to its lips.

Riley's mouth slams closed.

"You're right," Jordan says. "I don't think we're going to get any better shots in here. It's not even that creepy."

With effort, Riley rips his gaze away from the windows. "Yeah."

Jordan sighs. The camera sags in her hand. "And downstairs had been so promising. All right, let's head to the auditorium. I wouldn't be surprised if Josh and Colton have returned already, flakes that they are."

Riley offers her a plastic smile. "After you."

She fiddles with her camera all the way to the door, talking idly. Riley's barely listening. He keeps his eyes on her back. She steps through the doorway, into the hallway, and, on instinct, Riley pauses.

The door slams shut in his face.

He stares at the battered wood an inch from his nose. He's not surprised in the least.

"Riley?" Jordan calls. The door shakes as she slams a fist into it. "Riley, what are you doing?" The knob rattles but refuses to turn. "Riley, let me in!"

Riley doesn't bother responding. Slowly, he turns back to the room.

There's no figure in the window anymore. Instead, there's one standing right in front of him.

The figure's skin is bleached to the bone, and dark bruises rim its eyes—eyes a beautiful blue, as familiar as the curve of his mouth.

Riley swallows. "Hello, Ethan."

Ethan smiles. "Riley."

He looks the same. He looks so different. Older, somehow. Riley hadn't expected that. There's something else, too—a draining of life from his sallow skin, the warmth from his face. They're standing close enough that Riley feels the ice of his presence like winter between them.

Riley wants to touch him like he's never wanted anything.

His hands stay firmly by his sides.

"Ethan," he says, helpless. "What *happened* to you?"

The smile slips from Ethan's face. He opens his mouth to answer, but no sound comes out. He closes it again. Confusion sweeps over his face. The blue of his eyes is darker now, more night sky than day, and Riley has the feeling Ethan's no longer looking at him so much as through him.

"Hey," Riley says, panic rising. "Hey, no. It's okay. You're okay. We're okay."

Ethan takes a step back. The distance between them aches like an open wound. "I shouldn't be here," he says.

"No, no, no. Fuck, don't do this to me, not now. Ethan, please—"

Ethan frowns. Again, like a realization, "I shouldn't be here."

"Ethan, *please*." Desperation makes Riley stupid. He reaches out. His fingers close around Ethan's wrist, and Riley braces himself to feel nothing at all—nothing but the memory of a ghost, a wishful delusion. Instead, he feels something solid.

Flesh, cold like iron, unyielding in his hand.

Riley's heart stops. He can't help but stare, eyes locked to the point where they're touching.

Ethan's staring too. His eyes are blue again. "Oh," he says. Softer: "*Oh.*"

Riley feels hysterical. "Yeah," he chokes. "*Oh.*"

Ethan hesitates and then lifts his other hand, folding his fingers over the back of Riley's hand. It's like dipping his hand in a frozen lake, and Riley shivers, desperate for it. Ethan's thumb strokes along his wrist, and Ethan's staring at it, riveted.

This isn't real, Riley thinks. *You're asleep. You're dreaming.*

He knows that's not true, though, because Riley's dreamed of this moment a thousand times, and it's never been like this.

"Ethan," he says again. "What happened to you?"

Slowly, Ethan lifts his gaze from Riley's hand. The confusion has ebbed now; his eyes look the clearest they have yet. He doesn't let go of Riley's hand. "I . . ." He pauses. Frowns. "I don't know."

"I don't believe you," Riley says. He chances a step closer. "Don't lie to me. You've never lied to me before. Don't start now."

Ethan's frown creases his face terribly. Riley wants to chase it back with his fingertips. "I'm not . . . I don't remember."

Riley's self-control is only so strong. He drops Ethan's hand and reaches up, setting his palms to his cheeks, cradling his face. Ethan's eyes flutter closed, mouth open in a soft O.

This is so fucked-up, Riley thinks and leans forward to kiss him.

Ethan's mouth is no less freezing than the rest of him, but the way his breath hitches warms Riley to the bones. Ethan's fingers come up to hold Riley's hands where they are, meeting the kiss as if he's been waiting for this just as long as Riley.

Riley never thought he'd kiss Ethan again. Truthfully, Riley's not sure he's even kissing him *now*.

It takes the effort of his life to pull away, but somehow he manages. Ethan blinks slowly, looking at Riley with a wondrous expression that does terrible things to Riley's heart.

"Ethan," he presses, one more time, "what *happened*?"

Ethan looks at him for a very long moment. The classroom is so cold now that Riley struggles to breathe.

Ethan says, "You need to leave."

Riley stares. "What's that supposed to mean?"

Ethan leans forward, forehead resting in the crook of Riley's neck. Riley braces for the feeling of ice as Ethan breathes on his skin. He feels nothing. It takes him a second to realize it's because Ethan isn't breathing at all.

"Riley. Riley."

Riley threads a hand through Ethan's hair. He's looking past him, out the dark windows now, because he thinks if he looks at Ethan, he might finally break. "Yeah. That's me."

Ethan shudders. "I didn't want to go."

Fuck. He might just break anyway. "I know that. Of course I know that."

Ethan's clutching at his shirt. His fingernails scrape Riley's skin, marking him like a brand. "I knew you'd come back for me." He pauses. "You shouldn't have."

Riley's heart is pounding. He wonders if Ethan can feel it. If he can hear it. "What was I supposed to do, then?"

"You shouldn't have come back," Ethan repeats again. Too soon, he pulls away, and Riley's not strong enough to hold him in place. Ethan's eyes are darker again, and Riley's beginning to realize that there might be more behind that than just the changes of the light.

"You've got to be kidding," Riley says. "Ethan, I'm not leaving without you. God, could you just—"

Ethan's hand snaps over Riley's mouth. Riley stares at him, taken aback, but Ethan's not looking at him—he's looking over his own shoulder, back to the windows. His hand on Riley's mouth is like steel. "He's listening," Ethan says.

Who's listening? Riley thinks, almost hysterical.

Ethan looks back at him. His eyes are like midnight, but when he speaks, his voice is clear. "You need to go. Don't stay. Be careful. He's listening." Ethan considers Riley for a moment and then he leans forward, and his lips brush Riley's temple. "Don't come back for me," he breathes. "Please."

The hand on Riley's mouth vanishes, and so does the ghost of the boy it was attached to. Riley stands there like a statue, the ice of Ethan's kiss lingering on his skin.

And then his legs give out.

He doesn't know how long he sits there staring at the windows across from him. Could be a single second. Could be a thousand. Time seems very far away right now. Everything seems very far away right now. Eventually, the door to the room crashes open, and reality rights itself.

The Spirit Seekers crowd the doorway, but it's Vee who sees him first. "Riley!" She swoops in, dropping down in front of him, uncaring of what the disgusting floor might do to her skirt, and throws her arms around him, squeezing him close. "God, Jordan said— And the door wouldn't— I was so scared."

Shakily, Riley raises his hands to her back. She's so warm. Compared to Ethan, it's like hugging a furnace. "I'm okay," he says, but even to his ears, his voice sounds weak at best. "Vee, I'm fine. I swear."

Her grip on him tightens, and Riley realizes she's shaking. Concerned, he cuts his gaze to the crowd in the doorway. None of them look any better than Vee.

Carefully, he eases Vee back so he can look her in the eyes. They're red-rimmed. Panic lances through him. "Forget me; are *you* okay?"

Vee shakes her head, rubbing at her face. "I'm fine, I'm fine," she says. "It's not me."

Realization sets in. "It's not me either," he says. "What happened?" Vee doesn't answer. She's crying again, sprawled across Riley's lap, hands fisted in his shirt. He glances past her to the others. "What *happened*?"

To her credit, Jordan doesn't blink. "It's Colton," she says.

"What about him?" Riley asks.

"That's just it," Jordan says. "We don't know. He's gone."

BEFORE

By the time the sun had well and truly set, they'd filmed every inch of Dominic House and walked twice as much.

"God, this is so much harder when there's a whole mansion," Vee said, knuckling sleep from her eyes. "I think I'm going to pass out at this rate."

The group had retired back to the chapel, despite Riley's reluctance after Ethan's initial reaction to it when they'd arrived. They'd unloaded their sleeping bags from the car, but it was too hot to even consider crawling inside. Instead, the bags had been unzipped and piled in the middle of the floor like a nest, an effective barrier between them and the splintered floorboards. Riley's camera sat atop the stand in the pulpit, ready to keep watch through the night. They had a single flashlight on, illuminating the chapel in a wash of pale light.

"I thought you wanted to do another walk-through at three a.m.," Colton said, sprawled on his stomach as he fiddled with the spirit box, determined to fix it. "The devil's hour and all that."

"I do!" Vee protested. "I just think . . . I might need a nap first."

Riley was on his back, head pillowed in Ethan's lap, drowsy and fighting it. "I'll go with you, so long as you wake up."

"Me too," Ethan said, carding a hand through Riley's hair. "It's a big house. I'm sure we've missed things."

"Maybe we could break down some of those locked doors," Colton suggested.

"I'm sure we've missed things that don't require destruction to find," Ethan amended, and Colton grinned up at him, unapologetic.

Despite himself, Riley was feeling the pull of sleep. His eyes were bleary, and the rhythmic stroking of Ethan's fingers through his hair made him feel safe. "Maybe just for an hour or so," Riley relented. "We'll set an alarm."

Vee swiped through her phone. "Done," she announced, flopping down on her back. "God, I didn't realize walking through the same house a dozen times telling ghost stories could be so exhausting."

"Yeah, I'd have thought you'd be used to it. You already talk so much," Colton said and barely managed to dodge the sharp jut of Vee's elbow.

"Maybe Colton should sleep in the car," she said. "Or alone in the house."

"At least I wouldn't have to deal with your snoring."

"Kids, I *will* turn this car around and no one will go to Disneyland," Ethan said.

Riley laughed. "Even me?"

Ethan pulled at his hair gently. "Even you," he said, but he was smiling.

"All right," Vee said. "Flashlight is going out. Everyone go the fuck to sleep."

The flashlight clicked off. The chapel plunged into darkness, broken only by the moonlight seeping through the open doors and stained-glass windows. It painted patterns across the floor that made Riley's head spin.

Even with that, the darkness was deep. Suffocating. A black hole. Riley's heart sped up without his say-so.

Colton cleared his throat. "Maybe—?"

"Yeah," Vee said and turned the flashlight back on in a hurry.

"Okay," Colton said. "Good night for real, assholes."

✗ ✗ ✗

Riley dreamed deeply and he dreamed strangely.

Dominic House was alive around him but in muted colors with muted noises. He stood in the middle of the foyer and watched as people bustled about. When he turned, the front door was closed, its window clean and clear, the handle unblemished by age.

He reached for it. It rattled in his grip but did not open. He tried again. Again. Again. Again—

In the window, somebody was watching him. Dark hair. Dark eyes. Riley opened his mouth to say something.

The figure brought a finger to its lips.

Riley's eyes snapped open. For one bleary moment, he was confused, and then he heard the blaring of Vee's alarm, and reality reasserted itself. It was dark. At some point, the flashlight must have gone out.

There was a rustle of movement beside him followed by cursing. "Vee, turn your phone off or I swear to god—"

"I'm getting there, hold on." The alarm cut out. More rustling, and then searing light as Vee flicked the flashlight app on. She looked sleep mussed and exhausted, her mascara smudged in spiderweb patterns on her cheek. "I feel like hell."

Colton struggled upright, running a hand through his hair. "Yeah."

Riley rolled over, blinking up at the ceiling. His head was throbbing, and he had the notion that he'd dreamed of something particularly awful. On instinct, he reached beside him but encountered nothing but sleeping bags. "Ethan?"

Vee flashed her phone in his direction, illuminating . . . nothing.

Ethan was gone.

ELEVEN

Colton is not in the dormitories, the kitchen, the dining room. He is not upstairs, somewhere Riley knows he would never have willingly returned to regardless, and he is not, Josh swears, anywhere on Dominic House's grounds where he'd last been seen.

Josh is almost as inconsolable as Vee. "He was right there," he insists, frantic in his worry. "The whole time, he was right behind me, and then when we came back to the house, he was just . . . gone. I barely took the camera off him—I barely took my *eyes* off him."

They're in the auditorium, Alejandro religiously rewinding through Josh's footage for any sign, supernatural or otherwise, of Colton. Jordan sits in one of the shitty folding chairs, legs crossed as she taps her fingertips atop her knee. Despite the dust in her hair from tromping around a haunted house in search of a wayward teenager, she's unshakable, the eye of the storm. "We can't rule out the possibility of a prank," she says. "If anyone would do such a thing—"

"He wouldn't," Vee interrupts, vicious. "Not in this house. Not to us."

Alejandro and Josh exchange a look Riley does not miss, and Jordan's mouth purses. "I understand you're upset—"

"You don't understand anything," Vee snaps. "Something happened to him, and we're wasting time just sitting around."

"Vee." Riley lays a hand on her elbow. "We'll keep looking, okay? We're not going to stop."

Just like that, the fire that had chased her tears burns out. "He wouldn't prank us," she insists. "He *wouldn't*."

"Yeah," Riley says. "I know."

In the wake of Colton's disappearance, Jordan seems to have forgotten the episode upstairs. Nobody's asked him a thing about it, as if Riley locking himself away in a derelict classroom is nothing out of the ordinary.

Ethan's lips still linger on his skin. Riley can't think about it. He can't stop thinking about it.

Ethan Hale had felt so alive for a boy everybody had told him was two years dead.

Riley glances over his shoulder to the windows lining the auditorium. They're pitch-black. Nothing stares back at him. Not Ethan. Not Colton.

Riley doesn't know if that's a good thing or not.

You shouldn't have come back, Ethan had said. *You need to go.*

"I can't find anything," Alejandro says, voice tight like a bowstring. He tosses the camera back to Josh, the most careless he's ever been. "The footage is all the usual shit. Josh was right: one second Colton's in it, and then he's not."

Josh looks to Jordan. "Boss . . ."

Jordan sighs. "I know," she says, scrubbing a hand over her face. "I know, okay?" She turns to Riley. "Looks like you'll finally get your wish."

Riley frowns. "What wish?"

She smiles thinly. "Shoot's over. Missing kid trumps haunted house tour. I'm going to call the authorities, and then I'm going to call our agent and let them know that the most anticipated episode of our whole season has just been canceled."

"That's what you're worried about?" Vee says. "Your fucking *show*?"

"No," Jordan says, getting to her feet. "But it's easier to be mad about that than it is to think about the fact that one of the kids under my supervision just vanished."

Vee blinks, taken aback, and Jordan crosses the room, pulling her phone from her pocket and dialing. Vee glances to Riley.

Tired, Riley says, "She's not a bad person, Vee."

Vee's shoulders sink. "It's not like that. It's just . . ."

Riley wraps an arm around her shoulders. "Yeah. I get it."

She leans on him, staring at the far wall. Quietly, she says, "It's happening again, isn't it?"

Riley doesn't know how to reply to that. "Vee," he says. "There's something I need to tell you."

Vee frowns, turning her head to look up at him. "What?"

Riley tightens his arm. "Upstairs. Before. I—"

"What do you mean you don't have signal? You have a fucking satellite phone!"

165

Alejandro and Jordan are arguing, Josh circling them like an uncertain shark. "Alejandro, calm down—"

Alejandro thrusts his phone in Josh's face. "I haven't got a signal, Jordan hasn't got a signal, the emergency satellite phone doesn't have a signal, and you want me to *calm down?*"

Vee and Riley exchange a look. Riley's phone is in his pocket still, and when he slides it free, he knows what he's going to find before he flicks the screen on.

His wallpaper stares back at him. A generic black texture that came as the default. He has no messages, no calls. Contained in its little black bar, the signal is punctured by an exclamation mark.

Vee says, "How long did that take?"

Riley thinks back to their arrival. "I don't know. How long have we been here? Four hours? Five?"

Vee smiles. It's more resigned than anything else. "Quicker than last time."

Last time most of the night had passed before they'd realized anything was wrong, too focused on the camera instead of their phones. By the time Riley was screaming Ethan's name in the courtyard, their phones were as alive as anything else in the building.

The floor creaks and Riley looks up to see Jordan stomping back over to them, face grim. "Get up," she says. "We're leaving."

Vee startles. "We can't leave—"

"The nearest town is half an hour out. We're heading there now," Jordan says. "You kids can't stay here. We can get some help. Josh, Alejandro, and I will come straight back, okay?

166

We're not leaving Colton behind, but there's not much more we can do at this moment."

Vee looks fit to argue, but Riley grabs her hand. In the back of his head, he hears Ethan, the ghost of a ghost.

Leave. Don't come back.

Riley doesn't want to do either of those things. He doesn't want to leave Colton behind any more than Vee does. He doesn't want to leave *Ethan* behind.

The way Jordan is looking at him tells him he doesn't have much of a choice. Riley gets to his feet, numb all the way to his toes. "Okay," he says. "Okay."

✗ ✗ ✗

They don't bother to collect their equipment from the house; the LEDs stay in the auditorium, and Josh's prized thermal cameras remain where they've been left. Jordan surges down the hall and to the front door, one bag of spare gear slung over her shoulder and the other over Alejandro's.

Riley feels disconnected from the moment. As they step out onto the porch, he can't help but glance back, but the window of the front door is as dark as every other one he's seen.

Outside, the LED Josh left by the van has gone out. None of them seem remotely surprised by this. Instead, their flashlights cut ghastly paths through the gloom. Everybody follows in Jordan's footsteps, barely an inch between them. Vee's hand is sweaty in Riley's grip, but he refuses to let go.

The van is right where they left it, parked crookedly several feet from the house. "Oh thank god," Alejandro hisses and drops his bag to sprint the remaining distance, overtaking Jordan. He slams into it with a thump, hands already ripping the front door open.

A hand lands on Riley's shoulder and he jumps, but it's just Josh. "We're fine," Josh tells him. "We'll be out of here in a moment, and then we can bring a search party for Colton. Everything is going to be fine, yeah?"

Vee and Riley exchange glances. "Yeah," Riley says.

He does not say what happened the last time they left a friend behind to come back with a search party.

The sound of Alejandro shouting makes all of them flinch, and Riley whips around to see him retreating from the van, face creased in frustration. "It's ruined! The whole van's ruined!"

"What do you mean, 'it's ruined'?" Jordan demands, dropping her own bag and beelining for the driver's seat.

Alejandro steps aside for her. "Somebody's been in here. They've ripped the whole dashboard out. It's a mess."

Josh's hand falls from Riley's shoulder. "You can still get it to start though, right? Just try it!"

Alejandro shoots him a look of pure venom. "Even if I knew where to put the damn key, I'd have a hell of a time getting the engine to turn when every wire in the car is mangled." He runs frustrated hands through his hair, pivoting on the spot. "Fuck! *Fuck!*" He slams his boot into the tire, and the whole van rocks with the movement. "Fuck this van, fuck this stupid fucking house, and fuck *you* for making us come here."

Jordan steps back, slamming the door closed. "I didn't *make* you come anywhere," she hisses icily. "We're a team—we decide where to go together or not at all. Do *not* put this on me."

Alejandro bristles, and before the argument can escalate, Riley drops Vee's hand, lurching in between them. "Hey, the last thing you should be doing right now is picking fights." Riley levels Alejandro with a look. "That helps nobody."

Alejandro's fury holds him righteously tight for a second—two—but then it leaches out of him all at once. His face falls, and he passes a tired hand over his eyes. "Shit. Yeah. You're right. I know you're right." To Jordan, "Sorry. I didn't mean any of that. I'm just . . ."

"I know," Jordan says, reaching past Riley to squeeze Alejandro's arm. "It's okay."

"Well, if you two are done bickering," Josh says, "can we figure out what the fuck we're going to do *now*?"

Vee folds her arms, looking pensively down the winding road to the gates. "I could walk to the highway for help," she says. "Somebody will pass by eventually."

Riley's stomach lurches at the idea of letting her out of his sight. "No," he blurts.

She glances back at him, but the dark of her eyes is steel. "I can do it. I did it last time, didn't I?"

She had. And by the time Riley had gotten to see her again only a few hours later, they were both different people entirely. He doesn't know if he can live through that again.

"Don't be ridiculous," Jordan says. "I can't let either of you do that. You're under my care right now; you need to stay where I can see you."

Unable to help himself, Riley snaps, "Oh, like Colton?"

Jordan flinches, but she doesn't back down. "You'll stay with me. Nobody is leaving anybody's sight."

"Jordan, that's great team spirit and all, but it doesn't solve the issue," Josh says. "Somebody needs to go."

Alejandro holds up a hand, stepping away from the van. "I'll do it."

Jordan spins on her heel to glare at him. "Because splitting up is always the best option in situations like this."

"What situations would those be?" Josh asks. "Situations where either we're being harassed by some kind of psychopath or—"

"Don't—"

"—the haunted house we're messing around in might be *actually* haunted?" Josh hoists up his bag, camera poking from the unzipped pocket. "The shit I've caught on film tonight really makes me think we might be leaning one particular way on this one."

Riley can see the stress fracturing Jordan's perfect foundations. "There's no reason to jump to conclusions."

"Are you serious?" Vee asks, cutting in. "Are you fucking serious right now? Colton's gone, *something* happened to Riley upstairs—we've been here for *hours*, and everything has been a mess the whole time. And you want to look me in the eye and say that we're jumping to conclusions."

Jordan grimaces. "That isn't what I said."

"No," Vee snaps. "It's what you *implied.*" She turns to Alejandro and says, "It's about an hour to walk back to the highway. Last time, it took two more before somebody would stop for me."

Alejandro nods, grim faced and serious. "What are my chances of it taking half that?"

"Hopefully better than mine were," she says. "Stick to the road and you'll be fine."

"Right," Alejandro says with a weak grin. "Be prepared for the long haul, got it."

Jordan sighs, pinching her nose in frustration. "Alejandro—"

"I'm going," Alejandro says. "Somebody has to, and it shouldn't be the kids. Josh is better in a crisis than me anyway. I'll be back with help, okay? If you want to stop me, you're going to have to sit on me, boss."

Jordan rolls her eyes. "I was going to say, 'For the love of god, be careful.'"

Just out of sight, Riley feels the looming cross of the chapel watching them, and he shudders. "Let's not bring God into this," he says. "I don't know how welcome he is here."

"With that cheery thought," Alejandro says, stooping to pick up his bag and sling it over his shoulder, "I'll be off. Try to all be here when I get back, yeah?"

It's a joke that falls flat. The absence of Colton is a fresh bruise between them, and Riley's had more than his fair share of experience in how long those take to heal.

The Spirit Seekers trade a few things among themselves— two phones go to Alejandro, in case he stumbles upon a signal, and anything that might weigh him down stays with the crew. Vee and Riley huddle together, watching the trio talk in soft voices.

"He'll be fine, right?" Riley asks, not loud enough to be overheard.

"I was," Vee replies, which doesn't sound like an answer at all.

Josh tugs Alejandro in for a hug, slapping him on the back, and Jordan squeezes his elbow with more affection than Riley is used to seeing from her. Finally, Alejandro pulls away. He offers Riley and Vee a smile. "You'd think I was going off to war or something, huh?"

Riley doesn't deign to give that a reply. "See you soon."

Alejandro's smile dissolves. In its place is something else, something grim and tentative. "Yeah, buddy. See you soon."

"Remember," Vee says, "stay on the road, keep your eyes forward."

"I know, I know." Alejandro glances past them to the gates, ajar on their creaking hinges and hinting at a world beyond the inescapable grasp of Dominic House. "Stay safe, everyone."

He goes, and the group swarms together by the van to watch him; unable to look away until he's through the gates, down the road, and out of sight, claimed by the distance.

Alejandro had been wrong. It doesn't feel like sending someone off to war; it feels like freeing someone of it.

BEFORE

Riley had torn through the chapel, the courtyard, fervently searching through all of the ground floor. He'd half expected to find Ethan in every room he burst into, standing by the windows that overlooked the chapel, a specter of a presence.

He hadn't been there. He hadn't been anywhere. Fear climbed Riley's ribs like a ladder, lodging sharp claws in the softest parts of him.

Their phones had no service. Clouds had rolled in while they slept, and Colton swore up, down, and sideways that when they cleared, they'd be back in business.

Riley knew better. Not that anybody would listen to him. It had taken both Colton and Vee to calm him down.

"He's probably fine," Colton promised, hand on Riley's shoulder, as if without it to ground him, Riley might just float away. Riley wasn't so sure he wouldn't. "He probably just wandered off again, yeah? We'll find him."

They were in the house, bunched in one corner of the auditorium, breathless from their searching. They'd taken a moment to regroup, but every second that ticked by felt like an eon, time they could be searching wasting away.

"You don't understand," Riley said. "He's been— God, all day. He's been off. Haven't you noticed? Something's wrong with this place, and it's getting to him."

Colton and Vee exchanged a look over Riley's shoulder. He read the meaning clear as day.

"I'm serious!" he insisted. "Something's wrong!"

Colton stepped back, relinquishing him to Vee in a smooth transition. When she spoke, her voice was low, as if soothing a spooked child. "We'll find him, Riley. And when we do, I'm going to kick his ass for worrying us all, okay?"

Riley shook his head, arms crossed. He didn't know how to get them to understand—he didn't know that *he* understood.

"I'll check upstairs," Colton said. "You keep searching down here. Someone should stay in the chapel in case he comes back."

Low enough that Riley knew he wasn't supposed to hear it, Vee said, "I don't think Riley should be alone right now."

"None of us should be alone," Riley insisted. He shrugged Vee's hands off. "I'll go with you."

Colton shook his head. "Go back to the chapel. He'll probably be back before I am anyway. Wait to see if you can get a phone signal."

Riley wasn't so certain. "Colton—"

Colton turned, his flashlight bobbing as he strode away, and Riley was helpless but to watch as he vanished out into the hallway.

"Hey," Vee said, snagging his attention. She pushed Riley's hair from his face. "You're letting this place get to you, okay? How many places have we been to that were *actually* haunted?"

Frustration consumed Riley. "Breaking into a few cemeteries and a few empty buildings around town has nothing on this, and you know it."

Vee's patience was endless. "Let's go back to the chapel. When Colton returns, we'll—"

A crack resounded throughout the house, and Colton screamed.

TWELVE

"Well," Jordan says after the silence of Alejandro's departure has lingered long enough to become uncomfortable, "the way I see it, we have two choices."

The snap of Josh's lighter breaks through the air as he sparks a cigarette. "Can't wait to hear 'em."

Jordan holds up a finger. "One: We stay out here until Alejandro brings the calvary back."

Josh fogs the air with smoke. "Why did you have to start off with that one?" he complains. "Whenever you lead with the best option, I just *know* I'm going to hate the next one."

"And option two?" Riley prompts, ignoring him.

Jordan flicks up another finger. "Two: We head back inside and see if we can find Colton ourselves."

"Of course we're going back inside," Vee says. "I've already lost one friend to this stupid house, I'm not about to lose two."

"I mean, if you *had* to lose a second friend, Colton seems like a reasonable choice," Josh offers.

Vee sends him an acid look. "That's not funny. Do you know what happened last time somebody vanished here? No, because *nobody does*."

Josh holds up his hands defensively. "You're right, sorry. That wasn't funny. Shit, I just make bad jokes when I'm nervous, okay?" He shoots Riley a glance. "Give me a hand here."

Riley doesn't respond; he's too busy deliberately avoiding everybody's eyes. Ethan's touch lingers on his skin, cold as a deathbed.

If he was going to tell them what happened, now would be the time to do it. Now might be the *only* time to do it. Once they go back inside the house, who knows what might happen.

Be quiet, Ethan had whispered. *He's listening.*

Riley opens his mouth. Out of the corner of his eye, he glimpses the inside of the van for the first time. His mouth slams shut again. He tears toward it, ripping the door open, ignoring Vee's startled call of his name. What he sees makes his guts go cold.

Alejandro had been right, the entire dashboard seems to have been torn apart; wires dangle from beneath the wheel, from the broken gearbox, from everywhere wires might dangle from. The keyhole is smashed to ruin, the metal twisted.

He hadn't mentioned the scars.

Claws marks rend the seats, spilling stuffing into the foot-well like guts. The steering wheel has the impression of sharp fingertips ripped through its cover, and the plastic that covered the dashboard is split in the echo of four crooked claws.

Riley's own scars burn, and his hands tremble like a leaf.

"Riley?" Vee latches on to his elbow, tugging him back, and Riley allows it. She turns him to face her, expression tight with concern. "Riley, what's wrong?"

Ethan's voice in his ear, whispering in fear. *He can hear us.*

Riley shakes his head. "Nothing," he says. "Nothing at all."

Vee looks him up and down. She glances over her shoulder to Jordan and Josh and asks, quieter, "You sure?"

It's so open outside. It's what had allowed Riley to feel safe out here before.

He doesn't feel safe now.

"Vee," he says, "do you trust me?"

Her frown deepens. "You know I do."

"All right," Riley says. "Then trust me when I say I've got nothing to share right now."

She stares at him. Riley holds her gaze. Doesn't blink. Doesn't look away. The hand on him is warm.

"Okay," she says, slow but firm. No deeper meaning—all the deeper meaning. "You've got nothing to share right now."

She always was the smart one. Riley loves her so much, he could kiss her.

Vee doesn't linger, turning back to the others. "All right," she announces loudly. "We're accomplishing nothing out here. Let's go find Colton."

Josh drops his cigarette, grinding it beneath his heel. "I've always wanted to rescue a maiden in distress," he says. "Guess this is as close as I'm going to get."

"Everybody's getting cameras," Jordan informs Vee, holding up a hand to stall her protest. "*Not* for content. Because between the issues with the lights and the incident with the spirit box, any possible sign of paranormal activity has manifested itself as electromagnetic activity. If this really is something supernatural, the cameras might pick it up first."

Vee doesn't look pleased, but she holds out a hand. "I hope you know I'm not prioritizing your equipment over my life, no matter how much it costs."

Jordan laughs, and it sounds only slightly on edge. "Fuck, that only mattered when everybody was here and accounted for and I was aiming for a Pulitzer. Now I'll be lucky if production doesn't axe my show entirely. If you need to, throw everything at a specter's head and make for the nearest door."

That finally pulls a small smile from Vee. Jordan passes a camera to Riley, and he takes it with reluctance. The snap of it opening is as familiar as it is distressing. "So just to clarify," he asks, "you're giving us blanket permission to break everything you own?"

"Only if you want to explain it to Alejandro," Josh says. In his hands is a clip-on flashlight, like the rest of the Spirit Seekers have been wearing. "Now, both of you hold still and let us clip these on, will you? I think it's about time you got upgraded to your own special-made, hands-free flashlight."

"Oh thank god." Vee sighs. "You don't know how long I've waited for you to say that."

Jordan snorts, beckoning Riley in. He goes obediently, and she snaps one on the front of his shirt. "Try not to break these, at least. You two are wearing the only spares we have, and once we run out of light, we're out for good."

Riley tries not to think about how ominous that sounds. "I'll try my best."

"That's all I've ever asked." Jordan steps back, assessing them with her hands on her hips. They've been out here long enough now that she's ironed the nerves from her expression, in charge once more. "All right, we ready to venture back in?"

No.

"Yes," Riley says.

Jordan smiles at him, setting one hand on Vee's back, the other to his. "Well, here we go. Once more into the breach it is."

They follow Jordan back up to the porch, but as they do Riley's new flashlight sweeps over the front of the house, and he's drawn up short.

Before, the flower beds had been thick with wild poppies, sprouting from fluffy green bushes. He'd noticed them when they'd arrived and then again when he was sitting outside.

Some of them are still cheerful and bright. Most of them are not.

A stretch of the flowers are wilted, the bushes they hang from browned and limp. As Riley stares at them, he realizes they line up with the window in the hallway near the dormitory—the one Josh had sworn he saw somebody walking past.

Riley doesn't know what could do that. Suck the life from a living thing like poison in the veins. He doesn't think he wants to.

Ahead of him, Jordan calls, "Riley?"

Riley wrenches his gaze away. "Yeah," he says. "I'm coming."

And once more, he follows Jordan into her fabled breach.

✗ ✗ ✗

With both Colton and Alejandro gone, the house abruptly feels quiet and still. Without the abundance of voices to chase back its oppressive energy, Riley feels its sinister pull on every inch of his skin.

He stands in the foyer, uncertain what his next step is supposed to be. A part of him fears that if he moves at all, the inky blackness of night will open and swallow him whole, just like it's done to Colton.

Like it did to Ethan.

A hand lands on his shoulder and he spins, heart in his throat, but it's just Jordan, watching him with concern. "Are you okay?"

Riley is sick of people asking him that. "No," he says. "Are *you*?"

Jordan blinks and then huffs out a laugh. "Fair," she concedes. She glances over Riley's shoulder, and her flashlight beam dances up the steps to the second floor. "I'm taking Evelyn to look around the courtyard. Stay with Josh, and for god's sake, don't wander off."

Before Riley can respond, footsteps announce the others. Jordan asks, "Is everyone clear on how we're doing this?"

"Stay together, no wandering, meet by the van in thirty." Josh taps his watch. "We've got it, boss. The kid is safe with me." A pause. "This time I mean it."

Jordan doesn't comment on the last part. Instead, she says, "If we find Colton, be prepared to carry him out. He might have fallen somewhere in the dark; he could be injured. This is not a safe house to be lost in without a light."

Riley doesn't want to think about Colton falling. He doesn't want to think about the state Colton may be in if they find him.

When. When they find him.

His expression must be something to behold, because when Vee looks back at him, she says, "We'll figure it out, okay?"

Riley wants to believe her more than he actually does. "Yeah. Sure."

Vee's face dips into a frown, but Jordan is already moving, steering her down the hall and toward the auditorium door. Riley watches her go, the shine of her hair vanishing into the dark.

Josh nudges him in the shoulder. "C'mon," he says. "I want to go through and check the thermal cams. They might have something we missed."

Riley doubts it, but it's not like he has any better ideas. He glances toward the staircase to the second floor, the classrooms.

You need to leave, Ethan had said. *Don't come back for me.*

He knows Riley well enough to know that was never going to happen. Riley came here for Ethan, and now that he's found him, he's not leaving without him.

He turns to Josh. "Lead the way."

✗ ✗ ✗

They start in the dormitory, Riley planted in a corner, absently scanning the room with his handheld while Josh reviews the footage from the thermal.

Without the others, the room feels so much bigger. The dark eats into the corners, and no matter how many times Riley turns, his light sweeping over cobwebs and dust, he can't shake the feeling they're being watched. By whom, he doesn't know. Ethan, maybe, angry about Riley's continued presence. Or something worse, angry about another thing entirely.

Riley shivers and looks down at the camera screen. It offers him nothing of interest.

Josh sighs, aggrieved, and abandons the thermal camera. "There's nothing here. The only time Colton set foot in this room was when we were all together. And the footage from then isn't all that interesting either. Spirit box aside."

Both their eyes flick to what remains of the box in tandem, nothing more than a shattered nest of plastic and wires. Josh grimaces. "You know what? That whole thing was a lot more exhilarating two hours ago."

"For you, maybe." Riley closes his camera. "Where do you want to head next?"

"We'll go through the rest of the first floor, and if nothing turns up, I guess we'll try upstairs again."

"He's not going to be upstairs," Riley says.

183

Josh frowns. "You both keep saying that. What has he got against the stairs?" A flicker of a smile, trying for levity. "Afraid of heights?"

Irritation chases along Riley's frayed nerves before he can stamp it down. "You've seen the broken railing."

"Yeah," Josh says. "And I'm not an idiot, so I don't go the fuck near it."

"Well, it wasn't broken two years ago," Riley hisses. "It only broke when Colton fell through it and snapped his leg in three different places."

Silence falls, awkward and heavy. "Oh."

"Yeah," Riley says. *"Oh."*

Josh sighs, rubbing a hand over his face. "I didn't know," he says apologetically. "It wasn't in any of the research we had."

"Of course it wasn't. Colton didn't talk about his injury with the media."

"That's not what I meant," Josh corrects. "Just . . . he didn't say anything. Nobody would have ever suggested he go any-where near the second floor if he'd *said* something."

"Colton doesn't talk about what *really* happened that night," Riley says. "Not ever."

Josh raises a brow. "Not even to you?"

"We haven't spoken in over a year," Riley says. "So no, not to me either."

Josh says, "Would have thought going through something like that would have brought you all closer together."

Riley sinks down on the nearest mattress. "That's why."

"What's why?"

"'Something like that,'" Riley says with accompanying air quotes. "How are you meant to bond over surviving something if you can't even talk about *what* that something was?"

Josh eyes him with consideration for a second and then, without warning, snaps his camera closed and tosses it to the mattress beside Riley's. He drops a hand to his belt. It takes Riley a second to realize he's fumbling with his mic pack.

Riley frowns. "What—?"

"There," Josh says. "No cameras. No recording. Just you and me. Hopefully."

"Jordan will be furious," Riley remarks.

"Jordan's not here," Josh says shortly. "Riley, what happened two years ago?"

Riley's stomach turns. He goes cold—his scars burn. "You think I'm going to give you an answer this time just because you hit some fucking buttons and made a production out of it?"

"No," Josh says. "I think you're going to give me an answer because whatever happened two years ago seems to be happening again, and you've seen enough people disappear in this house to last a lifetime."

Josh's blunt honesty hits Riley low and leaves him winded. He stares at Josh and Josh stares back, as serious as Riley has seen him. "Wow." Riley breathes out. "I think I liked you better when you were pulling your punches."

That tugs a small smile from Josh. He drops down beside Riley, nearly bouncing the cameras to the floor. The mattress squeals, and Riley is uncertain whether the bed frame is going to hold their weight.

"Look," Josh says, "at least tell me you understand why I'm asking you."

Riley glances down to the stained carpet. "I know. I get it."

"I'm going to be real with you, man," Josh says. "I've been to a lot of haunted houses over the past few years, and none of them has ever been like this. I'm scared as *hell*. I don't care if we never film another episode again—I just want to make it to sunrise, you know?"

Riley knows that, too. He doesn't lift his gaze from the carpet. His stomach feels like a ship loose in a storm. "You're not going to believe me. Nobody believed me then."

Josh's hand lands on his back, warm against the chill of his spine. "Riley," he says seriously, "you could tell me that Santa Claus is boning the tooth fairy and I'd believe you right now."

Riley laughs, but it doesn't feel like it comes from him. He tangles his hands together in his lap to keep them from shaking. They're not yet. They will. "Dominic House isn't just some urban legend."

"Yeah. I'm beginning to see that."

Riley glances up. Josh is looking at him, puppy-dog earnest. Riley could keep his mouth shut. He has for two years, after all. And now he's certain that there's something in the house listening.

If he keeps his mouth shut and Josh disappears too, he'll never forgive himself.

Fuck it, he thinks.

"Ethan didn't just vanish," Riley says. "He didn't run away. There's something in this goddamn house, and it took him."

Josh hesitates. "When you say 'something' . . ."

The scars on Riley's face are hot enough to scald. He raises a hand to them, pressing his fingertips along the furrows, feels the way they fit to his fingertips. "Something." Riley hesitates too and then corrects, "Someone."

Josh's eyes flicker to Riley's scars. "'Death touched me,'" Josh quotes. "'He wouldn't let go.'"

"I was high off my face on morphine when I said that," Riley says.

"Did you mean it?"

He did. He thinks about it all the time. He dreams about it. A burning cross, eyes like a tar pit, sticky and bottomless. "It had Ethan," he says. "In the chapel. Colton was already injured by then, and Vee had left to find help. It had Ethan, and I knew if I didn't try to stop it, I'd never see him again."

Josh breathes in deeply. Holds it. Lets it out. "What had Ethan?"

Riley shakes his head. His hand falls from his face. "I don't . . . I don't know."

"Bullshit, you don't know," Josh says. "You're one of the smartest kids I've ever met. Riley, what took Ethan?"

Riley closes his eyes. The chapel is waiting for him, as it always is. He can feel the warmth of the fire on his skin. "It wasn't alive. I couldn't see it, not in the dark. But I could feel it." Riley opens his eyes, mouth twisting into a tight smile. "You heard of the uncanny valley?"

"Something that looks human but isn't?"

"Sure," Riley says. "Or something that used to be but isn't anymore."

Josh looks at him. Then he leans back, hands on the mattress for support, and considers the wall. "Ghosts, huh?"

If Riley had the energy, he'd laugh. "Not like you didn't know what you were getting into."

"I chase ghost *stories*, not *ghosts*," Josh huffs.

"I thought you were a believer."

Josh shakes his head. "I am. I was. God, I *am*. But in the same way you believe you might win the lotto when you buy a ticket. This is above my pay grade."

"Yeah," Riley agrees. "And I was sixteen when a ghost tried to rip my face off, broke my best friend's leg, and spirited away my boyfriend."

Silence. "This is so fucked," Josh says.

This time Riley does laugh. It hurts like hell all the way up and sounds worse. He gets to his feet and holds out a hand. "Come on," he says. "We've got most of the house to go yet."

Josh considers his hand like a man who very much does not want to take it, but he sighs and lets Riley pull him to his feet. "Yeah. Sure. I'd love to search through the house of a murderous ghost. Why not."

Riley smiles at him. "That's just what I thought you'd say."

BEFORE

Colton was in the foyer. No, more accurately—Colton had fallen into the foyer.

He was on the floor, sheet white, gasping for breath that wouldn't come. He'd curled into an awkward ball, his hands wrapped around his leg.

Above, the railing that separated the first floor from the second was broken.

"Colton!" Vee was at his side in a heartbeat, wrenching his hands out of the way as gently as she could. "Colton, you have to let me look, okay?"

Colton howled. The house rattled with the sound of it, and Riley, who was standing frozen in the doorway, wished he could unhear it.

Vee managed to pry Colton's hands away. His palms were bloody. Vee gripped the denim of his jeans and tore. Beneath it, Colton's leg was a wash of red. Something white stuck through the skin. It took Riley far too long to realize it was bone.

Tears were streaming down Colton's face. "How bad is it?"

"It's fine," Vee lied. "You're fine, Colton. Don't be a baby, okay? It's just a flesh wound. Riley, get over here."

Colton laughed. It sounded worse than his scream. "You're such a fucking liar."

Vee didn't falter. "Riley, *now*."

Riley's feet took him to her on autopilot, already shrugging out of his flannel. Vee snatched it from him without

189

taking her eyes off Colton, bundling it against the gaping wound in his leg. "I need you to hold this, okay? Keep pressure on it."

Colton fumbled. It took him two tries to get his hands there, and they were shaking like a storm. "Fuck me," he said. "Holy shit."

Vee tried to stand, but her knees buckled, and Riley rushed to catch her. When she grasped at his shirt for support, she left smears of blood behind. There was a thumbprint of it on her temple where she'd pushed her hair from her face. "We need to call 911."

When Riley checked his phone, there was still no signal. Vee's was the same.

Vee cursed. She turned back to Colton. "Shit, okay. Colton, where's your phone?"

Colton shook his head. "I don't know. Dropped it, I think. Upstairs."

Immediately, Vee set a hand to the banister to climb. Quicker than Riley thought he should be capable of, Colton seized her ankle. "Don't!"

"We need to—"

Colton squeezed. His grip left bloody fingerprints on the delicate curve of Vee's ankle. "Don't go up there. Don't, please, shit, don't—" He cut himself off with a cry, both hands jerking down to hold Riley's shirt to his leg as it slipped.

This time, Vee and Riley exchanged a look. Vee crouched down. "We need to get help," she said. "Riley and I still don't have signal. Maybe your phone does."

Colton was already shaking his head. "You can't go up there," he insisted, barely coherent. "There's somebody *there*."

Riley went cold, warm only where Vee had left him marked by Colton's blood.

"Who's up there?" Vee pressed. "Colton, what happened?"

Colton didn't answer. His hands went slack. He was gone, pulled away by the pain, the shock, something else entirely. His ragged breathing was the only sound in the foyer for a long moment.

When Vee stood again, her hands were shaking. "Help me carry him to the car."

Riley stared at her. "We can't leave. What about Ethan?"

"What about *Colton*?" Vee snapped. "Riley, that's a compound fracture. We have to do *something*."

"So you take Colton and I'll stay to look for Ethan," he said.

Vee's face crumpled. "Riley, you *can't* stay here alone—"

Riley ignored her, bending down to gently rifle through Colton's pockets. It was a trial, being mindful of his leg, but Riley was petrified to wake him when he knew all he would be welcoming Colton back to was pain and uncertainty. He was so careful that, at first, he thought he'd missed what he was looking for. He searched again.

There was nothing in Colton's pockets. When Riley looked back to Vee, she could read it in his face.

"Fuck!" She spun on the spot, hands tearing at her hair. She looked toward the stairs. From there, they could see the glimmer of Colton's flashlight by the railing. "Maybe he dropped them."

"He said not to go up there," Riley said.

"We need the keys," Vee insisted. "I don't know how to hot-wire a car, do you?"

Riley stood. "Let me check," he said, but Vee was already moving, taking the stairs two at a time. Riley considered going after her, but by the time he caught up, she'd be at the top anyway.

With great reluctance, he turned his attention back to Colton. Carefully, he wound his flannel around the fracture in his leg, tight enough for pressure and no tighter. The hint of bone piercing through reminded him keenly of the chapel's cross in a way he couldn't explain.

How long had Vee been gone? How long did it take to search for keys? She'd been too long. Riley needed to—

Vee's footsteps thundered down the stairs, and Riley looked up just as she threw herself down the last few steps. She lost her balance and nearly tumbled to the floor but managed to throw a hand to the wall in time to keep upright.

Alarmed, Riley asked, "Vee, what—?"

"I'm going to walk to the highway," she said. "Get help. We can't stay here. We can't. I have to—"

Realization hit like the swing of an axe. "You saw something."

Vee was shaking her head, but that wasn't it; her hands shook, her legs, everything that made her Evelyn Cho, rattled to the core. "We shouldn't have come here," she said. "Riley, *we shouldn't have come here.*"

"Hey, hey." Riley squeezed her shoulders. "Tell me what happened."

She shook her head again, eyes squeezed shut. "I can't find the keys, and we can't waste time looking for them. I have to get help, okay? You stay here with Colton. Don't leave him alone."

Riley wasn't sure he could promise her that. Instead, he said, "If anything happens, come straight back, okay?"

Vee laughed. It sounded hysterical. "I think I'll be safer out there than in here."

"Thanks," Riley said. "That makes me feel a lot better."

She threw her hands around him, squeezing for all she was worth. When she pulled back, her eyes were damp. "Don't go upstairs," she insisted. "Don't go anywhere without a light. And . . ." She hesitated, but decided against whatever was going to follow. "I'll be back soon, okay?"

A lie. Without the car, who knew how long it'd take to find help.

"Okay," Riley said.

Vee glanced to the stairs one more time like she couldn't help herself, and then she left, her flashlight beam bouncing off the hallway walls as she headed to the kitchen, where they'd broken in what felt like eons ago now.

Riley waited a long, long moment to see if she'd change her mind, if she'd come back.

She didn't.

On the stairs, something creaked. Riley's head snapped up. There, at the top step where the light faded, a figure slipped into the shadows.

"Ethan?" Riley called.

Nobody replied.

Riley thought he was going to be sick. His heart thundered a hundred miles an hour. He kept his eyes fixed on the stairs, waiting to see movement, waiting for the next creak of the steps.

He saw nothing. The steps didn't creak.

He closed his eyes, turning back to Colton. His hands, supporting the flannel wrapped around Colton's leg, were numb from fear.

With nothing else he could do, he sat there, watching his friend bleed out, waiting for help that did not come.

THIRTEEN

Downstairs gives them nothing. The kitchen, the dining room, all the rooms where they'd been before pass like a blur. Josh finds nothing on their stationary cameras, and Riley stands in the corner, filming nothing.

In the priest's quarters, they find three fresh dead rats, curled up in a huddle right by the tripod. Josh nudges them out of the way with the toe of his boot, looking more scared of a few dead rodents than he had been of the literal revelation of the supernatural.

"You know they can't hurt you," Riley points out. "Of all the things in this house to be afraid of—"

"You have *no idea* what kind of diseases they could have," Josh says and then busies himself fussing with the camera.

Riley rolls his eyes but gives him space. It's not really about the rats, he knows. Josh does a good job of hiding nerves behind his Irish charm, but he's shaken, and even Riley, who reads people poorly, can see it.

He gives Josh space, circling the room curiously. They hadn't gone in here last time. The door had been locked.

Looking at it now, Riley knows that the Riley of two years ago would have been ecstatic with the aesthetic of it all.

A cross is mounted on the wall above a bed made with military discipline, even after all these years. The sagging drawers of the dresser show moth-eaten clothes, and a rosary is puddled on the bedside table by a shattered lamp.

It doesn't look like the room has been touched since its owner disappeared. Riley skates his fingers atop the dresser, rubbing the dust between his fingers. "Did the school really close down right after the disappearances?"

"That's what all the reports Jordan could find said." Josh glances up at the room as he flicks through the camera. "Guess the poor father didn't have anybody to come calling for his things."

Riley thinks of Ethan's mother, of the police officer on the phone saying, *Mrs. Hale? Mrs. Hale?*

He wipes the dust on his shirt, mouth sour. "Seems like it."

Josh is distracted with the camera, so Riley allows curiosity to guide him to the half-open bedside table. He rattles open the drawer, and a Bible stares back at him, battered from love and dusty with disuse. Unable to help himself, Riley brushes it off, lifting it from its coffin.

It cracks open in his hands, falling to what had obviously been a much-read psalm, eager to please with its broken spine. Passages are underlined with enthusiasm, and Riley's eyes are drawn to them like the irresistible magnetic pull of the universe.

In him we have redemption through his blood, the forgiveness of sins, in accordance with the riches of God's grace.

A chill runs through Riley. He flips through the pages, landing on another dog-eared passage.

I have swept away your offenses like a cloud, your sins like the morning mist. Return to me, for I have redeemed you.

There's writing crammed in the margins. The pages are yellowed from age, and the ink is smudged. He can't read it, but in several places, the pen has torn through the thin paper in its eagerness.

"What have you got there?" Josh asks, sweeping closer.

Riley snaps the Bible closed and offers it to him. "Proof that whatever else happened here, the good father took his mission to rehabilitate really seriously."

Josh winces, holding up a hand. "No thanks. If you grow up Irish Catholic, you read that enough to last a lifetime."

Riley glances down. The text on the cover is a deep gold against the black leather, like not even the endless dust and grime of abandonment could touch it. Once, somebody had loved this Bible more than life itself. "Yeah. Not exactly my thing either."

"You can take it with you if you want," Josh says. "Could be good for scaring off spooks."

Riley snorts. "Thanks, but no."

Josh shrugs, turning for the door. "Suit yourself."

Riley goes to toss the Bible on the bed but pauses without

knowing why. His thumb passes over the cover, the worn leather. Against his better judgment, he tucks the book inside his jacket pocket.

When he turns around, somebody is standing behind him.

Ethan looks as real as he did upstairs. Pale but real. Blue-eyed, golden-haired. Older than he is in Riley's memories.

Not a hallucination, then. "Hey, stranger."

The corner of Ethan's mouth curls up, but it flattens almost immediately. "I told you to leave."

"Yeah," Riley says. "And you know firsthand just how well I follow instructions."

"Riley." Ethan sighs, and it makes Riley want to punch him and kiss him in equal measure.

"I'm not leaving Colton," Riley insists. "And I'm not leaving you. Not again."

Ethan's shaking his head before Riley's even done speaking. He reaches out, and the ice of his fingertips brushing Riley's hand makes his heart jolt. "You have to," he says. "Don't worry about Colton. I'll take care of him."

Riley's stomach turns. "What," he says, "does that mean?"

From the hallway, Josh hollers, "Riley, what's the holdup? Don't wander off. I can't take losing another one of you right now."

Riley calls back, "I'm coming. Just—just a minute."

The touch of Ethan's fingers on his disappears. When Riley looks to him, Ethan is gone.

Riley stands there for long enough that Josh pokes his head back in, frowning. "Seriously, stick with me, yeah? You're going to give me a heart attack at this rate." Then, seeing Riley's face, he asks, "Is everything okay?"

Riley folds his hand into a fist. "Yeah, everything's fine."

Josh's frown deepens. He looks about the room and then to Riley again. Cautiously, he says, "Would you tell me if it wasn't?"

What's Riley supposed to say to that? *The ghost of my boyfriend keeps trying to kick me out of this stupid fucking house?*

Riley plucks his camera from the bedside table and shoulders past Josh into the hallway. "Let's go," he says. "We need to find Colton, and soon."

✗ ✗ ✗

Riley's second trip upstairs is far less rewarding than the first.

The classroom is just how he and Jordan left it, and Josh trawls through it at the pace of a snail, filming with his handheld like he expects something to jump out at any moment.

Riley tires of waiting for him and checks the thermal camera himself. It takes a couple of tries to figure out how—technology evolves fast—but before trauma robbed him of his enthusiasm, Riley was a textbook technophile.

"God." Josh sweeps his camera across the room. "Tell me the truth: Is this place more or less creepy than the first time you were here?"

"Trick question." Riley doesn't glance up. "It's equally creepy because the same fucking things keep happening."

Josh's camera drops to his side. "We'll find Colton," he promises. "This place is only so big. And even if . . ." He hesitates. He still can't make himself talk about ghosts as anything

199

more than an abstract, Riley's noticed. "Even if," Josh continues, "something happened, he has to be here *somewhere*."

"Yeah," Riley says, still not looking up. "That's what they said about Ethan."

Silence falls like a hangman's noose.

Riley scrubs through hour after endless hour of empty classroom footage. He checks his watch. It's nearing two in the morning now—that's five or six hours of film to look through. Riley grits his teeth, determinedly speeding through the footage. It's so blandly predictable that when the door on the tiny screen cracks open, it makes Riley frown—then the warm outline of Jordan steps into the room, and it clicks.

He'd forgotten that his and Jordan's brief stint would have been caught on film. He hadn't even been thinking about it when—

Riley heart stumbles on the next beat. He fast-forwards.

Jordan struts through the room at double speed, painted in glowing red. Riley trails after her. Like a practiced dance, they retreat to the door, and just like Riley remembers, Jordan's warmth vanishes behind it, but Riley's does not.

A moment later, Ethan appears.

On the screen, Riley and Ethan sway to each other like reeds caught in the wind, blurs of moving color. Riley stares, speechless. He rewinds. He watches. Ethan appears, just as before, real as anything.

Ghosts don't appear on film. Not like this. Not solid, undeniably human shapes.

The shock is the only reason it takes Riley so long to notice the obvious.

Film-Riley sets a hand, dyed sunset orange on the thermal, on Ethan's cheek. Ethan leans into it, and so does the mass of bruised violet and blue that defines him.

Riley feels numb from head to toe.

From across the room, where he's sitting in one of the abandoned desks, Josh calls, "Anything useful?"

Riley looks to him and then back at the camera. The rainbow of color makes his eyes hurt.

He turns off the screen. "No," he lies. "Nothing at all."

Josh sighs. "How can so much go wrong and leave so little trace behind?"

Riley has his back to him, setting the thermal back down on its stand. Something glimmers in the windows, and he glances up sharply. Nothing looks back at him except his own reflection, streaked and smudged.

"Riley?"

Riley makes himself turn around. "Get used to it," he says. "This place is a hellhole."

Josh looks pained. "Thanks, Riley. That's real reassuring."

Riley shrugs. He picks his camera up, glancing over his shoulder and back to the windows before he can help himself. "You adjust."

Before Josh can reply, there's the sharp sound of Jordan yelling. They're too far away to make out what she's saying, it seems as if she's still in the courtyard, but her tone is frantic.

"Fuck," Josh says, getting to his feet in a hurry. "That can't be good. Come on."

Heart in his throat, Riley follows him as they beeline out of the classroom and over to the stairs. Worst-case scenarios flash before his eyes, and as they approach the landing, he clings to the banister to keep upright.

Josh looks to him, sees his face, and doubles back. "Hey," he reassures, hands on Riley's shoulders. "It's okay. Whatever it is, we'll figure it out."

"You *know* that's not true," Riley says. "God, what if—?"

"Let's get downstairs," Josh says firmly. "And then we'll figure it out, okay?"

The banister beneath Riley's hand creaks, and he forces himself to let go. "Okay."

Josh smiles at him. "Okay," he says. He drops his hand.

Both their flashlights go out.

Riley reaches for the banister again immediately. The darkness that swoops in is so sudden and pervasive that it leaves him blinking, trying to see anything beyond it. "Josh?"

Josh doesn't answer. He doesn't make a single noise. Riley can't even hear him breathing. Blindly, he reaches out a hand to where Josh had been only a moment ago and finds nothing. "Fuck, Josh. *Josh!*"

He takes one step forward. Two. Where do the stairs start? He can't remember. He can't see *anything*. Dominic House is a void, swallowing everything inside it, and Riley feels it laying greedy hands on him too.

Fumbling, he reaches up, fingers grazing the light strapped to his chest. After several false starts he finds the switch and flicks it. Nothing happens. Again, frantic. Nothing.

Again. Again. Again.

Riley can't breathe. He's suffocating. "Josh, please—"

Again. Again. Again. *Again. Again*—

The light clicks back on. The relief is short-lived. When he sees what's in front of him, his heart trips to a standstill.

It's Ethan, back to him, pale in the flashlight. He has a hand around Josh's throat, holding him a half foot above the ruined carpet. Josh is clawing at him, white-faced and wide-eyed. His camera is on the ground, filming his dangling feet.

Riley takes a step forward. "Ethan—"

Ethan's head snaps to him, and Riley freezes where he stands.

There's no blue in Ethan's eyes. He looks right through Riley, empty of recognition, of love, of all the little things that are intrinsically Ethan Hale, even in death.

Riley stares at him and, finally, has the realization that the thing looking back at him isn't Ethan at all.

Josh's eyes snap to his. His fingers are wedged into Ethan's fist, struggling to break his grip. He can't speak, has no air, but his mouth forms Riley's name.

That grabs Riley like a hook between his ribs and jerks him into action. He braves another step forward and somehow his legs do not give. "Ethan," he says. "Please. Let him go."

Ethan stares at him. Not-Ethan, he means. Then he looks back to Josh. He's seconds away from passing out entirely. Ethan's mouth curls into a smile. Riley realizes what's going to happen, too late.

He lurches forward. *"Don't—"*

Ethan lets Josh go. He falls right through the split in the railing—there one moment and gone the next. He doesn't even have the breath to scream.

Thud goes his body as it hits the rotting floorboards of the foyer.

Riley stays where he is, one hand pressed over his mouth to stop himself from letting out the scream Josh hadn't. He feels like he's going to be sick. He can't make himself look over the railing to the foyer below.

"Riley," Ethan says in a voice like silk.

Riley looks to him. Ethan's eyes are like pitch. On a gamble, he asks, "Jacob?"

Ethan blinks placidly. The smile on his face is peaceful, at odds with the fact that he's just thrown a man over a balcony. Riley's skin crawls to see it. Ethan doesn't answer.

Riley has *no* clue what to make of that expression, that silence. "Whoever the fuck you are," he says, "*whatever* the fuck you are—leave my boyfriend alone."

Ethan considers that. "No," he says, and before Riley can say anything else, he melts back into the darkness.

Riley's legs are rubber, and his lungs are frozen. There are no sounds coming from downstairs. He swallows. "Josh?"

Silence.

He needs to look. He needs to look over the fucking railing. He needs to—

Unbidden, he thinks of Colton, the white of his bone, the red of his blood.

He can't. He can't. Not again.

Riley sinks to the floor, clutching the railing for strength. *Get up*, he coaches himself. *Get up, get up, get up, get up—*

He gets up. Then, one painful footstep at a time, he forces

himself down the creaking staircase. It feels like walking to the gallows.

The foyer is bright from Josh's flashlight, illuminating the dust motes drifting aimlessly past, and Riley follows the source of it down, down, down until he finds the crumpled figure lying almost exactly where Riley had found Colton years ago.

Riley kneels beside him, hand on Josh's arm. His skin is clammy. It hadn't been upstairs, when their lights had gone out and Josh had reached toward him to chase back the smoky fear choking them both.

He's sprawled on his back, arms and legs askew like a doll that has been cast aside. Riley can't tell if anything is broken, not like he could with Colton. Josh's face is pinched, sheened in sweat, and when Riley calls his name, he doesn't wake, he doesn't blink, he doesn't do anything at all.

Terrified, Riley presses an ear to his chest. He hears the rattle of Josh's breath and relief punches him to near tears.

"Fuck," he says. "Jesus, Josh."

The door to the auditorium bangs open, and Riley flinches, spinning around to come face-to-face with Jordan.

She blinks at him, opens her mouth to say something, and then catches sight of Josh. She sucks in a breath so sharp, Riley imagines it must cut her to pieces deep inside. "Is that—?"

Riley's tongue is stuck to the roof of his mouth. He can't speak. He gets to his feet and Jordan blows past him, sinking to her knees, calling Josh's name over and over like a radio on loop.

Mrs. Hale? Mrs. Hale?

Riley stares behind her at the smudged glass of the front door, arms folded, hands tucked close. He's cold as ice. He doesn't know where his camera has gone. Upstairs with Josh's, probably.

He feels disconnected from this moment, from his body. This is all happening to somebody else.

He felt like that last time too. It hadn't been true then, either.

In the door's glass, something glimmers. Riley stares at it.

It's Ethan. Or maybe it isn't. His eyes aren't black, but they're not exactly blue either. He's looking right at Riley, finger to his lips like a secret.

"What do you want?" Riley asks, voice a whisper. "What the fuck do you *want*?"

Not-Ethan's finger falls. He looks past Riley. Over his shoulder. Not to the auditorium, Riley knows. To the building that lies beyond it.

He thinks of Jordan's notebook.

Chapel, chapel, chapel, chapel, chapel—From where she kneels on the floor, Jordan's voice breaks over Josh's name.

BEFORE

Riley sat with Colton for what felt an eternity. Both their hands were clammy, and when Riley pushed Colton's hair from his face, it was damp with sweat. His leg bled through Riley's shirt, steady as a river flowed.

The house creaked and groaned around them. Things moved in the corner of Riley's eye, but when he turned to look, there was nothing there. There was never anything there.

He didn't look back to the stairs. He couldn't.

It was just Colton, Riley, and Dominic House. Riley was starting to think that it had always been that way—that it always would be.

Colton didn't wake. A relief for both of them.

When Vee had been gone for an hour, maybe more, Riley squeezed Colton's hand one last time, drawing strength, as if Colton had any to spare. "I'll be back," he promised. "Vee and I, we'll be back, okay?"

Colton didn't answer. Riley was glad for it. He didn't know what he'd say.

Riley got to his feet. In the corner of his vision, something shifted in the glass of the front door. When he turned to it, he caught a passing glimpse of watchful eyes, gone as quick as they'd appeared.

They'd been looking over his shoulder, and just like that, Riley knew precisely where to be.

FOURTEEN

The red of Jordan's jacket draped over Josh's chest makes his skin look sallow.

Jordan sits beside him, holding his hand. Without the armor of her leather jacket, she looks strangely smaller. Life-size instead of larger than. When she speaks, her voice is rough. "What happened?"

Riley says, "You know what happened."

Jordan's mouth pulls tight. She looks to the broken railing. She hasn't been able to look away. "I thought . . ."

I thought we'd be okay, she doesn't say. *I thought nothing could touch us.*

Riley knows how that feels. He knows how it feels to be wrong. "Where's Vee?"

Jordan shakes her head. The hand not holding Josh's is pressed over her eyes.

"Jordan, what happened to Vee?"

"You know what happened," Jordan echoes.

Riley had expected it. At this point, of course he had. It still hits him like a gut punch.

Ethan. Colton. Vee. Dominic House had taken from him every single friend he had, unsatisfied unless he was wretchedly alone and miserable.

Behind Jordan, the door to the auditorium is open. Beyond that, looming outside the darkened windows, is the one place Riley had always hoped he would never again set foot in.

He looks to Josh. He's pale as sin, and his forehead is beaded with sweat. But he's alive. "Look after him," Riley says. "I'll be back soon."

Jordan's hand drops from her face. "Where are you going?"

Riley backs away. "Don't leave him," he says. "Stay together."

"Riley. *Riley!*"

Riley goes. He does not look back.

✗ ✗ ✗

The path to the chapel is bracketed by rosebushes, grown wild without a hand to tend them. Every single one of them is rotted, weeping dead petals to the ground. Gravel crunches beneath Riley's boots, and as he approaches the doors, he's certain he's not alone.

Behind him, Dominic House watches. In front of him, the chapel waits.

Riley expects to be scared. To be unable to do more than stand still as stone, another statue littering the courtyard.

He isn't scared. He isn't still. He's just ready for this to be over.

The chapel doors are chipped and cold beneath his hands. Riley skates his fingers up, wrapping them around the handles, and shoves with everything he has.

The doors don't budge an inch. If Riley couldn't see flickering light through the thin gap between them, he'd think they'd been welded closed.

Something doesn't want him in the chapel.

Well, Riley thinks, *that makes two of us.*

It has his friends, though. Once, Riley let the specter of Dominic House steal his friends—his family—from him. He's not about to let it happen again. And by freezing him out of the chapel like it has, it has let Riley know one very important fact.

It considers Riley a threat.

He steps back, assessing, and a loose rock catches the heel of his boot. He considers it for a moment and then stoops to pick it up. It weighs about as much as a brick, and Riley hefts it once, twice, and pitches it through one of the lovely stained-glass windows on either side of the door.

It shatters instantly, glass spraying everywhere in a rainbow of shards. Riley neatly steps back a split second before the doors fling themselves open with such force that the building shakes. Crumbling stone drips free of its mortar.

An icy chill sweeps over Riley, something unnatural and unwelcoming, incongruent with the golden candlelight glimmering inside.

He grins. It feels just as cold. "Didn't like that, did you?" he asks.

The chapel does not reply. Riley doesn't need it to. From somewhere inside its cavernous entrails, a frozen fury emanates like a blizzard.

Riley sucks in a deep breath and then, in what might be

the most courageous thing he's done all night, steps over the threshold.

The doors slam shut behind him, and this time Riley knows no matter how many windows he smashes, they will not open until Dominic House is done with him.

That's fine. Riley will walk out of here when *he's* done with Dominic House, too, and not a moment fucking sooner.

Inside, the chapel is a derelict wreck bathed in gold. The stone walls are blackened, and despite the years, it reeks of smoke from the last time Riley was here.

The candles are all burning. Every last one of them. The wax has burned down to stubs, and the flames they cast waver, ready to go out at a moment's notice.

Above, the cross looms on the wall. Jesus hangs from it, eyes watchful, soot smeared over the burnished bronze of his cheeks.

It looks exactly like Riley remembers.

He takes a tentative step forward, and the floorboards creak but do not crack. He chances another step, and then another, until eventually he's standing at the pulpit, near enough that if the cross were to fall it would take him out on the way down.

He looks at Jesus and says, "Guess you couldn't escape this place either, huh?"

No answer.

Riley looks around. The stained glass makes it impossible to tell if anybody's watching him. "I'm here," he says, spreading out his arms. "Where the fuck are *you?*"

Silence. For a second, Riley thinks he'll get no reply, and then a glimmer in the corner of his eye catches his attention. He turns. There's nothing there. Frowning, he turns back.

Next to him is a boy, sixteen at most. He stands an inch from Riley's elbow, looking at him with pale eyes. His hair is a mess, cheeks painfully gaunt. He looks so different from the newspaper clippings that Riley almost doesn't recognize him.

"Jacob?"

Jacob Smith stares at him, and Riley is helpless but to stare back. A dim pounding starts in his head, just behind his temple. He has the feeling he's seeing something his brain isn't equipped to handle, like pulling a scene from a photo negative.

Riley shivers. "What are you— What happened to you?"

Jacob raises a finger to his lips, and Riley's spine prickles as he recognizes the gesture, recognizes it from mirrors, windows, dreams—from Ethan.

A warning. A promise. A guiding moment across two different nights when Riley was lost in the dark and so, so alone.

Jacob lowers his finger slowly until he's pointing at the step they're standing on, the one that ascends to the pulpit.

Riley shuffles back, glancing down. "What?"

No answer. He looks up. Jacob is gone. It's just Riley alone in the corpse of the chapel. Riley had never realized the absence of a ghost might be more frightful than its presence until this moment.

"Shit," he mutters, scrubbing a hand through his hair. "Fuck me, I don't know what I'm doing here."

He wishes Vee were here. Colton, even.

He wishes, as he has every day for years, for Ethan.

That's enough to get him moving. He told Ethan he wasn't leaving this house without him again, and he'd meant it. He rolls up his sleeves, crouching down where Jacob had pointed, running his fingers along the wooden step, searching for . . . god knows what.

Dust coats his fingertips. Down here, Riley can smell the dampness and rot of the chapel clear enough to wrinkle his nose. But if Jacob wanted him to look, Riley would look.

His fingers catch on something. Frowning, he presses down and feels part of the wood give. *Click* goes the step, and Riley watches, amazed, as he slowly slides it away to reveal it hadn't just been a step at all. A trapdoor, cut from the same wood as the step surrounding it. As it rattles back, it unearths several steep steps into the bowels of the chapel. The bottom step ends at a steel door, battered and bowed toward Riley, as if somebody on the opposite side had kicked it with force. A metal bar holds it closed.

Riley stares, open-mouthed. He'd seen blueprints for Dominic House before. This wasn't on them.

"Oh my god," he marvels. "I'm in a fucking horror movie."

The candles flicker and Riley glances over his shoulder but sees nothing. That doesn't make him feel any safer. He looks back to the steel door and takes a deep breath. "Fuck. Okay. I'm really doing this."

He goes down the stairs slowly. He has to skim the first few on his ass. There's not enough room to stand, but by the fourth step, he manages to get to his feet, so long as he hunches over. The gold of the candlelight recedes behind him, and his flashlight washes the world in pale yellow.

When he presses his hand to the door, it's cold as ice. His breath fogs in front of him. He half expects the trapdoor above to close, but it doesn't.

"Okay," he says. "Okay, okay, okay."

The bar is on a hinge, set to be levered up and off. Riley grips the bar and heaves at it. It resists him, fused in place by age, and Riley experiences a moment of fear that he's not going to be able to move it—then it gives, snapping clean off its hinge in his hand, and Riley nearly staggers beneath the weight of it.

It clangs to the floor. Without the bar, the door handle turns in his grip, and the door gives a discordant shriek as Riley pries it open.

Behind it, the stairs continue. A dozen more, maybe. Riley sees where they open into a shallow room, dark as a tomb.

Riley does not want to go down there.

He glances to the steel door. From this side, he can see just how hard somebody had fought to open it. Dents mar it from top to bottom, and pale scratches frame the handle.

Riley's scars ache looking at them. Unable to help himself, he places his hand to the scratches, and his fingers fit perfectly.

Somebody had wanted out more than they'd wanted anything in their life. Looking down the stairs, Riley doesn't blame them.

"*Fuck*," he says, once more with feeling, then picks up the metal bar, places it to keep the door wedged open, and descends.

It takes a lifetime to reach the bottom. Eight steps, at least eight thousand years. When his boots hit dirt, something rattles against his heel. Frowning, Riley looks down, and his flashlight illuminates a skull staring back.

Riley swears and tries to scramble up the stairs, only to lose his footing. As he falls, he throws out a hand to catch himself. It plummets right through a skeletal rib cage at the foot of the stairs.

Bones crunch beneath his palm. He feels dust between his fingers.

I'm going to be sick, Riley thinks, but there's nothing left in his stomach, and when he yanks himself free and curls into a ball, all he can do is pant for breath, staring at the dirt floor. He's keenly aware of the bone chips that once belonged to a human being lodged beneath his fingernails.

His breath is so loud down here. Like being trapped in a coffin.

It's that thought that levers him upright, so quickly he gives himself a head rush. Spots dance before his eyes as his vision hurries to clear. Finally, he gets his first real look at the hellhole Dominic House's poisonous roots sprout from.

It's a cellar. Or it was once, anyway. The floor is dirt, and the stone walls look sturdy and solid, interspersed with hefty wood reinforcements to keep them stable. Shelves line one of the far walls, although they're dusty. An empty tub of rat poison sits on its side, its label peeling.

The room itself isn't nearly so empty.

The skeleton Riley had tripped over stares up at him, its bare face ghoulish, what's left of its ribs concave. The clothes that cling to it are rotted scraps—the white collar circling its throat the only thing to survive.

Well. At least he's solved one mystery. Whatever happened forty years ago, Father Thomas went into this forgotten cellar, and he never climbed out.

The empty eye sockets unnerve him, and unable to help himself, Riley turns the skull so it's staring at the wall. A sizable crack at the base of the skull flakes at his touch. Riley eyes it and then looks back toward the stairs.

Two mysteries, maybe.

He gets to his feet, brushing dust from his jeans, and as he does, his flashlight beam jumps across a shape in the corner. Riley turns to it. He's expecting Ethan, Jacob.

It's not.

Colton slumps against the wall, limp all the way through, eyes closed. There's dirt in his hair, and his clothes are covered in cobwebs like he's been dragged across the floor. Beside him, Vee lists against his shoulder, face doll-like in slumber.

Riley crosses the room in a heartbeat, sinking to his knees before them. "Hey! *Hey!*"

Neither of them wake. A vision of Josh on the floor flashes behind Riley's eyelids.

Riley grits his teeth. "Sorry about this," he says and slaps Colton clean across the cheek.

Colton jerks awake with a hurricane gasp. His hands shoot

out, fisting in Riley's shirt as he blinks frantically against the burn of Riley's flashlight.

"It's just me," Riley hisses, shaking him gently. "Colton, hey. It's Riley."

"Riley?" Colton stops struggling, clinging to him as he gasps for breath. Shakily, he scrubs one hand across his eyes. "Shit, where . . . ?"

"You're in a cellar beneath the chapel," Riley says.

"The chapel?" Colton looks bewildered. "No, I was in the courtyard. With Josh. And then—" The bewilderment fades. Fury replaces it. His gaze snaps back to Riley. "Your fucking boyfriend is a piece of work."

"That wasn't Ethan," Riley says grimly. "Come on, I don't have time to explain. Can you wake Vee?"

For the first time, Colton seems to realize they're not alone. He shakes her shoulder far too gently to be of any use.

"You're going to have to be more forceful than that," Riley says.

Colton squints at him, as if remembering. "Did you slap me?"

"No," Riley lies and backs away, surveying the cellar as Colton gives Vee a more vigorous shove.

After the theatrics upstairs, Riley had been certain he was walking into a viper's nest down here, but as far as he can tell, they're alone. Father Thomas rotting by the stairs, and Riley's friends bleary in the corner.

No ghosts. No Ethan.

Riley looks over his shoulder. Vee is half-awake now, one hand to her temple as she blinks uncomprehendingly at

Colton. They'll be leaving any minute, and Riley knows once they do, he'll never come back again.

There has to be *something* here. Ethan didn't disappear into thin air.

"Fuck," he mutters under his breath. "Ethan, c'mon, *please*."

He cuts a circuit around the room, trailing a hand along the mossy stone wall. The ground is uneven beneath his boots, and his flashlight casts everything into uncomfortable shadows. The whole cellar is maybe a dozen feet in either direction, bigger than his room back home but not by much.

He makes it to one corner. Turns to another. His light glimmers on something on the ground

It's a chalice. Rusty with age. When Riley comes closer, he realizes it's not alone. Bones gleam beside it.

For a moment Riley thinks he's found Ethan, but as he draws nearer, he realizes all he's found is another skeleton. Slightly smaller than Father Thomas but just as rotted. It's curled up in the fetal position, the white of its bones a beacon in the dark.

Riley stares at. There's nothing about it to recognize. He does anyway.

"Jacob?" he whispers.

Upstairs, the cellar door slams closed. Riley's flashlight goes out. The room plummets into darkness.

BEFORE

Riley found Ethan in the chapel, gazing up at the crucifix.

The clouds had cleared and the moonlight painted his hair silver; the shadows hollowed the highs of his cheekbones. His hands were clasped in front of him, as near to silent worship as Riley had ever seen from him.

The candles were burning. Every single one.

Looking at Ethan, Riley couldn't recognize him at all. Riley stood with one foot in the chapel, the other frozen in the courtyard outside. Across the room, his camera blinked at him from the pulpit, beckoning him closer.

Riley swallowed. His hands were stained with Colton's blood. Somehow he found the strength to step inside. "Ethan?"

Ethan's head cocked, as if listening to him. He didn't reply. He didn't move. The shadows of the chapel consumed him.

Riley's heart was a rabbit inside his chest, beating heavy feet on the cage of his ribs. Ethan's back was broad, his shoulders loose and relaxed. It occurred to Riley that he'd never paid much attention to Ethan's back before—Ethan had so rarely turned it to him.

In a panic, Riley moved closer, reached out, snagged Ethan's arm. When he pulled, he expected Ethan to resist.

He did not. He allowed Riley to turn him without a fight.

His expression was as empty as the blue of his eyes. Riley was standing half a foot from him, but he might as well have been a world away. Ethan wasn't looking at him; it didn't seem as if he was aware of Riley at all.

Riley squeezed his arm hard enough to bruise, shaking him. "Ethan! *Ethan!*"

Ethan blinked. His brows drew tight. Confusion burgeoned across his face, and relief swept through Riley like a tide.

It did not last long.

The shadows behind Ethan shifted, and when Riley looked, his heart froze.

There was a hand on Ethan's shoulder.

FIFTEEN

"Riley, put your light back on!" Colton snarls.

Riley doesn't bother replying. He stays stock still, conscious of the dead child at his feet, his friends at his back. The rest of the wide, empty space. He waits for his eyes to adjust.

Vee, more uncertain, says, "Riley?"

Riley turns toward her voice without meaning to. "I'm here," he says. "Be quiet, okay? Just . . . don't say anything."

Riley's not sure if that will help the situation. So far, none of his ghosts tonight have seemed to care one way or another how silent he was, how still.

He's not a child, and nightmares can't be chased away by hiding beneath the covers. Somehow Riley can't help but try.

There's a rustle of movement. Colton sucks in a breath to say something else but lets out a sharp hiss instead, like Vee has struck him in the ribs.

The darkness looms. Riley waits.

A hand lands on his shoulder. Solid. Cold. Riley very deliberately does not flinch.

In his ear, Ethan says, "You shouldn't have come down here."

Relief tastes like iron on his tongue. Riley reaches up to squeeze Ethan's fingers. "Where else would I go?"

Ethan's other hand lands on his waist, and with aching gentleness, he pushes Riley forward. Riley loses his grip on Ethan but finds Vee in the darkness. She lets out a surprised noise, but when she realizes it's him, the outline of her shoulders sags in relief. Her hand envelops his. "What do we do?" she says, no louder than a whisper.

"Riley and I could break the door down," Colton offers. His hand brushes Riley's other one briefly in the dark, and Riley seizes it before Colton can try anything stupid.

"Trust me," Riley says, "if something wants that door shut, we're not going to get it open."

A shiver chases through Colton. Riley wouldn't have even noticed if they weren't touching. "Then what the fuck do we *do*? God, I don't want to die here, Riley."

"We won't," Riley says, far more confident than he feels. "Ethan will get us out."

"*Ethan*?" Colton hisses. "He's the one who dragged me down here!"

Riley stamps down on his impatience. "I told you, that wasn't him—not really. I think—I think the other ghosts have been possessing him. Or one of them, at least."

"Other ghosts? Ghosts, *plural*? This gets better and better."

"Colton, shut up," Vee says. "I think I can hear something."

Riley can't hear a thing, but before he gets the chance to say so, his light flickers back on.

Riley is expecting Ethan.

It's not.

He's expecting Jacob.

It's not.

Behind him, Colton sucks in a breath. Vee's hand trembles like a leaf. It takes all Riley has not to back into the wall.

Death has rendered Father Thomas a shade of the person he was in life. His pale skin is near translucent, and his dark hair is plastered to his skull with blood, the white of his priest's collar spotted with it.

His eyes are black pits, like the shadows of the decaying skull by the staircase.

"Oh my god," Colton says. "What the *fuck* is that?"

Riley has an idea, and the idea amounts to *nothing good.* "Colton, Vee, get to the stairs," he says, as calmly as he can, which is not that calmly at all.

"Riley—"

"*Go.*"

They scramble along the wall, Vee holding Colton up when his bad leg threatens to give. Riley keeps his back to them, walking sideways to slot himself between Father Thomas and his friends.

Father Thomas moves with them, turning in a half circle to follow their movements, watching them. At least, Riley thinks he's watching them. It's hard to tell when his eyes are more an idea than a reality.

Riley passes by Jacob's bones. His heel catches on something, and he stumbles, hand out to the wall to keep himself upright. He glances down and immediately wishes he hadn't.

A skeletal hand pokes from the dirt. The soil around it is uneven, shallow in more places than not. With dawning horror, Riley looks along the wall.

White gleams through in places, bright in Riley's flashlight. Jacob is curled up alongside it all, as if a sentry, forever watchful.

How many students went missing? Four? Five, including Jacob? How many shallow graves is Riley walking on? How many children's remains rot beneath his feet?

Colton and Vee are nearly to the staircase. Father Thomas is watching them, unworried, silent.

Riley says, "Did you kill them?"

A beat. Father Thomas looks to him. His hands are folded neatly behind his back. His cassock inspires worship.

Riley has never wanted to kill somebody who was already dead so much in his life.

He picks up a rock and throws it with all his might. It passes through Father Thomas and clatters against the far well. Father Thomas turns to look at it and then glances back at Riley, unfazed.

"I said," Riley snaps, "did you fucking kill them?"

He's not expecting a reply. He never is in this place.

Father Thomas says, "I did not."

Riley stares at him. Colton and Vee are frozen by the doorway, watching them, so still Riley isn't sure they're breathing. He wants to tell them to move, to get going while Father

Thomas is focused on him, but Father Thomas's attention cuts like a laser beam.

"I don't believe you," Riley says. "Fuck, I don't know why nobody figured it out sooner. It's always the priest, isn't it?"

Finally, Father Thomas's face pinches. "The children were lost souls," he says. "Dominic Savio's was a salve to their wounds, but it couldn't heal them. Their sickness—"

"Sickness?" Riley repeats, incredulous. "They weren't fucking sick, they just needed *support*. They were teenagers—just kids. Who knows how they would have turned out when they grew up, if they'd been allowed to grow up at all."

Father Thomas continues as if Riley hasn't interrupted him. "—made their lives painful. Their parents recognized that. If left to fester, it would spread, and then they and everything they touched would be beyond saving."

Riley looks to him and then to the dirt, to the bones littered at their feet. "You call this saving? Are you listening to me at all? They were *children*. Just fucking children."

Father Thomas says, "In him we have redemption through his blood, the forgiveness of sins, in accordance with the riches of God's grace."

Riley thinks of the Bible, dusty and devout, stored in Father Thomas's bedside drawer. "I don't think God was asking for you to murder in his name."

"They went peacefully," Father Thomas says. "And our Lord was waiting to welcome them into his arms."

Riley's mind stalls on that. He turns his head, eyes landing on the ancient tub of rat poison atop the shelf, the empty goblet overturned in the dirt. His brain spits out a realization.

Across the room, Vee presses a hand to her mouth, cheeks bleached white.

"You poisoned them," Riley says numbly. "They were kids. They didn't . . . You took them down here, and what? You told them to take communion? And then they—"

Father Thomas smiles. His hands fold serenely in front of himself. "Into the Lord's arms, as he intended."

There's a clatter from the stairwell and Riley glances up to see the door swing wide open. Standing behind it is Ethan, the metal bar in his hands. The glow of the chapel candles haloes him like something vengeful.

"Ethan?" Vee starts for him, but Colton yanks her back.

"Careful," he warns. "How do we know he's *him*?"

Ethan ignores them both. He's looking right at Riley. His eyes are blue.

Jacob's eyes had been, too, Riley realizes. And Father Thomas—he looks back to the priest, the awful blackness sunken into his sockets, the same blackness that had stared back at him from Ethan's during his worst moments.

"It's him," Riley says.

That's good enough for Vee. She grabs Colton firmly by the arm and begins to haul him up the stairs, uncaring for the hitch in his breath as his bad leg begins to crumple beneath him. Ethan moves to help them, but he barely has one foot on the step before Father Thomas calls his name.

Ethan pauses. His knuckles bleached white against the metal bar in his grip.

As if commenting on the weather, Father Thomas says, "Get them off the stairs, please."

The temperature in the cellar dips. Riley's light flickers. At the top of the stairs, Ethan's eyes glaze over, darkening. He raises the metal bar.

Vee, seeing what's about to happen, curses and swerves, yanking Colton down. They both barely keep their footing, but the bar Ethan swings slams into the wall where Vee's head had been a moment ago.

"Fuck!" Colton's leg gives out, and he topples down the stairs, landing heavily on his side. Vee rushes down to pull him away from Ethan, back into the cellar, toward Father Thomas and Riley.

Ethan stays where he is, expressionless.

"I thought you said it was him?" Colton snaps.

"It was," Riley says, heart choking him. "I thought . . . so long as Father Thomas was here, he wouldn't be able to . . ."

"Looks like you thought wrong," Colton says, stumbling to his feet.

Ethan had been down here with Father Thomas for two years. Two. Years. Maybe the ghost they'd first met in the burning chapel had only had enough strength to claw at Riley's face or push Colton from the stairs, but this version of him had been possessing Ethan for a long time, and Riley was willing to bet that for all that humanity Ethan had lost underneath his influence, the priest had gained something in return.

"You said there was another ghost," Vee says. "Could he—?"

Riley's already shaking his head. "No, Jacob wouldn't do that."

"*Jacob?*" Colton asks. "Isn't he the one they originally thought was behind the whole shit show?"

Vee punches him in the arm. "Look around, dickhead. Do you *think* he was behind it?"

Riley ignores them both. Father Thomas is watching them all passively, but Riley remembers the smile on Ethan's face before he dropped Josh over the balcony—he knows how very little it'd take to stir that passivity to something worse entirely.

Forty years ago, Father Thomas might have done what he did under the guise of misguided moral judgment and zealousness. Riley doesn't think any of those things guide him now.

Whoever—whatever—death has turned Father Thomas into, morality has little to do with it at all.

As loud as he dares, Riley says, "Ethan. Can you see me? You can, right?"

Ethan turns toward the sound of his voice as if on instinct. That's fine. Riley can work with that. Riley's worked with less, after all.

"It's just me. It's us. I told you I was going to get us all out, didn't I?"

Ethan's listening. At least Riley thinks he is. His grip on the metal bar sags. After a moment, the bar drops to the floor, clattering down the stairs, coming to a rest beside Father Thomas's skeleton.

Something about that jerks Father Thomas into action. Riley's light flickers again, and when it comes back on, Father Thomas is gone. Riley spins on the spot. "Where—?"

Vee cries out, a cutting sound in the dark. Father Thomas has her by the wrist, dragging her away from the staircase. The white of his hand stands out like a shackle on her skin, and Vee struggles, digging her heels into the dirt, pulling with everything she has.

Colton's closer than Riley, and he lurches forward desperately. Before he can reach them, Father Thomas wrenches particularly hard and a sickening *pop* tears through the air.

Vee's face blanches, and the noise she lets out borders on inhuman. She sags against him, and without the resistance, Father Thomas drags her back toward the shallow graves. Colton misses them, slamming into the wall and sinking to the floor as his leg refuses to hold.

Riley doesn't know what Father Thomas plans to do. He doesn't want to find out.

He remembers the rock, the way it sailed right through the priest, untouchable so long as he wishes, now that the grave has claimed him.

Riley's one kid. He can't fight a fucking ghost.

The light flickers again, and Riley frantically reaches for the flashlight on his chest, desperate to keep it from going out. As he does, something bumps against his palm.

Hope blossoms like a wild rose in the hollow of his rib cage.

Riley turns, dashing for Colton, dropping to his knees to pat him down frantically.

"What are you doing?" Colton hisses, pushing at him. "Go—Vee needs—"

"I know," Riley snaps. "Just let me—"

He finds what he's looking for in Colton's left pocket. "Fuck, thank god for your stupid smoking."

Colton's lighter is a welcome weight in his left hand, and when Riley gets to his feet, he pulls Father Thomas's Bible free from his jacket with his right. He flips it open to a random page, holding it by the corner of the cover, and flicks back the lid of Colton's Zippo with the other.

"Hey," he calls, "Father. How do you feel about a bit of holy fire?"

Father Thomas's eyes slide to him like an oil slick. Vee dangles from his hand, Father Thomas still as a statue. He doesn't say anything, but Riley knows he's watching—can feel the weight of it on every inch of his skin.

"Are you sure about that?" Colton pants.

"No," Riley says honestly and clicks the lighter.

A flame springs to life. Father Thomas drops Vee. He rushes toward Riley like a shadow, in one place one moment and another the next. Cold fingers brush like cobwebs along his wrist, and Riley jerks back, holding the flickering flame a half inch from the crumbling pages. "I don't think so," he says. "Touch me and it burns. And you should remember just how good I am at that."

Up close like this, the fire paints Father Thomas's face into the abstract of a human being. Shadows where there ought to be light and light where they ought to be shadows.

He looks furious. He looks like he wants to rake his fingers along Riley's face and tear it from the bone.

Riley's scars burn beneath the force of his expression, but

he ignores it, taking a half step back. Father Thomas follows him like a stalking lion. From the corner of his eye, Riley sees Colton crawling forward to Vee.

He can't see Ethan. He hopes that's a good thing right now.

"I'm thinking you're still pretty attached to this," Riley says, jiggling the Bible. A half-attached page nearly slips free. "Must get pretty boring stuck down here all these decades on your own. Could do with some light reading."

The corner of Father Thomas's mouth curls. Like a smile. Like anything but a smile. "Not alone."

Riley doesn't allow that to shake him. "Yeah, about that. We're taking Ethan with us too."

"You can't," Father Thomas says. Not like a plea. Like a fact. "He's mine."

Riley snarls. "He was mine before he was yours, and I'm not giving him up."

The lighter's flame hisses out. Frantically, Riley clicks until the lighter spews up another one.

Father Thomas's fingers are a bare inch from Riley's chest. From his heart. Riley can feel the ice of them. He stares Father Thomas right in the eyes and does not flinch. Slowly, Father Thomas lowers his hand.

"You're not getting Ethan," Riley says. "You're not getting anybody. I'm going to make sure nobody ever sets foot in this place ever again. You can stay down here and rot for the rest of your miserable existence."

He seems to hit a nerve. Father Thomas's teeth glimmer behind his lips, sharp and feral. "The Lord—"

"Get it through your head," Riley says. "The Lord doesn't want you. Does this look like heaven to you? No, the Lord's locked the gates on you. The only place you're going is hell."

Riley realizes a second too late he's gone too far. The fury in Father Thomas's eyes peaks and tips over into something that on somebody more human might be anguish. His hand shoots out, and Riley stumbles back, but not quickly enough to avoid the bite of the priest's fingers ripping into his chest.

The lighter catches on the Bible, and both fall from Riley's hands, tumbling to the dirt.

Riley scarcely notices. Father Thomas's fingers rend through his flesh, and pain rolls in like a storm front, clouding every one of his senses until it's all Riley can do to writhe in the priest's grip, struggling for breath.

He slams into the wall, upsetting the shelves behind him. He barely notices that, either.

He tastes blood in his mouth. The world wavers black.

Somebody calls his name. Riley doesn't know who. He blinks. All he can see is Father Thomas's face, filling his whole view.

He can smell smoke. Feel fire on his skin. He doesn't know where he is. He doesn't know *when* he is.

Fuck, Riley thinks. *I'm not ready to die.*

An iron bar swings clear into Father Thomas's head, and Father Thomas dissolves like mist. The grip on Riley vanishes. He falls to the ground, hand to his aching chest, gasping for breath he can't believe he's actually breathing.

Colton stands in front of them, the iron bar from the door in one hand. "Huh," he says, looking at it contemplatively. "I didn't think that would work."

Riley's eyes are watering. "Colton."

Colton bends down, hauling Riley upright. Pain rips through him again, and Riley cries out, pressing one hand to where it blooms. His palm comes away red. "Oh," he says, surprised. "That's not good."

"Fuck," Colton grunts. "You've got to move with me, man. I can barely hold myself up, and you're nowhere near as light as you look."

They stagger forward, Riley leaving a bloody smear along the wall. The smoke smells worse now. Riley turns his head, glancing over his shoulder.

Father Thomas's Bible is alight like a bonfire. One of the support beams next to it has caught fire too. Flames and smoke are filling the cellar, climbing along the wooden struts hungrily.

A hand loops through his elbow. "Move," Vee says. *"Now."*

"Where's—?"

"I don't know," Vee says. "But he can't be far, and I want to be out of here before he comes back."

Together, they manage to stagger up the steps. Riley half expects the door to slam in their faces, trapping them down here to burn with all the other dead and dying things, but it doesn't.

They crawl out of the passage, back into the chapel. The cellar must not be as airtight as Riley had thought, because smoke rings the ceiling and the whole building groans around them.

Colton's leg gives out, and he takes Riley down with him. Alarmed, Riley tries to get to his feet to check on him, but his spinning head sends him stumbling to his knees.

He blinks against the smoke. He can see blood on the floorboards beneath him. He's almost certain it's his.

"You have to get up," Vee urges. "Please, I can't carry both of you out of here. Please, c'mon."

Riley's lost too much blood. It's a familiar feeling. Fumbling, he drags the neck of his shirt down.

Gashes run down from beneath his right collarbone, coming to a stop right over his heart. A matching set to the scars on his face. He looks like he's been caught in a bear attack. He's bleeding like it too.

Riley looks up. Vee has Colton on his feet, helping him hobble to the door. She glances over her shoulder, and Riley can tell the exact moment she realizes Riley isn't going to be able to follow her.

Riley tries one last time to get to his feet, clutching at the nearest pew for stability. He takes one step, two. His knees give out.

Somebody catches him before he can fall.

"I've got you," Ethan says.

It's the smoke that's making his eyes water, but if Riley had anything left in him, he thinks he might cry anyway. "If you let me go, I'm going to fucking murder you."

Ethan slings Riley's arm around his shoulders and curls his own around Riley's waist. He's gentle, but the movement sends fresh sparks of pain kindling along Riley's nerves anyway, and he nearly passes out. When he comes back, they're halfway to the door, and the flames have eaten their way into the chapel.

Voice hoarse, he says, "This really wasn't how I wanted us to walk down the aisle one day."

Ethan glances at him and smiles, that golden-boyish one that always made Riley's toes curl. "Till death do us part?"

Riley clings to him harder. "Not even then."

Colton and Vee are out the door. Ethan and Riley are so close, Riley can almost smell the fucking roses.

The door slams shut.

BEFORE

Riley had never seen a ghost.

For nearly a year now, he and his friends had been skulking through town, chasing local legends and ghost stories for their channel. Riley had paced cemeteries at midnight, crept through creaking empty warehouses, camped at haunted creeks.

He'd seen nothing he couldn't explain. When he posted videos, they were carefully edited to show a reality Riley had yet to grasp.

He grasped it now. He wished he didn't.

Riley hadn't realized he'd stepped back until the distance between him and Ethan grew like a chasm. The hand on Ethan's shoulder was as reliable as a mirage. In the shadows, Riley could only see a faint outline, a shifting shape as absent as it was present. He could see eyes. Dark, dark eyes, glimmering in the candlelight.

Carefully, Riley extended a hand. "Ethan," he said. "Come on, come over here, okay?"

Ethan didn't respond. The hand on his shoulder tightened, the shine of clean white nails digging into his skin.

The message was clear. Ethan wasn't going anywhere.

For a ghost hunter, Riley did not think he was a particularly brave person. He didn't like watching horror movies alone. When he walked late at night, he kept a hand on his phone. And when he went ghost hunting, he took his three closest friends with him.

Ethan hadn't liked the house, the chapel, the hunt.

He was here because Riley was. And Riley wasn't going to leave him behind.

Riley surged forward, snagging Ethan around the wrists. "Fuck you," Riley snarled. "Let him go, you undead piece of shit. I swear to god—"

The shadow behind Ethan moved like a striking snake, and Riley, who was focused only on trying to drag Ethan free of its grip, failed to move out of the way in time.

Fingers scraped across his face, icy cold, and pain like he'd never known exploded through him. He staggered back, barely managing to grab at a pew for balance. When he pressed a hand to his face, blood seeped between his fingers, dripping to the floorboards. The world spun around him, and dark spots fluttered behind his eyelids.

When he looked up, the hand on Ethan's shoulder had returned, tipped with blood, drawing him back into the shadows.

Helplessness clawed through Riley, and not thinking straight, he lurched forward again. He missed Ethan, but he upset the candles lining the pulpit, wrenching them free of their wax puddles.

Behind him, something caught alight. Riley barely noticed. Ethan was so close, being led away like a lamb to the slaughter. "Ethan! Ethan! *Ethan!*"

Slowly, Ethan looked to him. His gaze was as empty as the eyes on the cross above, and when the hand on his shoulder tightened, he turned away.

Heat battered at Riley. Flames licked at his heels. When he

glanced over his shoulder, he saw half the chapel was alight; the thin runner down the aisle had guided the fire to their sleeping bags, to the rotting wooden pews, to the Bibles.

The chapel was kindling, and Riley was just another piece to be devoured. If he stayed here, he would be eaten.

Frantic, he turned back around, but by then it was too late. Ethan was gone.

SIXTEEN

Ethan's hold on him tightens, and Riley's too woozy from blood loss to do anything but hang on as Ethan spins them around to face the pulpit.

Father Thomas looks worse than he did downstairs. Riley didn't think that was possible. The priest's thin veneer of humanity has slipped. He barely looks human at all now. His shape flickers in and out of focus, and every time it does, Riley sees through his skin to the crumbling skeleton beneath it. Riley can see the hole he punched into his rib cage.

"What do you even want?" Riley asks. He's too exhausted to be scared now. He just wants it all to be *over*. "What did we ever do to you?"

It's Ethan that answers. "He's trapped. He can't leave. He's bound to the place he died."

Realization settles like a shroud. "That's why he wants you. So long as he's possessing somebody who's alive . . ." Riley trails off.

Ethan smiles at him. Not so boyish now. Gentle but painful all the same. "I'm not so alive anymore," he says. "Not really dead, either."

Riley can't think about that right now. Not if he wants to get them both out of here before the chapel falls around their shoulders. To Father Thomas, he says, "If you keep us locked in here, we're all going to die. You won't have anybody left to possess then."

Father Thomas flickers. The flames climb along the back wall to feast on the cross above him.

It's enough to give Riley déjà vu. He clings harder to Ethan.

Ethan says, "You can't reason with him. He's been dead too long. He doesn't understand things the way you or I do anymore."

Riley grits his teeth. The door is so close behind them. "What do we do?"

"If I let go of you, can you make it outside?"

Riley straightens, as if struck by electricity. "Don't you even *think*—"

Ethan squeezes him tight. "When the door opens, run."

"Ethan—"

The weight holding Riley up disappears. Without its support, he staggers. He doesn't know where Ethan's gone. He can't see Father Thomas.

The world spins around him.

The door flings open. Riley looks at it. Through the wreath of smoke, he can make out Colton and Vee slumped on the path outside.

He looks back inside. There's movement down the steps to the cellar.

"Fuck," Riley says and laboriously limps his way back down the stairs to hell.

He almost can't make it. The heat down here is intense. The smoke makes him dizzy. The fire hasn't reached the doorway itself, but he knows it can't be far. He clings to the wall and stumbles down the last two steps.

Inside, he finds Father Thomas and Ethan. It's not nearly the situation he'd hoped it would be. Father Thomas has Ethan pinned to the wall, both hands wrapped around his throat. Ethan's fighting him off, but it looks like he's losing. Neither of them even hears Riley come in.

"Hey!" Riley calls. "Hey, fuckface!"

Father Thomas doesn't even glance at him, but Ethan's gaze jerks to his over Father Thomas's shoulder. When he sees Riley, his eyes go wide.

Something touches his elbow, and when Riley spins around, he comes face-to-face with Jacob.

Like Father Thomas, Jacob's ghost seems more unstable than it had upstairs, flickering in and out of focus. Unlike Father Thomas, he seems as human as ever.

Jacob points to the ground. Riley glances down. The bar from the door lies by his boots; the same one Colton had put through Father Thomas's head earlier. Riley bends down and seizes it. The iron is surprisingly cool in his hands, a soothing parallel to the crisp burn of the flames.

Riley tightens his grip on it. When he goes to stand, what

blood isn't leaking all over the floor rushes to his head, and he nearly passes out again.

Cold hands on his elbows hold him up. Riley blinks away the black spots in his vision. Jacob is still there, waiting. He looks at Riley and then back down—to Father Thomas's skeleton.

It takes Riley a moment, but it clicks. "You want me to . . . ?" Jacob's hand doesn't leave his arm. Riley swallows. His chest throbs. He can barely stand upright. "I don't know if I can. Physically, I mean."

Jacob moves closer. He raises a hand, setting it on Riley's cheek, startling him. Like this, they're eye to eye. He doesn't say anything. He doesn't speak. Riley knows what he's asking for all the same.

Across the room, Ethan makes a choked-off noise. It sounds like Riley's name.

Riley closes his eyes. He takes a deep breath. He opens them again. "Yeah," he says. "Yes, do it."

Jacob holds his gaze for a long moment. He nods. His hand falls from Riley's cheek. He vanishes—and Riley feels control of his body leave him.

Being possessed is like nothing at all Riley has ever experienced. He's cold. The world is distant. The fire of the room doesn't frighten him anymore.

His hands tighten around the bar. It's burning in his grip. Riley can feel it singeing his palms.

Like a lifetime ago, Riley remembers Vee saying, *Ghosts don't like iron.*

Jacob brings Riley's arms up high—and then he swings down.

Father Thomas's skull crunches. Splinters of bone fly like shrapnel. One of them nicks Riley's cheek on the way past, and Riley can't even flinch. Jacob swings again. Again. Again.

Jacob's fury is endless. Riley feels it like a possession in its own right. As Jacob smashes in Father Thomas's skull, he's thinking of that night, of being shepherded from bed, to the chapel, to the basement below that none of them had even known existed.

There had been one chalice. Jacob had been the last in line, and his hands had shaken as it was passed to him. He'd never liked communion. The stink of the wine reminded him of home.

One of the boys started to choke. Father Thomas held his hands and began to pray.

Jacob's memories wind him. Riley tries to pry control back, to escape from them, but he can't. In his hands the bar swings down, down, down. The skull is rubble now. Jacob doesn't stop swinging.

When he dropped the chalice, the wine foamed on the dirt. Jacob tried for the stairs. Father Thomas caught him at the top. They struggled, all elbows and knees, until Jacob managed to get his hands on Father Thomas's shoulders and push.

It'd been too dark to see him fall, but Jacob heard his skull hitting the bottom step. He did not get back up.

The door wouldn't open. The bar had fallen back across it during their struggle. For days, Jacob begged and screamed. Nobody came. The cellar was too deep. If any search parties tromped through the chapel, he couldn't hear them and they couldn't hear him.

The bodies in the cellar began to rot. It no longer stank like wine. It stank like death. There was a shovel in the corner. It took Jacob days, but he buried his classmates as deep as he could. He left Father Thomas to rot where he lay, empty eyes staring at nothing.

It did nothing to help the stink.

Thirteen days after Jacob had been led into the basement, he lay down and closed his eyes. When he opened them, he was dead. And he was not alone.

Forty years of that. Of death. Of only the company of the man who killed him.

In death, Father Thomas had wanted life.

In death, Jacob Smith had only ever wanted freedom.

Riley's crying. His vision swims. At his feet is a shattered mess. He tries to swing the bar again, but something catches the end of it.

"Riley," Ethan says. "It's over. He's gone. They're both gone."

Riley blinks. His head is aching, set to split from the force of it. There is nobody inside but himself.

The iron bar clatters to the floor, and Riley follows it down, his body finally pushed to breaking point. Ethan catches him effortlessly.

Riley sags into him, wrapping his arms around Ethan's neck and burying his face in his shoulder. "Shit," he chokes out. "He was just a kid."

Ethan's hand on his back presses him closer. "I know."

"He was just a kid." Then, because it's been killing him slowly for years: "*We* were just kids."

"I know." Ethan sighs. "But it's over now. Whatever Jacob did, Father Thomas is gone."

Somehow Riley finds the strength to look over Ethan's shoulder. He's right. There's no trace of Father Thomas, of Jacob. Nothing but a burning cellar, fit to collapse at any moment. "We should probably get out of here, shouldn't we?"

"Very much yes. Can you walk?"

Riley thinks about that. A crack sounds and one of the support beams in the ceiling gives way. Dirt and brick pour through into the cellar. "I don't think so."

"I've got you," Ethan says, and for the first time all night, Riley allows himself to believe it.

✗ ✗ ✗

Ethan carries him out of the chapel. Riley, who's been relegated to holding his bunched-up jacket to his own gaping chest wound, can do nothing but cling to him, watching over Ethan's shoulder as the building burns.

Vee sprints for them the moment they're outside. "Is he okay?" she asks frantically. Then, seemingly coming to a realization: "Are *you* okay?"

Ethan gingerly lowers Riley to the grass beside Colton. "He needs a hospital."

"Join the club," Colton says. He looks at Ethan, assessing. "So, are we going to have to fight you too?"

"Colton," Riley snaps.

"It's a valid question," Colton protests.

Ethan sinks to his knees beside Riley, adjusting his legs so Riley's head is in his lap. He cards a hand through Riley's hair. Riley should tell him to stop. He's a greasy, bloody mess. He doesn't. "I don't think you have to worry about that," Ethan says.

A resounding snap rings through the night. Riley turns his head just in time to see the roof of the chapel cave in. The glow of the fire casts dizzying patterns through the remaining stained-glass window.

Above, the cross creaks. When it falls, the flames pull it under and away. In its absence, the sky seems brighter; clear skin beneath an old wound.

Riley doesn't realize he's said that last bit out loud until Colton says, "That's just the sunrise, dipshit."

They're quiet for a long moment, the four of them watching the chapel burn.

If Riley closes his eyes, it's kind of like a bonfire. His head in Ethan's lap, his friends on either side of him, the summer heat warm on his skin.

Something normal. Something safe.

Somewhere in the distance, the wail of sirens breaks through the dawn.

Vee sighs in relief. "Alejandro made it."

Riley opens his eyes. Reality settles back in. He goes to sit up, but pain lances through him and Ethan eases him back down quickly. "Don't move," he says. He's taken over holding pressure to Riley's wound, and the ice of his hand helps soothe the burn of it. "You'll open it up again."

Riley looks at him. Out here, with the dawn cresting on the horizon, his hair is paler than Riley remembers. Less blond, more white. The only color on his skin is the smears of Riley's blood.

Riley reaches up, wrapping his hand around Ethan's wrist, and says, "If you're not dead but you're not alive, what does that make you?"

Ethan smiles. The corners of his eyes crinkle. "I don't know," he admits. "I still feel like me. I just . . . feel like more than that, too."

"It doesn't matter what he is," Colton says, propped up on his elbows. "He can't be here when the cops arrive."

Riley bristles, but Vee hovers a hand over his chest to keep him down. "No," she says. "Colton's right. What do you think is going to happen when the paramedics try to treat him?"

Beneath him, Ethan is still like stone. Riley brushes his thumb along the dip in Ethan's wrist, his pulse point. Nothing beats back at him. "I'm not leaving without him. Not again."

"It's not for good," Ethan says. "Once you're healed up, you can come back for me." He pauses, glancing to where Dominic House shadows over them all. "Believe me, I'm as done with this place as you are."

It's not good enough for Riley. "I'll stay with you," he insists.

Ethan looks at him with both fondness and exasperation. "Half an hour ago, a ghost tried to claw your heart from your chest. You need medical attention."

Riley opens his mouth to protest, but Vee's good hand slaps over the top of it. "Listen to me," she says. "You're going to the hospital. We're *all* going to the hospital. And then we'll see Ethan again. You're not the only one who's missed him, and I promise if anybody tries to get in the way, I'll make them regret it."

A pause. From the ground, Colton sighs. "Fuck. Yeah, me too."

The sirens are closer now, the earsplitting wail of them makes Riley wince. Flashing lights bathe the dark sky in red and blue.

Riley, who's already struggling against the grip of unconsciousness, feels as if he's dreaming.

Ethan tucks a strand of Riley's hair behind his ear. "Go to sleep," he says. "Be good for the hospital staff. I'll see you soon."

Riley has more to say to that. He wants a promise. He wants an oath. He wants to hold tight to Ethan until nothing in the world can crack them apart.

He squeezes Ethan's hand tight enough to break. "God, I hate you," he says and reluctantly lets unconsciousness claim him.

BEFORE

They found him in the courtyard, bleeding out as the chapel burned.

Hands hauled him to his feet, pressed at the wreck of his face, pulled him away from the blaze. Riley let them, too confused to do anything else.

People talked at him, the buzz of their voices lost beneath the crackle of fire.

"What?" Riley asked, trying to blink away the fog ruining him. "What did you say?"

The face in front of him swam into view. Some no-name police officer. The man frowned, but didn't repeat himself, ushering Riley gently into the hands of a nearby paramedic.

Riley was walked through Dominic House. In the foyer, Colton was swarmed by medics, already being levered onto a gurney. Riley caught his eye as he walked by, and when Colton saw his face, what little color was left in his drained.

Out front, Dominic House was alight with red and blue. Squad cars sat crooked along the driveway, and two separate ambulances parked by the fountain. Riley was deposited in the back of one, a blanket dropped over his shoulders.

He didn't need it. The summer heat, the chapel fire—he felt scorched in his skin.

Somewhere, he could hear Vee crying, but when he turned to search for her, a firm hand guided his face back.

"Don't move," said the paramedic. "You'll make it worse."

It took Riley too long to realize she meant his face. Feeling strangely disconnected, he asked, "Is it bad?"

She paused. The look she leveled at him was concerned. "It's bad enough."

Riley laughed. It hurt every inch of him and then some. "Yeah. It is."

Footsteps sounded nearby, and when Riley looked up it was the officer from before, the one who'd pulled him away from the chapel. He paced back and forth, phone to his ear. "No, I can't call back. We need you here. There is the possibility that we could be looking at a missing person case."

Riley closed his eyes. Behind them, he could see the chapel, the cross, Ethan bright against the shadows. He could hear the wail of another approaching siren, and as he looked, a fire truck trundled up the hill.

The officer's boots clattered against the flagstones. "Mrs. Hale? Mrs. Hale? Mrs.—"

SEVENTEEN

Riley wakes briefly as they roll him towards the ambulance. It is not a kind waking, given the immense pain he's in. He gasps, shooting upright on the gurney only to be forced back down by a nearby paramedic.

"Hey," says a familiar voice. "Calm down, you're okay."

Riley blinks. The world swims into view. "Jordan?" he croaks.

She smiles down at him, looking at least half as bad as he feels. There's dried blood on her hands. "Yeah, it's me."

He stares at her. "You're bleeding."

"It's not my blood."

Riley keeps staring. He's missing his shirt, and there's a compression bandage wrapped around his ribs. "Oh."

"Yeah, 'oh,'" Jordan says.

"Where's...?" He wants to say "Ethan." At the last moment, he remembers he shouldn't.

Thankfully, Jordan misreads him. "Josh went in the ambulance before you. Alejandro is with him. Colton and Evelyn are being looked over by the paramedics. They'll get the ambulance after yours."

"Send them now," Riley insists. "We can share."

Jordan looks at him pityingly. "The drugs are really getting to you, huh? There's not enough room for all three of you. Don't worry, they're in good hands. Compared to you and Josh, they got off lightly."

Riley remembers the snap of Vee's wrist in the cellar. Colton crawling along the floor when his leg couldn't hold him up. He remembers Ethan's frigid touch, keeping the warmth of Riley's blood where it belonged. "I don't think any of us got off lightly."

Jordan seems surprised, but her expression softens. Somebody nearby says something, but he doesn't catch it or Jordan's reply. Turning back to Riley, she says, "They need to take you now. Listen to the paramedics and let them do their job, okay?"

People keep saying that to Riley tonight. He struggles to keep his eyes open. A minute awake, two at most, and he's ready to go under again. "Okay," he agrees.

"If only you were this agreeable without the morphine," Jordan says, which makes no sense at all. She steps back and says to somebody out of Riley's eyeline, "Take care of him, okay?"

"Yes ma'am."

The gurney rattles as it slides into the ambulance. Behind the paramedics, Riley catches one last glance of Dominic House, its cladding bathed in red and blue, swarming with people. On instinct, he lifts his gaze to the sky.

The cross does not greet him. All he sees is the rising sun.

Uncaring for the blood on his teeth, he smiles. One of the paramedics looks at him and frowns. They ask him a question.

Riley doesn't hear it. This time, when unconsciousness pulls him under, he goes peacefully.

✗ ✗ ✗

The next time Riley wakes up, he's in the hospital and a nurse is patting his face to rouse him.

"Wake up, dear," she says cheerfully. "Surgery went well!"

"Surgery?" Riley slurs. "What . . . What surgery?"

"I see we're still not completely back," she says. "Here, up we go."

Baffled, Riley lets her help him so he's propped up on his pillows. She holds a cup steady for him as he takes sips from a metal straw, and once he's done, she tucks him in like his mother hasn't done since he was five and afraid of the monster under his bed.

Memories seep back in. The chapel burning, Father Thomas's skull crushed to dust at his feet. Sitting with Ethan and the others in the courtyard while they watched it all burn.

His stomach lurches. "My friends," he blurts. "Are they—?"

"They're fine," the nurse reassures him. "A bit worse for wear but fine."

Riley droops in relief. "Can I see them?"

The nurse shakes her head. "You just got out of surgery. You need to recover."

"I need to see my friends," Riley corrects. "Are they in the waiting room? They are, aren't they?"

Her cheerful smile disappears. In its place a stern frown rises. It's an expression with which Riley is very familiar. "The doctor wants you to rest," she says. "You should—"

Riley's done listening to her. He slings his legs out of bed, reaching for the IV plugged into his arm. It has the desired effect. She rushes to stop him, hand closing over the crook of his elbow. "Do not," she warns, "*do that*. I'll talk to the doctor about sending your friends in."

Riley smiles at her. "Thank you."

She shoots him an unamused look, helps him back into bed, and disappears out the door.

For the first time, Riley glances around. There's no other bed in here. A private hospital room. A nice one, too. The walls are beige, not white, and a plush couch sits in the corner, ready to receive guests. Riley wonders who's paying for all this luxury, because it sure as hell isn't him.

The door to the room bangs open. He flinches, glancing up just in time to receive a lap full of Vee as she throws herself on top of him, arm around his neck. She's aiming for gentle, but her enthusiasm causes her to miss the mark. "God," she says. "I thought you'd never wake up."

Riley clings to her, the familiarity of her touch grounding him. It doesn't offset the painful throb in his ribs though. "Yeah," he says. "Sorry, could you . . . ?"

"Oh!" She leans back in a hurry. She's dressed in fresh clothes and looks like she's showered since he saw her last.

One of her arms is tucked into a sling, and he can see the plaster of a cast poking out of it. "Are you okay?"

"Peachy," Riley says. "Are *you*?"

"Broken wrist," she says. "Some bruises. I'll live."

Behind her, Colton says, "I'm fine, too, if anybody wants to ask."

Vee rolls her eyes but steps back as Colton hobbles into the room on a crutch. Riley stares at it. "Did you break something new?"

Colton smiles thinly. "No, but being dragged down stone steps and being forced to crawl out of a burning building isn't great for chronic pain issues." He considers Riley. "Still doing better than you."

Riley glances down at himself. He's clean, mostly. Less like he's showered and more like somebody has given him a hasty scrub-down with a sink and sponge. The hospital gown he's wearing has teddy bears on it. "Why am I dressed like a *Sesame Street* character?"

Colton grins. "The hospital ward was running low on gowns, so the pediatric department chipped in," he says. "Be glad it wasn't the one with clowns."

Vee reaches up, taking one of Riley's hands. "Ignore him," she says. "He's been ornery since he had to talk to the police."

Riley winces. "And what did you say?"

Colton settles onto the couch, bouncing slightly as if testing the cushions. "That I got knocked out like four hours into the night, and the next thing I remember everything was on fire and the paramedics were there."

Vee says, "That we were kidnapped by ghosts."

Riley stares. "You said *what*?"

She rolls her eyes. "Trust me, nobody believed me," she says dryly. "Nobody believed me last time, either. I believe the police labeled me an 'unreliable witness.'"

Riley grimaces. "Still. Risky."

"Forget me," Vee says. "You need to think about what you're going to say when the police interview *you*."

Riley frowns. "They've already spoken to you. Why do they need to talk to me?"

"I *know* you're not that naive," Colton says. "You remember what a circus it was last time? Now throw in a B-list celebrity and see where that gets you."

Hazily, Riley remembers Jordan leaning over him outside Dominic House, talking to him in a soft voice before the paramedics spirited him away. "Where is she? And Josh, is he okay?" Colton and Vee exchange a look. "What?"

"The police have been interviewing Jordan since they found us," Vee says. "The way they see it, three teenagers were under her direct supervision, and now all three of them are in the hospital."

"They have to know that wasn't her fault," Riley insists.

Colton shrugs. "What they think doesn't matter. None of us are going to press charges, no matter how much they want us to, just so it fits their neat little narrative. She'll be fine."

"And Josh?" Riley pushes.

Vee squeezes his hand. "They won't let us see him," she says. "But I spoke to Alejandro, and he says that considering the fall he took, he's doing well."

"'Considering,'" Riley repeats. "What does that actually mean?"

Colton says, like ripping off a bandage, "He broke his back. Still too early to tell for sure, but he'll probably be in a wheel-chair for the rest of his life."

All the air leaves Riley at once. Vee spins on her heel, hiss-ing, "*Colton.*"

"He's not a baby," Colton snaps. "He deserves to know."

"There are gentler ways to say it!"

"No," Riley says, numb. "Colton's right. I asked. I wanted to know."

Vee looks fit to disagree, but there's a knock on the door, and the nurse from before is back, frowning at the lot of them. "Miss Cho? There's a call for you at the nurses station."

Vee sighs. "My mother?"

"Yes. This is the third time. You *do* have a cell phone, I assume?"

Going by Vee's face, Riley can guess it's been turned off. "I'll be right there," she promises.

The nurse eyes them skeptically. "See that you are," she says, disappearing again.

Riley looks at Vee. "How long has it been?"

"Two days," Vee says. "She won't stop calling. She nearly had a meltdown when I said I wanted to wait in the hospital for you to wake up."

Two days. Riley takes a moment to digest that. His mother must have been in and out while he was asleep. Probably couldn't afford to take any more time off work. He's sure once he gets his phone back, she's going to have some choice words to share with him.

He doesn't blame her. They're still paying off the hospital bills from his last stint in the ER.

To Vee, he says, "She's only calling because she cares."

"I know," Vee says, pained. "And I love her, but . . . I can't be around her right now. She means well. I know that. But she just . . . She doesn't understand."

Riley gets it. He wishes he didn't. "Go talk to her," he says.

Vee leaves, but very reluctantly. Colton keeps his position on the couch. Silence dips between them, broken only by the hush of noise outside. Riley lets his eyes close.

He's tired. He doesn't know how he could sleep for two whole days and still feel like he's been run over by a truck.

Into the quiet, Colton says, "I never got the chance to apologize to you."

Riley cracks open his eyes. "About what?"

Colton shuffles, reaching into his pocket for his smokes. He taps one out, holds it in his hand, and then frowns. He slides it back in. Riley can't help but ask, "Thinking of quitting?"

"No," Colton says. "You lost my lighter."

Riley had forgotten about that. "When you think about it, it kind of saved our lives."

"No," Colton says. "Pretty sure that was you."

Riley says, "No, most of that was Ethan, actually."

Colton hesitates. "That's what I wanted to apologize for. Before everything went to hell. When I outed you to Jordan."

Oh. It'd happened so long ago, comparatively speaking, that Riley can't even spare the energy to be mad about it. "It's fine."

"It wasn't," Colton says. "I mean, I genuinely didn't realize I was outing you, but still. If I'd thought about it for two seconds, I'd have known to keep my mouth shut."

"Yeah," Riley agrees. "But thinking's never been your strong suit."

Despite himself, Colton smiles. It smooths out some of the rough edges the years have scraped onto his face. It makes him look younger. Makes him look his age. "Yeah, fuck you too."

A pregnant pause. Riley thinks about not saying anything. Knows he'll regret it if doesn't. "If we're having a heart-to-heart, you want to tell me what last time was all about?"

Colton frowns. "Last time?"

"When you went on a press junket telling every tabloid a bunch of bullshit and lies," Riley says bluntly.

Colton's shoulders tense. "I didn't *lie*."

Riley refuses to take the bait. "That's not my point. You know that's not my point."

For a moment, Colton looks so mad, Riley thinks he might get up and walk out. And then it leaves him. He sighs, head falling back on the sofa. "Hell, okay. Why the fuck not, I guess." He takes a deep breath. "I needed the money."

Riley stares at him. "It was about *money*?"

"How much did your little hospital trip cost you?" Colton says. "Now imagine needing three surgeries over two years to piece your leg back together. And that's without accounting for the fact I couldn't walk for a year. I couldn't work. I needed a *wheelchair*, Riley. My mom had to take time off to look after me. I have three younger sisters. That's a lot of mouths to feed *and* pay my medical bills."

Riley doesn't know what to say.

Colton lifts his head, meets Riley's eyes. "I know some of the shit that got printed was bad, but every other word I said got misquoted, and eventually I just stopped fighting it. It wasn't worth it. So yeah, it was about money. It's always about money when you don't have it."

Riley closes his eyes. He has never in his life felt like such a piece of shit. "Why didn't you say anything?"

Colton shrugs, picking at a stray thread on the sofa. "I knew how it looked. And Vee was really, *really* angry." He pauses. "I love her, but she's kind of scary sometimes."

Despite himself, Riley smiles. "Yeah. She is."

Colton glances at him and then away. He sets his jaw. "So. Are we okay?"

"Yeah, Colton," Riley says. "We're okay."

The tension seeps from him. A comfortable silence settles. Riley glances to the door. Still no sign of Vee. Cautiously, he asks, "Have any of you . . . you know?"

"Gone back to the house?" Colton asks. "No. Fuck. I figured that was your job."

"Somebody should check on him," Riley insists. "See if he's okay."

"Riley, he survived two years being possessed by Father Voorhees, I'm sure he can survive a few days more." Colton thinks. "Is 'survive' even the right word?"

Riley had been trying not to think about that part. "He's still human."

"Sure," Colton says. "But how much of him is, you know, alive?"

The ice of his touch lingers on Riley's skin. "It doesn't matter. Whatever happened to him, we'll figure it out."

Colton studies him silently, and Riley thinks he's going to protest. After a moment he gets to his feet, leaning heavily on the crutch. "Your boyfriend, your decisions," he says. "I'm going to go find something to eat that didn't come out of a vending machine. You want anything?"

Riley shakes his head. Colton rattles the door open, vanishing out into the hallway, and Riley is left alone in the fancy hospital room in his teddy bear gown.

✗ ✗ ✗

The police, when they interview him, are forced to do it from Riley's hospital bed.

It turns out they want a statement more than the hospital wants him to recover uninterrupted, and Riley, who really just wants to wipe the blight of Dominic House from his life, lets them do it with only minimal fuss.

Depending, he supposes, on your definition of "fuss."

"Let me get this straight," says one of the interviewing detectives, a stern woman called Detective Knox who so far has greeted everything Riley's shared with a healthy dose of suspicion. "You don't remember how you found the cellar beneath the chapel, you don't remember how you wound up injured, and you don't remember who started the fire that burned it to the ground."

"Is that what happened?" Riley asks. "I wouldn't know. I don't remember."

Knox exchanges a look with her partner. He shrugs. Her lips purse. She turns back to Riley, and Riley strives to look the part of the exhausted victim. It's not hard. He *feels* the part of the exhausted victim. "You realize this is the second incident you've been involved with at Dominic House, the second fire started that you 'don't remember.' If I didn't know better, I might ask if you feel an inclination toward arson."

"And if you did, my answer would be I really, really do not," Riley says, honest for the first time. "If I never have to see a fire again in my life, it'll be too soon."

Knox's pen taps against the notepad in her hand. She looms over his bedside. She hadn't asked for a seat, and Riley hadn't offered. "You should know that Ms. Jones has offered to take full responsibility for the damages of that night."

"What?" Riley struggles as upright as he can when laid low in bed. "No, she had nothing to do with anything."

"Interesting," Knox observes, "considering you don't remember any of it."

Riley jams his mouth closed. The silence hangs between them.

Knox sighs, snapping her notebook shut. "Nobody is being charged with anything," she says. "All we have is a bunch of inconclusive testimony and some damage to an abandoned building that was set to be demolished anyway."

Riley stares at her. "Wait, they're demolishing Dominic House?"

"Apparently historical significance does not outweigh reputation," Knox says dryly. "It's starting to give the county a bad name. It's been on and off the council debates for years. After this, I can't imagine there will be any holdouts."

Dominic House gone. Ethan had said all he wanted was to leave and never see it again. Riley hopes it's really as easy as that, because if he's as stuck on those stupid grounds as Jacob and Father Thomas were, Riley can't even begin to comprehend the amount of trouble they're in for. "Oh."

Knox eyes him. "Nothing more to say about that?"

Not to her, anyway. "No."

"Thought as much." She pulls out her wallet, slipping a card free. She holds it up for a moment before setting it down on his bedside table. "In case your memory comes back."

"My memory isn't very good. I wouldn't hold your breath," Riley says.

Knox snorts. "Of course not. Try to stay out of trouble, Mr. Fox. Let's not meet again, shall we?"

"Let's not," Riley agrees, and when she leaves, he crumples her card into a ball and tosses it in the trash.

BEFORE

Overnight, Riley's life made international headlines.

LOCAL TEENS SURVIVE HORROR HOUSE, said the front page of every newspaper in the state.

GHOST HUNTERS BECOME GHOST-HUNTED, said the trending page on YouTube.

HAVE YOU SEEN ME? said the posters that went up around town in the weeks following. Ethan smiled out of the paper, boyish and alive. *LAST SEEN JULY 12*.

No reward was offered. As the weeks turned to months, the posters yellowed and curled, pasted over by band promos and help-wanted ads.

By some small miracle, nobody put together the missing poster with the headlines. Everybody in the world knew four wannabe ghost hunters had walked into a haunted house and only three had walked out. Nobody outside the police department knew who they were.

Six months after the tragedy, Colton sold the story to the first tabloid.

The media circus, which was only just beginning to die down, was renewed once more. Reporters found Riley's address and set up camp outside his apartment building until the neighbors called the police. He started getting fan mail, from psychics and fanatics alike. Once, while buying milk in the supermarket, a reporter materialized from nowhere and shoved a microphone under his nose.

"When will you share the footage of Dominic House?" she asked as Riley stood frozen to the spot with his 2% going warm in his palms. "Since Mr. Pierce's article came out, your YouTube channel has hit over one million subscribers; how do you feel about that?"

Riley hadn't even known. He hadn't checked the channel once since everything happened. He shoved the milk into her arms and backpedaled out of the store before she could even think to follow him.

Eight months after the tragedy, Colton sold his second article. It was a lot less generous than the first.

There were no ghosts, it said. *I fell and broke my leg. I had no clue what was going on. We were scared teenagers; whatever the others think they saw, I can promise you they didn't.*

Vee took it about as well as Riley had thought she would.

"He thinks we're lying," she hissed, curled around a pillow on his bed, mascara smudged from crying. "After all that— and he says *we imagined it*."

"He wasn't even awake for most of it," Riley pointed out, as kindly as he could. "And he's half right; he *was* hurt, Vee. He probably doesn't even know what he remembers."

"What do *you* remember?" Vee pushed.

Riley didn't allow himself to think about that. For eight months, he'd dreamed of smoke and Ethan's empty eyes. *Mrs. Hale? Mrs. Hale? Mrs.—*

"I remember my boyfriend is gone," Riley said. "And none of this is going to bring him back."

Nine months later, the media turned on Colton, as it was

wont to do. Why was he the only survivor to speak out? Why did his story change on a dime? Why, why, why—?

Colton the Coward: Crazy or Criminal? trended as Buzz-Feed's top article for two months straight. Riley didn't read it, but he knew Colton had by his incredibly terse texts. He thought, now that Colton had become the internet's new punching bag, that might be the end of the saga.

A month after that, Colton sold his third article, and Vee stopped speaking to him. When Riley read it, he followed suit.

EIGHTEEN

It's another two days before the hospital agrees to discharge him. Given the lack of parental supervision Riley has to return to back home, he knows the staff aren't exactly thrilled. But he's eighteen and excels in the fine art of making a nuisance of himself.

"You're going to have to keep on top of wound care," his nurse says his last night there as she rewraps his bandage for him. "If it gets infected, it'll be nasty."

"I know," Riley says, sitting on his hands to stop himself fidgeting. "It's not like it's my first rodeo."

His nurse pointedly does not look at the matching scars on his cheek. "Yes," she says, smoothing the end of the bandage down. "Well, hopefully you'll keep out of trouble for some time now."

Riley doubts that. He's itching to get back to Dominic House, but only so he can put it in the rearview mirror once and for all.

If Ethan's not waiting for him there, Riley thinks he might do something drastic.

When the nurse leaves, Riley waits the appropriate amount of time to appear respectful of the doctor's orders before he slips from his bed, shuffling into a plush dressing gown and equally opulent slippers Vee had bestowed upon him from the gift shop downstairs.

"You deserve a little comfort," she'd said when Riley had tried to turn them down. "Besides, as far as hospital fashion goes, they're practically chic."

Riley hates to admit that she has a point. They're unbearably comfortable, and compared to the teddy bear gown he woke up in, the suave navy fluff is much more his style.

He shuffles out into the corridor, sparing tentative looks down both ends. Nobody is watching. The nurses station is out of sight around the corner. Riley tucks his hands in his pockets and strides off through the hospital.

It takes him some time to find what he's looking for. He hasn't had much cause to leave his hospital room, and worried about potential reporters lurking in hallways, he hasn't ventured any farther than the cafeteria.

He doesn't have to go that far now. Three more hallways and two turned corners. The door to a private room identical to Riley's looms before him.

He doesn't knock. When he tries the handle, it's not latched. The door creaks open.

Josh is propped up against a mountain of pillows, eyes closed in peaceful sleep. Beside him, Jordan is settled in an armchair, magazine creased open atop her knee. When she sees him, her face creases into a smile. "Riley. What a surprise."

Compared to the last time Riley laid eyes on him, Josh looks radiant. He's a little paler, but he still has the warm glow to him that Riley is used to. He doesn't seem like he's in pain. There's not even a morphine drip hooked into his arm. Riley takes that as a good sign.

Jordan doesn't look nearly so good. Her hair is a mess, and her makeup is smeared as if she'd knuckled sleep from her eyes more than once.

"Wow," Riley says as he steps inside. "You look like hell."

Jordan raises a finger to her lips. A chill ghosts down Riley's spine, but then Jordan tilts her head to the left and he realizes there's one more person in the room.

Alejandro is sacked out on the couch in the corner, laptop open on the floor beside him, a pilfered pillow shoved so awkwardly beneath his head that Riley just knows it wasn't there when he passed out.

"The idiot's barely gone home since Josh was admitted," Jordan says. "I've had to drag him out to eat and shower because he was starting to stink up the place."

Quietly, Riley eases himself down in the much-less-comfortable plastic chair on Josh's other side. "Who's been dragging *you* home, then?"

Instead of answering, Jordan snaps the magazine she'd been reading closed, and Riley gets a glance at the cover for the first time.

It's a cheap tabloid. The kind of shit Riley's mom leaves sitting out on the breakfast table after long hours of working the night shift. The headline reads *HOAX OR HORROR STORY? HAUNTED HOUSE HOWLS AGAIN!*

Riley's distaste must show because Jordan smiles ruefully. "Sorry. Reading material around here is kind of scarce." Her fingers beat against the glossy cover. "Kind of interesting to be on the other side of this, though. Usually, I'm the one narrating other people's tragedies."

The picture that accompanies the headline is a shot of Dominic House, alight with blue and red. Riley can make out a grainy ambulance with his gurney being loaded into it. They've paired it with a zoomed-in photo of Jordan's face as she leans over him, weary and rattled.

Riley wonders if he ought to be grateful that it's her and not him. He wonders what the article says. He wonders if, this time, the denizens of the internet have deigned to treat them with a modicum of compassion instead of fascination.

Jordan offers him the magazine. "Want to borrow it?"

"No," Riley says decisively.

Jordan laughs quietly, setting the magazine down. Riley notices for the first time her nail polish is chipped. He doesn't think he's ever seen it anything less than perfect. "God," she says, cracking her neck. "I'd kill for a decent cup of coffee."

"I wouldn't call it decent, but I could probably smuggle one from the cafeteria if you wanted," Riley offers.

"Yeah?" Jordan asks, eyebrow raised. "And how much would that cost me?"

"Eight bucks," Riley says.

"For a single cup of coffee?" Jordan asks. "Your prices just get steeper and steeper. A girl could go broke around you."

"She still could yet," Riley says. "I got the feeling the police were *really* hoping there were some charges I wanted to levy against you—and if they couldn't find them, they'd be happy to make some up."

Jordan pulls a face. "At the very least, I'm guilty of gross negligence—"

Riley pitches his voice up. "'Don't worry about that—that's what we have insurance for.'"

She looks at him dryly. "Mimicry isn't your strongest talent. Don't give up your day job."

Riley kicks his feet up on the corner of Jordan's chair. "My day job fired me, so it seems like I'm free to pursue whatever I want right now."

Jordan's face drops in dismay. "What? Didn't anybody call to say you were in the hospital?"

Riley had missed two shifts while recovering from surgery, and once he'd finally been reunited with his phone, his messages had been full of increasingly frantic calls culminating in a stern "If you can't be bothered to come in, don't come back."

Chantelle had sent him over a dozen messages. The first one featured nothing but a photo of the tabloid Jordan had been reading followed by a string of question marks, so any hope she didn't remember Jordan's visit had died a quick death. Riley had deleted the rest of her messages without reading them.

"Anybody who might have thought to call was also in the hospital," Riley points out. "It's fine. If they hadn't fired me, I was going to quit."

Jordan doesn't immediately reply. Riley's gaze slips back to Josh. Finally, he says, "The others told me he broke his back. That he won't be able to walk again."

Jordan sighs. "*May* not be able to walk again," she stresses. "Spinal injuries are complicated."

"How's he holding up?" Riley asks.

"You know what? Surprisingly well." Jordan huffs out a laugh. "He always was the strongest out of the three of us." Then: "It probably helps that he doesn't remember jack shit."

Riley's head snaps back up to her. "What?"

"It turns out falling from the second floor of a derelict house can wreck more than just your spine." She pauses. Riley wonders if he's supposed to laugh. He's rarely heard something less funny. "Doctors say he might get the memories back over time. Might not."

Riley takes a moment to digest that. "Good."

"Good?" Jordan repeats skeptically.

Riley thinks about what the past two years have been like, the long nights of staring at the ceiling, wondering how much of what he remembered was fact or fiction. The nightmares that sank their claws into more than just the delicate skin of his face to leave their scars behind.

He thinks about what it might be like to have the privilege to live in a world where he didn't have to worry about what may live in the haunted corners of every place he stepped.

"After everything we all went through," Riley says, "somebody deserves to sleep easy at night."

Jordan doesn't answer immediately. Her fingers knot together in her lap, white at the knuckles. "I feel like I have a lot I should be apologizing to you for."

"Maybe," Riley allows. "But I needed to go back. I'm glad I went back."

She doesn't look like she believes him. "I know you probably think you needed closure, but—"

"It's got nothing to do with closure." Ethan flashes through his mind, the warmth of his smile. "Well, not in the way you mean, anyway."

Jordan's quiet for a second. "The police wanted all the footage we filmed."

Riley had anticipated that. "Did you give it to them?"

Jordan leans back in the seat. "No. I wiped it all shortly after you lot were sent off to the hospital. Alejandro regaled them with the tale of his terrifying walk from Dominic House, and I took the distraction to sneak away."

That, Riley hadn't anticipated at all. He suddenly understands the police's fixation with her. "That's evidence tampering."

"You call it evidence tampering—I call it covering our asses."

Riley snorts. "So. Still feeling agnostic?"

Jordan laughs. It sounds painful. She runs a hand through her hair. "I don't know. I don't know what I am. What I do know is that if people saw the things we caught on film, most of them would think it was a prank. But some of them wouldn't. And some of them would want to go there to find out themselves."

The idea of *anybody* deliberately seeking out Dominic House ever again makes Riley's stomach turn. Even now, with Father Thomas and Jacob gone, it feels . . . sacrilegious. Like playing with fire. "Some places men weren't meant to tread."

"Some places," Jordan says, "have a body count I don't want to add to."

"What are you going to do now?" Riley asks. "With the show, I mean."

"Keep ghost-hunting," she says instantly. "And if the channel wants to axe us, we'll go back to being independent."

Riley raises a brow. "And if you wind up in another place with a body count?"

She grins at him. "Then I guess our equipment will malfunction again."

That's good enough for Riley. He gets to his feet, casting one final glance at Alejandro, asleep in the corner, Josh passed out in the bed. Then he looks back to Jordan. "About that twenty-five grand," Riley says. "Is that still being honored?"

"Of course it's still being honored." Jordan frowns. "Hell, I told the suits we should have doubled it as hazard pay, but they said insurance was already on their ass for paying for private hospital rooms for the lot of you."

At least that answered that. "How soon?"

"Should be in your account by the time you're discharged," she says. "Why? Have you got big plans?"

"Thinking of going on a road trip," Riley replies nonchalantly.

"Oh?" Jordan asks, interested. "Anywhere good?"

Riley smiles at her. "No clue," he says. "But the company sure will be."

BEFORE

Eventually, people stopped talking about Dominic House. They stopped talking about Riley. A school shooting two states over. A celebrity overdose in New York. Abuse allegations among the Hollywood elite. Riley's tragedy became old news, shoved aside to make room for fresh horrors.

Riley, who lived with that horror every waking moment, could barely fathom how much his life had stretched to accommodate the weight of it.

Every morning he woke from nightmares and stared at the ceiling until his alarm went off. He showered quietly, so as not to wake his mother, recovering from the night shift. Buttered toast for breakfast when there was bread. Nothing when there wasn't. One crowded bus ride into town and seven hours of making coffee, feeling the prickle of eyes on his face; TV-screen familiar but unplaceable, a dozen news cycles out of date, his scars a compulsion unto themself.

A bus ride home. Empty hours of watching TV on the couch, canned laughter ringing in the empty apartment. A text from his mom, the same as the one above it, and the one above that: can you pick up groceries tomorrow?

Sure, he texted back, the most they'd spoken in days.

The clock hit midnight. Like a robot, Riley undressed and climbed into bed. Beside him, Ethan smiled, trapped beneath his ageless glass.

Rinse. Repeat.

Repeat.

Repeat.

Every moment, Riley thought of Dominic House, of its smudged windows, its towering walls. The chapel's cross threatening the sky like the blade of a knife. His skin crawled with imaginary flame, and his scars ached beneath imaginary fingers.

I could go back, he thought every morning as he lay in bed, waiting to rinse and repeat. *I could go back. Ethan's there. He's still there. I know he's still there. I could—*

This alarm went off, and Riley rinsed and repeated.

Two years after Dominic House—after Ethan—Riley stood behind the counter jabbing the rusty buttons of the register. Next to him, Chantelle tugged his sleeve and said, "Why didn't you tell me you knew *Jordan Jones?*"

Jordan smiled at him, red hair, red mouth.

You can understand why I had to approach you, she said.

I can see that you need time to think about things, she said.

I'll be waiting to hear from you, she said.

And Riley went home, and he sat on the bed that carried him through a sea of nightmares every night. At his elbow, Ethan watched, waited.

In the morning, Riley would lie in bed. He would stare at the ceiling. He'd think sad thoughts about a happy boy. He'd suffocate beneath his misery. One step closer to brain death with every day.

Rinse. Repeat.

Riley picked up his phone. He called the number. He opened his mouth and said—

NINETEEN

In the morning, Riley stuffs what little has migrated to the hospital with him into a complimentary plastic bag, changes into a clean set of clothing Vee had ferried him, and stuffs his wallet and phone in his back pocket. His chest still aches, but the bandages are fresh, and he signs himself out without a backward glance.

Outside, the sun is searingly bright. Riley stands on the curb and blinks against it, hand held high as he tries to squint into the distance. There's a bus stop somewhere nearby. He recalls from last time he was here. For the life of him, he can't remember which direction it's in.

A horn blares and a car comes to a stop in front of him, right beside the *NO DROP-OFF* sign. The window rolls down and Vee leans out. She's wearing expensive sunglasses he knows she didn't own a week ago. "Get in, loser. We're going shopping."

"You know I haven't seen that movie," Riley tells her and cracks open the passenger door.

Inside, the air-conditioning feels like a blizzard. Riley pointedly turns the vent away from himself, but Vee ignores him, peeling away from the sidewalk too fast for the hospital parking lot. She's not wearing her sling, and her cast looks clunky against the steering wheel. He's reasonably certain she's not meant to be driving yet but knows better than to say anything.

"So," Vee says, "you want to tell me why I had to find out you were checking out from Jordan of all people?"

Riley would like to know that, too, considering he's reasonably certain he hadn't breathed a word to Jordan either. "Sorry. I was going to call when I was home."

She looks over her sunglasses at him, unimpressed. "Or you could have told me yesterday afternoon, when I spent three hours demolishing you at Scrabble in the hospital rec room."

Riley could have. He'd decided not to. "Sorry."

She sighs, the car slowing to a stop at a set of traffic lights. "I thought after everything, you might finally learn how to reach out. I guess that was a lofty wish."

"I didn't want to bother you," Riley says, and it has the advantage of being mostly true.

"Riley, if there's anything that the last two years have taught us, it's that things go better for all of us when we're there for one another, don't you think?" The light goes green. Vee adds, "If there's something else you want to tell me, now's the time."

Riley stares straight ahead, hands tangled in the plastic bag sweating in his lap. He teeters one way. He teeters the other.

From the corner of his eye, he can see a barely healed scab along Vee's jaw. A bruise above her eye, hidden by the wide lenses of her glasses.

Riley loses the fight with himself. "I'm leaving town." Vee's head snaps to him. The car swerves, and Riley clutches at the dashboard. "Eyes on the road! Eyes on the road!"

She looks back out the windshield, but her hands are clutching the wheel. "What?"

"You heard me," Riley says.

"But college—"

"I never applied."

Silence sits. Vee doesn't look at him, but he can tell she wants to. "You didn't tell me."

Riley lets go of the dashboard. "I didn't tell anyone."

"You've been planning to leave for that long?"

Riley hadn't thought so. The longer he considers it, the more he realizes he might have been. "I don't know."

Vee says, "And I assume you're not going alone."

Riley doesn't look at her. "No."

Silence again. Finally, they turn onto Riley's street, drifting to a stop in front of his apartment building. They sit for a moment, Vee letting the car idle, and then she sighs. "And you're sure?"

"Yes," Riley replies, instantly and without thought.

Vee nudges her glasses down to really look at him. Her excellent makeup can't quite cover the shadows Dominic House has left painted across her skin. "It's useless to talk you out of anything, huh?"

She sounds fond, though, and Riley chances a smile. She smiles back. Relief seeps through him. "I don't mean to make you worry."

"Sure you don't," she says, pushing playfully at his shoulder. "Get out of my car. I'll be seeing you soon, okay?"

"Soon," Riley promises and clambers out, plastic bag in his hand.

It takes him several tries to fish his keys out of his pocket. Vee stays parked the whole time. It's only when Riley finally sinks the key into the lock that she pulls away, car crunching on the road gravel. Riley turns. Hesitates. Waves to her. He can't be sure, but he thinks she waves back. The car revs, and then it pulls off down the street like a shooting star.

Riley stands on the doorstep, watching for a very long moment after she drives away. Then he goes inside to pack and say goodbye to everything he's ever known.

✗ ✗ ✗

Dominic House comes into sight like a mountain peeking over the horizon.

Riley sees it long before he's near, the blackened windows, the towering eaves. He expects it to look different, like a year has passed instead of a week.

It doesn't. It looks exactly the same. Except, for the first time in a long, long time, Riley doesn't feel as if it's watching him back.

The taxi driver pulls to a stop about halfway up the driveway, eyeing Dominic House dubiously. "Listen," he says. "Are you *sure* this is where you wanted to go? It looks like hell."

More true than he knows. It nearly pulls a smile from Riley. "I'm sure," he says. He paid an unreasonable amount of money for this little trip, but it'd been worth it to avoid an even more unreasonable hike. "Thanks for the ride."

The taxi pulls away as Riley strides up the last of the driveway, bag over his shoulder. The front gate, when he finally reaches it, is ribboned with fresh police tape. A sign proclaims it off-limits and dangerous. Riley snorts; they're three tragedies too late on that front.

He cracks the gate open and ducks under the tape, following the long, winding path. His feet trace out the pattern of dozens of tire imprints. He wonders how many were from last week. How many were nosy tourists in the days after.

A dozen more steps until he reaches the house. Half that. Three, two, one—

"I remember saying I would wait until you were *well*," Ethan says, fond and exasperated. "Would it kill you to listen to me for once?"

He's sitting on the fountain's edge. His pale skin stands out like parchment in the sun, and the blue of his eyes matches the sky. When he smiles at Riley, it rips the last of his strength clean from his bones.

Riley sinks down beside him. "I'm well enough."

Ethan looks at him, eyes dragging from Riley's scuffed boots to the tips of his ears. "Did you walk out here?"

Riley says, "Didn't have to. Haven't you heard? I'm rich now."

Ethan sighs. His arm drops across Riley, dragging him in.

Riley lets him, head resting on Ethan's shoulders. He's exactly as cold to the touch as Riley remembers. Ethan doesn't say anything else. Riley soaks up the familiarity of him, the sound of the wind rustling through the trees.

He closes his eyes. It's been a long time since he's felt such peace.

A strand of hair falls into his face. Gently, Ethan tucks it back behind his ear. "So," he says, "what's your big plan?"

"What makes you think I have a plan?" Riley asks.

"You always have a plan," Ethan says. "Usually, they could do with some improvement, but you always have one."

Riley cracks his eyes open. "Did you just call me reckless?"

"Of course not," Ethan says, smiling at him. "I would never."

It takes all his strength, but Riley manages to sit up, lifting his head from Ethan's shoulders. He stretches, and when his boots clear the shadows of Dominic House, he can feel the sun beating down on him. "I thought we could go away. Take a road trip."

"A road trip," Ethan repeats. "With what car?"

"We'll hitchhike," Riley improvises. "Just for a bit."

"You hate strangers," Ethan says. "Besides, that hardly sounds safe."

Riley sends him a look. "You spent two years possessed in a haunted house, and now you're . . . half dead or something. And you're worried hitchhiking might be too dangerous?"

"Not for me," Ethan says, with the endless patience Riley has missed. "For *you*."

"I can handle myself."

282

"I'd rather you didn't have to," Ethan says. "You never even learned how to throw a decent punch."

"Fine. You can throw the punches for me. How's that?"

Ethan shakes his head, but it's not a no, not when he's smiling like that. "I've missed you."

Riley's heart stumbles. "Did you? I mean, were you even capable?"

Ethan takes his hand, thumb stroking over the back of Riley's palm. He looks out, away from Dominic House, thoughtful. "I don't remember a lot before you came back," he admits. "Most of the time, I just remember being confused. Not sure where I was. It felt like I was dreaming."

Riley's been trying not to think about that, but he owes it to Ethan not to say as much. He wasn't the one trapped here for years, after all. "Most of the time?"

"I had moments. I think." Ethan frowns. "I'd blink, and I'd be standing in the dormitory, or the chapel, and I'd think, 'What am I doing? I'm not supposed to be here.'" He pauses. "They never lasted long."

"And now?" Riley asks.

Confidently, Ethan says, "I know I'm awake. I know where I am. Who I am." He pulls a face, and it crinkles his nose like a child's. "Maybe not so much *what* I am."

This is his chance. Riley takes in a breath. "About that," he says. "I was thinking maybe we could find out."

"What do you mean?"

"Dominic House can't be the only haunted place in America," Riley says. "And you can't be the only person to ever wind up like this. Somebody out there has to know *something*. Maybe they can figure out how to make you more . . ."

"Human?" Ethan supplies dryly.

Riley pinches him. "Alive," he corrects. "Less like an ice block without a heartbeat."

"I don't think ice blocks normally have heartbeats, actually."

"Ethan." Riley sighs.

Ethan smiles. "So. That's your grand plan. You want to go on a ghost-hunting road trip."

"It's hardly hunting," Riley says. "More like seeking, I guess."

Ethan contemplates that. "Back to our roots."

"I don't plan on *filming* anything."

"Maybe you should," Ethan suggests, surprising him. "Record it. For research, if nothing else."

Riley hadn't thought of it like that. The more he thinks about it, the more appealing it sounds. It's not like he'd ever been a great note-taker, anyway. "Maybe," he allows. "For now, let's just focus on the getting-on-the-road part." He hesitates. "I mean, if you want."

Ethan sighs. "A road trip with my boyfriend to find a way to cure my chronic case of undeadness, or a potential eternity of being stuck at the haunted house that made me this way to begin with. I don't know, Riley. It's so hard to choose." He squeezes Riley's hand before Riley can decide if he's offended. "Of course I want."

Relief sweeps through Riley. "Good. Because you were rid of me for two years, and that's long enough. You're not getting another out."

Ethan kisses him. It goes a long way to settling the knots in Riley's stomach. When he pulls back, Ethan says, "Should I take it you've already packed?"

Riley pats the duffel by his side. "Everything I need is in here. I figured we could squeeze in a shopping trip for you somewhere along the way." He gets to his feet, slinging it over his shoulder again, and holds out a hand to Ethan. "Let's get moving. We're burning daylight."

Ethan lets Riley haul him upright. The weight of him feels human enough, even if the ice of his touch does not. "What's the rush?"

Riley looks behind him to where Dominic House stands, a solitary presence without the chapel over its shoulder, its cross watchful. "I'm just sick of this place. Aren't you?"

Ethan follows his gaze. "There's nobody here anymore," he says. "Nobody but us."

Riley knows that. He can feel it. After experiencing the overwhelming presence of Jacob within him, his absence is like a hole. "I know. I still don't like it here."

Ethan stares at Dominic House for a moment longer. Then he turns away, to Riley. "Yeah. Me neither." He smiles, and this time he holds out a hand. "All right, this is your road trip. Why don't you lead the way?"

Riley takes his hand. "First things first: let's get the fuck out of here."

"Amen," Ethan says.

"That's not funny," Riley says, even though it is, just a little.

They leave the fountain behind, trudging down the drive to the gate. Ethan holds the police tape up for Riley to duck under, like a gentleman, and Riley pointedly returns the favor just to see the rueful smile on Ethan's face. Once they're out, Riley kicks the gate shut. The rusty latch groans as it falls into place. Riley hopes it never opens again. He looks to Ethan.

He's still there. Bright-eyed, pale-skinned, squinting at the sun. Free of Dominic House. Alive. Or mostly, anyway.

"I think I see something," Ethan says.

Riley is so busy having his moment that it takes him a second to process that. "Huh?"

"Yeah, can't you hear that?" Ethan points into down the road. "There."

Riley does hear it now. The grumble of a car engine as it trundles over a dirt path about a decade too old for its modern wheels. As he watches, a sleek car rounds the curve in the path, skidding to a stop about three feet out from running them over.

Riley stares. "I can't believe this," he says, although he can. "You've got to be shitting me."

The driver's window winds down. Vee beams at him. "Well, well, well. If it isn't my two favorite boys."

From the passenger seat, Colton snaps, "I'm sitting right here, you know."

"Two of three," she corrects smoothly. "The ones who don't get cigarette smoke in my car, anyway."

Riley doesn't know what to say. Disbelief has him stuck to the ground.

Ethan doesn't have that problem. He grins bright enough to put the sun to shame. "Vee! What are you doing here?"

Again, Colton: "I'm still here!"

Vee throws the door open and clambers out. She pulls Ethan into a hug at the same moment he reaches for her. "Riley told me about his plans. It seemed to me there were a few flaws in them, as usual."

"Hey!" Riley protests.

Vee ignores him, stepping back but keeping both hands on Ethan's arms. "Anyway, what's the fun of a road trip when it's just two people and no car?"

"You can't be serious," Riley says. "Vee, you can't."

The passenger door flings open and Colton climbs out, leaning on the roof. "She does what she likes. Thought you'd have known that by now."

"And you?" Riley says. "What are you doing here?"

Colton doesn't take the bait. "It's not like I've got anything going on. I've come into some money recently, you know? Feels like a road trip might be a good way to spend it."

"You hate road trips," Riley says dumbly. "You get carsick."

Colton sighs. "Get in the fucking car, genius. We haven't got all day." He folds himself back inside, slamming the door for emphasis.

Riley looks at Ethan. Predictably, Ethan doesn't look fazed in the least. He catches Riley's eye and says, "It'll be just like old times."

Vee snags his attention with a hand to his elbow. "Sorry," she says. "I know you don't like surprises, but I didn't want to give you a chance to run away before we got here."

"I wouldn't have run away," Riley says, and he's surprised to find it's mostly true. "I just . . . You can't take off like this."

"Why not?" Vee asks. "You and Ethan are."

"Undead men don't have a lot of responsibilities, and I'm a bad role model," Riley says.

"Riley's right," Ethan says. "My calendar isn't very full these days."

"Neither's mine," Vee says. "Or Colton's."

"What about college?" Riley pushes.

"I'll defer it," Vee says, as if it means nothing at all. At his expression, she says, "Riley, we're not doing this just for you. For either of you."

"Then why?" he asks.

She smiles at him, squeezing his shoulder. To Ethan, she says, "We're leaving in two minutes. You better be in the car."

Riley watches as she strides away, clambering into the driver's seat, arguing loudly with Colton as she goes.

Ethan says, "We could go by ourselves. If that's what you want."

Riley glances at him. "Is that what *you* want?"

"I think this could be good," Ethan says. "For all of us."

Riley sighs. "That's what Vee said about coming back to Dominic House."

Ethan raises a brow. "Was she right?"

Riley's scars ache: his face, his chest. He's bruised on every inch of his skin, and his nails are ragged from clawing his way up the stairs in the chapel.

He has nightmares every night. He doesn't think that's ever going to change.

For the first time in years, his hands don't shake.

"Fuck," Riley says, scrubbing a hand through his hair. "If we all wind up killing each other, that's on you."

Ethan grins at him. Bright. Sure. Everything Riley's missed. "I'll take my chances."

From the car, Colton calls, "Are you coming or not? I don't want to sit out here all day."

"Yeah, yeah, we're coming. Stop complaining." Riley throws open the back door and climbs inside, scooting along as Ethan follows him. "Would it kill you to shut up for just five minutes?"

"Yes," Colton says primly. "My cane's in the back seat. Don't break it."

The door slams closed. "We'll be careful," Ethan promises.

"All right, everybody buckle up," Vee says. "I'm getting us the fuck out of here, and I'm not making any pit stops on the way."

There's a mad scramble for seat belts, and when Vee hits the gas, the car lurches forward far too quickly for the gravel beneath them.

"Jesus, are you sure you don't want me to drive?" Colton says, clutching at the dashboard.

Vee smiles and sets her sunglasses down on the top of her nose. "Over my dead body, Pierce."

As they bicker, Riley can't help but twist, glancing behind them.

Dominic House sits like a fat, ungainly lord atop its hill, bloated with too many peaks, windows, walls. The path that wends its way through the forest to its gates is overgrown, and the car bounces every inch of the way down, unwelcome and aware of it.

Riley stares at it. He stares at it, and he feels . . . nothing.

From the front, Vee says, "What do you *mean* I can't choose the music? I'm the driver!" and Colton says, "I think we should let Ethan pick. He's the one who's been dead for two years. Riley, back me up here."

Riley looks a moment longer. Dominic House does not look back. It is, after all these years, just a house.

Riley turns away. "Ethan should pick."

There's more noise up front, Vee and Colton fighting over the radio. The back seat is quieter. Beside him, Ethan squeezes his hand, and when Riley looks to him, he asks, "Okay?"

Riley doesn't need to think about it. "Yeah. I'm okay. How about you?"

Ethan studies his face, looking for a lie. Riley lets him. Ethan smiles. "Good. I'm okay too."

Riley holds that gaze for a moment longer, soaking up his smile like sunlight. Then he turns, facing forward.

He does not look back.

ACKNOWLEDGMENTS

My agent, Madelyn Burt, who found something special in this book and understood every word I was trying to convey along the way. Thank you for weathering endless questions and championing *Trespass Against Us* relentlessly. I can't possibly begin to express how grateful I am for our partnership.

My array of editors, starting with Lily Kessinger, without whom this book might not have seen the light of day. Thank you so much for helping bring Riley and his friends into the world, and I'll never forget all the kind, beautiful things you have said about this story.

Alice Jerman, who stepped in to guide *Trespass Against Us* forward. I'm forever grateful for the way you never faltered at the unexpected and challenged me to polish this book at every step.

Clare Vaughn, whose commitment and belief have helped *Trespass Against Us* all the way to the finish line. Both this book and I have been truly privileged to have you on the team.

The rest of the team who've worked hard behind the scenes, including Heather Tamarkin, Mary Magrisso, Trish McGinley, Jessie Gang, Alison Donalty, Katie Boni, Audrey Diestelkamp, Marinda Valenti, and Ivy McFadden.

My incredibly talented cover artist, Kim Myatt. You breathed such life into Riley and captured the very essence of this novel in a way I could never have anticipated. I feel so blessed to have your work displayed with mine.

My dear friends! Pia Davis and Finley Hopley-Willcock, who get the honor of starting this lengthy list by virtue of being two of my oldest friends. You've both suffered literal decades of my raving and ranting about writing and met it with endless patience. Your unwavering belief that it would come to fruition has kept me afloat through many doubtful years.

Kaitlyn Hellwege and Artemis Fisher, just as loved, who've been sounding boards through novel after novel. You've helped me dig free of uncountable plot holes and read so many faltering manuscripts. You'll never truly understand what that has meant to me.

Demi McKay, who has never blinked when I locked myself away to meet deadlines and kept me fed and hydrated when I was too distracted to remember to do it myself. Your support is as underserved as it is appreciated.

Bek Conroy and Clo Dri! My Salty Pals! What to say except I adore you both fiercely, and even when time zones kept us apart, just knowing you were a single message away kept me sane on many nights when writing felt helpless. One day, I'll have a shelf dedicated to books just written by us, and I can't possibly wait.

Finally, June Williams. There is no adequate way to thank you for everything you've done for this project and for me. Without your gentle but loving bullying, I would never finish anything, and we both know it. You've been with me every step of the way, and I hope you know your DNA is as interwoven with this book as my own.

My coworkers from various jobs over the years—Rachel, Alana, Toni, and Hannah. Every single one of you met my shy confession of writing with such enthusiasm that it makes me smile even years later. Thank you for your support and making long shifts of doing nothing at all so much more bearable.

No acknowledgment is complete without touching upon family. Mitchell Kemp, my dear, annoying brother, who never doubted this book would be born, my sister Rhiannon Stojanovski, and my extended family, all of you, who supported me endlessly. A special thank-you to my Aunt Lyn Englefield—who isn't here to see *Trespass Against Us* publish, but I know would have been so proud.

Last but not least, my mother, Raylene Kemp. Not everybody is blessed with a mother like you, and please know I have never once taken it for granted. Long hours on the phone talking through sticky points in the plot, bouncing ideas back and forth, complaining when things don't go well, and celebrating when they do. You've read every book I've ever written, even the bad ones, until I finally got something right, and I never would have reached this point without you. Thank you for raising me to be somebody capable of chasing my dreams until I finally caught them.